We hope you enjoy this book. Please return or renew it by the due date.

You can renew it at www.norfolk.gov.uk/libraries or by using our free library app.

Otherwise you can phone 0344 800 8020 - please have your library card and PIN ready.

You can sign up for email reminders too.

First published in 2018 by Bloodhound Books

www.bloodhoundbooks.com

PRINT ISBN: 978-1-912604-81-4

Author's Note

While there are many similarities in practice between the jurisdictions of Scotland and England, one difference merits explanation. In England and Wales, the Crown Prosecution Service [CPS] is the principal public prosecuting agency for conducting criminal prosecutions, whereas, for the majority of crimes in Scotland a Procurator Fiscal [PF] or Fiscal Depute presents the case for the prosecution.

Prologue: The Lowther Hills, South Lanarkshire.

When the Passat pulled off the M74 into the Welcome Break petrol station outside Abington, he was waiting. The woman behind the wheel got out, walked towards him and introduced herself. They shook hands.

'Shall we get a couple of coffees to take with us?'

'Good idea,' he said, though it wasn't. The coffee from the machine inside was vile; he'd already tried a cup and poured it away.

'Great. What would you like?'

'Cappuccino, please.'

She smiled and went to fetch it. He watched her go: petite and bubbly; friendly and insincere. On the phone, two days before, he'd guessed she would be in her early thirties and she was. The ring on her finger and toys in the back seat told him there was a husband and maybe a couple of kids.

The coffee hadn't improved – if anything it was worse. He pretended to drink it to keep her happy and readied himself for the small talk which was sure to come. With females, control of the vehicle was well down their list of priorities. Inconsequential chit-chat was number one – always – that and taking their eyes off the road to look at whoever was in the car.

'What is it about this part of the country that appeals to you? Most folk find it too remote.'

He smirked behind his cup – it had taken less than thirty seconds for her to start. But without realising she'd answered her own question. He lied. 'It's peaceful.'

She laughed and he noticed a smear of red lipstick on her front teeth. 'It's that, all right.'

They took the country road on the other side of the motorway and drove into the Lowther Hills. Ten minutes later they still hadn't seen another vehicle. Today, this remote part of South Lanarkshire was undulating greens and browns and straw with the occasional patch of purple, and the air was muggy. In the sky, a dull sun dipped in and out behind low-lying clouds washed with grey, heavy with rain. What would it be like here in winter? He wouldn't be here in winter. Wouldn't be here at all if it went the way he wanted.

The estate agent prattled on. 'It seems farther than it is. Only six miles.'

With an effort, he stopped himself from telling her to shut up and just drive and settled in his seat while she droned on about the weather; it was going to be a long six miles.

They stopped in front of the Hopetoun Arms Hotel and surveyed the rows of miners' cottages from an age when there was lead in the ground. She spouted history which he filtered out. Finally she got to why they were here. 'I've identified three properties which may fit what you're after. The first is in Leadhills village itself.'

'Where? Can we see it from here?'

She pointed. 'At the end of the row.'

He dismissed it without getting out of the car. 'Too small. Let's go on to the next one.'

The cottage in Wanlockhead didn't meet the criteria either. His assessment, again, was instant so they drove on without speaking, the agent glancing at her watch, resigned to a wasted afternoon. Where they were going was close to derelict. Uninhabitable in its present state. A real no-hoper. So bad she'd almost left it off the list. 'It's a little further out, I'm afraid.'

He gazed at the countryside rolling by. Nothing but hills and more hills.

'No problem.'

The first thing he saw was the sign on a stake driven into the ground.

CUNNINGHAM AND McCLURE
ESTATE AGENTS
LANARK
01555 964142

The property was hidden from the road by a slope at the front and another to the rear. As they got closer, his pulse quickened. The agent turned the key in the rusty lock and made a face. 'Welcome to the Baxter house.'

She nodded at the horizon. 'Storm coming. May as well tell you before you find out for yourself, the roof leaks.'

She was joking: there was a hole the size of an armchair in the ceiling. Her client made no comment. Inside, in the semi-darkness, the smell of damp hit them immediately as they moved through rooms with boarded windows and peeling paint, gingerly picking a path across torn linoleum showing faded newspaper headlines, decades old. He knelt and fingered a dusty cable running to a grubby socket.

'The electricity isn't working, is it?'

The agent told him it wasn't.

'Needs complete rewiring, anyway.'

She apologised a second time and he caught coffee on her breath. 'I tried to warn you. It's worse than I thought. Sorry again. We've had this place on our books for years. As far as I understand, a family rented it in the late nineties. Hasn't been occupied since. No prizes for guessing why. The owner moved to Australia in the 1950s. Somebody in the office said he'd died and it's his grandson who's selling. He stays in the Caribbean. I haven't met him.'

She shrugged, regretting bringing anyone here. 'Getting a mortgage will be difficult with something in this condition, and even if you could, you'd need to completely renovate it. Would you be up for that?'

He grunted a reply which told her nothing.

'I'll email him. See if he's prepared to lower the price before the whole bloody thing falls down.'

The edge of a rotted floorboard crumbled in his hand. The agent watched, not comfortable with trying to sell something in such a bad state. Nobody in their right mind would buy this wreck. His question was casual, almost an afterthought. 'Your schedule said there's a cellar?'

Behind him, she coloured with embarrassment. 'Was afraid you'd ask about that. Not the best feature. Don't think it'll be good for much.'

'Show me.'

He followed her to an unlocked door at the end of the hall. She took a chrome torch from her handbag, switched it on and played a circle of light against the darkness. 'Be prepared, eh.'

He didn't smile.

They went down wooden steps which groaned under their weight. Apart from some cardboard boxes piled on the flagstone floor and rat droppings in one of the corners, there was little to see. Thick beams ran across the ceiling supporting the room above, some kind of fungus was growing on the rough plaster walls and it was noticeably cooler, cold even – he guessed they were ten or twelve feet underground. His eyes ran over the empty space, remembering how far they were from any other building, picturing where the heater, the chemical toilet, and the bed would go.

And the chain.

Back in the car she said, 'Shall I speak to the owner?'

He seemed distracted. 'Mmmm. What did you say?'

'I can contact the owner about doing something on the price.'

'Oh, yes. Yes, do that.'

'Can I tell him you might be interested?'

'Tell him to get real on the money or bring the bulldozers in.'

He wasn't serious; he wouldn't buy it at any price, he'd never intended to. But the decision was already made.

It was perfect.

Mackenzie Crawford had made a decision: today, she wouldn't have a drink.

Not the first time she'd made that pledge to herself or her husband – there had been dozens like it – too many to count. One by one, because she was feeling good or bad, happy or sad, she'd broken them, often with disastrous consequences.

" – We judge ourselves by our intentions. The world judges us by our actions – " she'd heard someone say. And, of course, it was true. If it depended on willpower – wanting to stop – she'd have quit years ago. The reality was more complicated: what was once a habit was now a need. At thirty-one, a figure that had turned so many heads was beginning to thicken, her skin losing its freshness, the long dark hair its lustre. Mirrors weren't friends anymore; she'd noticed the lines, like tiny cracks in porcelain on the once flawless complexion, running from the corners of her bloodshot eyes after yet another half-remembered night.

But this morning the sun was shining and she felt strong, stronger than she'd been in a very long time – strong enough to make promises.

She collected a trolley from outside the supermarket, thinking about Derek's refusal to accept she'd crossed an invisible line, that the days of choosing to drink or not were past. His solution was the same as his solution for everything: control. Two glasses of wine with their evening meal, poured by him, of course. When it didn't work because it was never going to work, he took it as a personal affront, got angry, and wouldn't speak to her. They'd rowed about it again last night and he'd slept in another room. It seemed they rowed about everything these days. Mackenzie had tried to get him to understand total abstinence was the only way – one drink was too many, a dozen wasn't enough.

Derek saw life in black and white. For him there were no grey areas. He didn't get it and sneered at the idea. 'You mean you can't drink at all? Not even at New Year? And what about our wedding anniversary? Are you seriously saying we won't be able to celebrate the best day of our lives? That's the most ridiculous thing I've ever heard. It's about discipline. Restraint. Accepting your responsibilities as a wife without hitting the sauce every time somebody says the wrong thing or looks at you the wrong way. You're weak. If you weren't, there wouldn't be a problem.'

Mackenzie had stopped trying to convince him.

In the supermarket she avoided the alcohol section and went through her list: chicken breasts for tonight, sirloin steaks for Sunday; milk and yogurt; breakfast cereal and vegetables. Did they have pasta? She tried to remember and got some anyway. Pappardella. Derek liked Pappardella.

She sensed she was being watched and turned. At the end of the aisle a man in a black coat was staring at her, his face expressionless. He was tall – almost as tall as Derek – with short fair hair and broad shoulders. And he wasn't just watching her, he was ravishing her with his eyes. It was obvious he didn't mind that she'd noticed. It didn't bother him. He didn't care, clearly trying to intimidate her. Mackenzie drew him a look and pushed her trolley past. He stood his ground and didn't move.

At the end of the cheese counter he was there again.

It spooked her and she hurried on, grabbing whatever came to hand. When she glanced back there was no sign of him and she relaxed, telling herself her nerves were getting the better of her. But in the next aisle he was waiting and Mackenzie knew she hadn't imagined it. It was possible he was just a man who'd taken a shine to her, chancing his arm, unaware he was freaking her out. She didn't believe it. There was a coldness to him, and the undisguised way he eyed her up and down scared her.

She rounded on him, forcing assertiveness into her voice. 'Can I help you?'

He didn't answer, unfazed by her directness, and continued his appraisal of her.

'Then stop following me. Just stop it.'

At the checkout he was behind her, then suddenly he wasn't. The young assistant noticed Mackenzie seemed flustered. 'Are you okay?'

She answered nervously. 'There was a weird guy following me. Did you see him?'

Concern furrowed the girl's brow. 'Did something happen?'

'No, it's all right, he just startled me.'

'Do you want me to call security?'

The suggestion was well-meant but laughable. 'And tell them somebody was looking at me? Don't think so. Knowing my luck the poor guy couldn't remember what he came in for.'

The girl started putting the items through the till. 'Most men are the same. Their wives ask them to pick up a loaf and they come home with half-a-dozen cans of Newcastle Brown Ale.'

They laughed, but the incident had rattled Mackenzie. Her hands shook as she packed the groceries into a bag. The words were out of her mouth before she could stop them, almost as if somebody else was speaking.

'Can I add a bottle of gin to this? A litre, please. Ring it up separately.'

Another promise was about to be broken.

Ring a ring o' roses,
a pocket full of posies;
atishoo, atishoo.
We all fall down.

Day One

Derek and Mackenzie Crawford

When they came out of Central Station into Gordon Street, the city looked fresh and clean in the spring sunshine and Derek was glad he'd suggested spending the day in town together, something they hadn't done in ages. Birds rose into the sky from a rooftop in Hope Street and flew towards George Square. Hope Street. Ironic. Because, for the first time in months, that was how he felt. A line of black taxis across the road made him think about his car, safely in the drive at home. Parking in Glasgow was a nightmare. All it took was some moron on his mobile not paying attention to scratch the paintwork and spoil the whole bloody look. Derek Crawford had learned the hard way. The world was full of fucking idiots: fact.

He took his wife's arm in his. 'Let's start with a coffee, eh?'

Her reply was dull and unenthusiastic. Mackenzie hadn't wanted to come. 'If you like.'

Her husband tried to ignore the apathy. 'Or would you rather hit the shops?'

'I'm not bothered.'

Derek felt impatience rise. 'Make an effort, will you? I am.'

Not the beginning he'd wanted.

For most of the morning they wandered aimlessly in Buchanan Galleries, her monosyllabic and uncommunicative, him scanning her face every few minutes for a sign she was enjoying herself and finding none. On the way out she stopped on the steps in front of the concert hall to drop coins into an old beggar's outstretched hand – a toothless emaciated man, shrouded in poverty and the grey days of age – certain Derek wouldn't approve. As he never tired of boasting, he'd overcome his own modest origins, and if *he* could, so could anybody who wanted to.

He waited for her to catch up and shook his head. 'If I've told you once I've told you a thousand times. Don't encourage people like that. Whatever you gave him will go on drugs.'

'Have a heart, he's old and he's sleeping rough.'

'And whose fault is that?'

She couldn't be bothered getting into it with him. 'Hardly going to change his life, is it?'

In a jeweller's, he encouraged her to buy a pair of earrings she hesitated over, offering to get them for her. They left without them because – apparently – they didn't suit. Further down the street, at the Lancome counter in the House of Fraser, a pretty dark-haired woman with 'Sharon' on her name tag described the fragrance notes of an expensive scent – sandalwood and amber were mentioned – and for the first time, Mackenzie seemed less distracted. Her husband stayed in the background and let her get on with it.

Perfumery took up a huge space on the ground floor of the cavernous and ornate department store. Chanel, Dior and Givenchy sat beside names he didn't recognise, and at every island the girls were lookers. Though not as beautiful as his wife.

Derek Crawford had everything he wanted in life and he'd made it happen all by himself. For a guy who'd left school at fifteen without a qualification to his name, he'd done all right. His teachers hadn't been sorry to see him go – they couldn't reach him. He wouldn't be told anything so he couldn't be taught. Mr Drummond, the head of the history department, predicted a 'brilliant' future ahead of young Crawford; on the graveyard shift, stacking shelves in Asda.

Mr Drummond was wrong. A series of dead-end jobs confirmed what the teenage Derek had always known: working for somebody else wasn't for him. But he had to wait until he was twenty-three – when a van bought at auction sold for twice what he'd paid for it – before the light went on with the realisation that there was money in this game. Two years later he had a second-hand car dealership on London Road and another on Ballater Street, near the Gorbals. In those days he'd paid his landlords by cheque, always adding 'Good luck with that.'

They'd laugh, thinking he was joking. Sometimes he was.

The smoothed-off accent – the big house and the polish – came later; he could buy them and he had.

At fifty-one, and close to six feet, he was happy with how he looked. His silver-grey hair added style to an otherwise unstylish appearance. Throughout his life women had found him attractive but he'd never been close to marrying. Not until he met Mackenzie.

From the moment he'd spotted her sitting with her friends in the pub in West George Street, he'd wanted her. Of course he knew her girlfriends laughed at him behind his back because he was older; they weren't laughing now.

Their wedding was without doubt the best day of his life. Derek had hardly been able to believe the vision by his side belonged to him. That first year had been bliss, she'd adored him. They rarely disagreed. When they did it was soon resolved. For a while, he congratulated himself on having found a wonderful partner.

Until the drinking started and everything changed.

He'd come home to find dirty dishes in the sink, the bed unmade, and Mackenzie slumped on the sofa. Slowly, he came to accept his wife had a problem. As a husband, his responsibility was clear: he had to help her. And he'd tried. God knows, he'd tried, allowing her just two glasses of wine per day. Some nights ended with her storming off to one of the spare rooms because he refused to let her have more. Derek tightened his already tight grip on their money. Every penny spent had to be accounted for, and while she visited her sister he'd search the house for hidden bottles and empty the contents down the sink.

Derek Crawford was used to being in control, but there was no controlling this. Threats meant nothing, her repeated promises to quit even less. The humiliations, public and private, came thick and fast – too many to count, too painful to remember, lying and deceiving him constantly.

One particularly embarrassing scene at the golf club gave him the excuse he'd needed to cut off their limited social life. Until Mackenzie straightened herself out the designer clothes would stay in the wardrobe upstairs, not needed. Apart from the odd unavoidable family gathering they wouldn't be going anywhere – it would just be the two of them.

Then, suddenly, around three months ago, the drinking stopped. It hadn't lasted, though while it did she started going out at night by herself, refusing to tell him where. The third time he'd followed and saw her get into a blue Vectra parked at the corner of the street. His brother-in-law, Blair Gardiner, drove a blue Vectra. Mackenzie couldn't be visiting Adele – Adele would've said – besides, there would be no need for secrecy if that was where she was going. And surely she couldn't be meeting him? He was a tosser, a nice tosser but a tosser nonetheless. Derek pushed the thought away. His instinct was to drag whoever was behind the wheel out and beat his head to a pulp. But apart from filling his neighbours' mouths, what would that change?

Around ten-thirty, she'd returned and gone straight to her bedroom without a word. He heard the door close. The perfect marriage had fallen apart; he was losing her, may have already lost her.

Finally, Derek had taken as much as he could stand and decided to have it out with her, whatever the cost. He cornered her in the kitchen and asked the question he didn't want the answer to.

'What's the game, Mackenzie? Who is it?'

Her reply stunned him. 'I'm leaving you, Derek.'

It was almost amusing. 'After the hell you've put me through?'

'My mind's made up. Trying to stop me is a waste of time.'

What could he say? He was living with a stranger.

She continued going out in the evening while he stayed at home worrying until she returned. Even if she didn't realise it, Derek was sure Mackenzie needed him. The worst part wasn't another man – lots of wives had affairs; they blew over. No, the worst part was doing what she was doing sober. Alcohol couldn't be used as an excuse. Any day he expected to come home from work and find his wife no longer there.

Until a month ago, when the drinking and the lies kicked off again.

She'd stopped going out at night, but wouldn't speak to him, sometimes for days. When she did it was to tell stories no one would believe.

'A man was watching me in the supermarket today. Every time I turned round, he was there.'

Derek pretended to accept what she was saying. 'What was he like?'

'He was wearing a black coat, I remember that, but it was his eyes. He just stood there staring at me. It was weird. He really scared me.'

Her husband had chosen his words carefully, things were delicate enough. She'd talked to him, that was progress. 'Maybe he was waiting for someone?'

'No, it was me he was interested in.'

'We'll report it to the police if you think we should.'

She hesitated. 'Maybe I was mistaken.'

Mackenzie didn't mention it again, the incident was forgotten, and the silent treatment returned.

This trip to the city was a desperate attempt by him to get them on track. That morning she'd been on edge. He'd recognised the signs and braced himself for the storm heading towards him. Coming out of the department store he tried to take her hand. She pulled away and barked at him. 'I'm not in the mood to shop. When're we eating?'

Derek resigned himself: food wasn't the attraction. His wife needed a drink.

'Whenever you're ready.'

'I'm ready now.'

They sat at a table in an Italian restaurant on the top floor of Princes Square, busy with the lunchtime office crowd gossiping and chattering. People like themselves, enjoying a day in town. He studied the menu. She didn't bother opening hers. Her voice was sly and provocative. 'Aren't you going to buy me a drink?'

'Mackenzie…'

'Don't give me a lecture. We're supposed to be having fun. That's why we're here, isn't it?'

'We're *supposed* to be here to try and work things out.' He shook his head. 'But who am I kidding?' He saw he wasn't getting through and used a softer approach. 'Look, I know it's difficult, but you can do this, Mackenzie. Just stick to what we agreed: two glasses, okay?'

She ignored him and called to a passing waitress. 'White wine, please.' When it arrived she asked for the same again, daring him to object. He did. 'We're going to your sister's tonight, in case you've forgotten – that's when you should be having your two drinks, not now.'

She reacted. 'You didn't tell me.'

'I shouldn't have to tell you. She's your sister, the only one you've got. We arranged it last month. It's her birthday.'

'Well, I'm not going. I don't want to.'

'She's expecting us. Gavin and Monica will be there.'

'Too bad.' Mackenzie finished the first glass and started on the second. Derek tried to steer the conversation on to safer ground. 'See anything you fancy?'

Her reply confirmed his suspicions she'd only been after booze. 'I've changed my mind. I'm not hungry.'

'Don't be stupid. You said you were ready to eat.'

'I've lost my appetite.'

He reached across and took hold of her hand. 'Eat something, please.'

The tenderness in his tone persuaded her and they ordered mushroom risotto for each of them. Mackenzie did no better than pick round the edges of hers in between the wine. Soon, she was signalling the waitress for another. Her husband placed his hand on top of her nearly empty glass. 'For Christ's sake. Haven't you had enough?'

She buried her face in her hands and burst into tears. 'I can't go on like this. It's too much. I can't stand it.'

He felt his cheeks redden. 'Mackenzie – get a grip. We're in the middle of a bloody restaurant.'

She took a tissue from her bag and dabbed at her eyes. 'I'm leaving you, Derek.'

'Not that again.'

'I mean it.'

She was leaving *him*. He wanted to laugh. People nearby were listening. Derek glared at them until they looked away and waited for his wife to calm down before raising the subject he'd rather have avoided. 'Who is he?'

'I don't know what you mean.'

'Yes, you do. There's someone else, isn't there?'

'No, of course not. Why do you always think that?'

'Because there is. Ever since you stopped drinking the last time there's been some guy in the shadows who's going to change your life. Well, I've got news for you. Nothing's going to change unless you deal with your drinking.'

She stood. 'I don't want to talk to you anymore. I'm going home.'

Mackenzie stormed away. Derek tossed money on the table and ran down the escalator after her, pushing past shoppers travelling at the speed of the moving stairway. On Buchanan Street, he caught up with her and grabbed her arm. She brushed it off. 'Let me go. Let me go!'

He tightened his hold and pulled her to him, whispering through gritted teeth. 'You're making a bloody fool of yourself. Of both of us. I mean it. Get a grip.'

The anger in his voice was enough to stop her struggling. Across the street, a man in his late-twenties, wearing a black coat, leaned against a shop doorway and stared over at them. He casually crushed the cigarette he was smoking under his shoe, smiling at some secret joke.

'Who's that?'

'I don't know what you're talking about.'

Derek pointed. 'The guy in the black coat.'

Mackenzie looked over his shoulder. 'It's him!'

'Who?'

'The one I told you about. The man in the supermarket. He's watching us.'

'The whole of fucking Glasgow's watching us.'

'He's following me. Oh my God. I knew I was right, he's following me.'

Black Coat waved and Derek's face twisted in a sneer. 'You really must think I'm an idiot. He isn't following you. He's waiting for you.'

Once, knowing she'd chosen him made Derek Crawford proud. Having a beautiful female on his arm was a boost to his ego. Three years on, pride had been replaced by other emotions. He turned on his wife. 'Was that the plan? Fall out with me and hook up with him?'

Mackenzie started to deny it when the stranger waved a second time. That was too much for her husband. 'Are you seriously asking me to believe he doesn't know you?' Derek laughed a brittle laugh. 'He knows you all right. He bloody *knows* you.'

He grabbed her arm again and half-dragged her up Buchanan Street. 'We'll discuss it when you sober up. As for your sister's party, you're fucking going.'

* * *

Gavin and Monica Darroch

Gavin knotted his tie and inspected himself in the mirror: not bad, considering he'd only managed a couple of hours sleep. The bags under his eyes which alarmed him two months ago had found a home on his face and seemed to belong there now, and earlier that morning he'd spotted a grey hair. Welcome to parenting. At this rate he'd be an old man before Alice hit her teens.

He had always taken his responsibilities seriously; as a student he hadn't spent his days in the bar, unlike so many of his peers. The result was a 2:1 degree in architecture from Edinburgh University, followed by three lost years in London, catching up on the fun he'd missed. Back in Glasgow, ready to put his education to work, he'd interviewed with the old established firm of Jamieson Coburn in the West End of Glasgow. They'd liked what they saw and offered him a job. All he needed to do was stay on the right side of the planning department and allow his flair to shine. Except, as he soon discovered, it wasn't so simple. Robert Jamieson, the founder's great-grandson, told him the facts of life on his very first day.

'You're young, bursting with enthusiasm, and that's good. We need your energy. But keep this in mind. Every office in the city will tell you a successful practice runs on great design. Not so. Invoicing is what keeps the lights on. Every hour a client's bill is delayed puts the firm at risk.'

He saw the new-start's confusion and placed an avuncular arm on his shoulder.

'Jamieson Coburn has been in business for close to four decades. I'm giving you the secret of our survival: don't get lost in the drawings, manage the project.'

Gavin took the advice to heart and ten years down the line was a junior partner: it was all working out.

One Friday night in Brown's Brasserie on George Square he'd met a girl with a very different world-view. Monica had just returned from a six-month trip around India and couldn't have cared less about paying the rent. Her blue eyes sparkled when she told stories about fishing off houseboats on the waterways of Kerala, camping under the stars in the Thar Desert or picking tea in Darjeeling, and by comparison, what he'd done seemed tame. She was the adventure he hadn't known he was looking for. When he took her home he was already in love with her. It was obvious they were right for each other and the romance moved quickly.

Light years ago, at least that's how it felt.

Before Alice was born he'd listened to his friends' jaundiced comments about fatherhood, making it sound like a living hell, and kept his thoughts to himself. Surely they were having a laugh? If it was as bad as they made out, why did some of them have three and four kids?

And he'd been right, they were joking. But they were also telling the truth.

Gavin put on his jacket and had a last look at his reflection. An older version of who he'd been stared back: a stressed-out guy who didn't laugh as much as he used to and, although he wouldn't admit it even to himself, worried about where his life was headed. He'd changed and so had his wife; the free spirit had gone leaving a stranger in her place. Being parents was turning out to be more of a challenge than either had foreseen. In the clinic, they'd listened to the lecture on postpartum, believing it had nothing to do with them, the way smokers believed lung cancer always happened to somebody else.

Alice was beautiful; he loved her. So much it scared him. But the tiny person they'd created together overwhelmed them, dominating and demanding more than they had to give. Gavin had taken time away from work to share the load. Not a great success. They got in each other's way and argued over issues which weren't really issues at all, in the end agreeing it would be better if he went back to the office. He did and they were both relieved, but it didn't solve the problem. The balance they'd taken for granted in their relationship eluded them, trying to find it pushed them further apart, and he began staying at his desk into the evening, dreading having to come home.

If this was how profoundly he – the man – was affected, what about his wife?

The gift Monica carried for nine months had become a curse. She felt inadequate as a mother, unattractive as a woman, and couldn't cope. Her mood swung all over the place, one minute joyful and excited the next anxious and irritable. Then came the depression. They'd been told the 'baby blues' could last for as long as two weeks. Three months on, things had deteriorated even further. Secretly they both feared the marriage wouldn't survive and avoided each other. They would die for their daughter – no doubt about that – but they were coming apart. Normal conversation didn't happen now and sex was a thing of the past.

He heard the doorbell, then Mrs McLeod's cheery Gaelic lilt drifting upstairs. She'd offered to watch Alice so they could go to Adele's birthday party. There wasn't much anybody could tell her about babies; she'd had five. Monica hadn't been keen and only agreed after Gavin promised they wouldn't out stay long.

Downstairs in the lounge the women were in discussion about feeding-times. He heard the concern in his wife's voice. 'If anything happens, anything at all. Call me.'

Shona McLeod was an old hand at the game. She understood. 'Forget about us, enjoy yourself, we'll be fine.'

On the journey across Glasgow, Monica stared out of the window, her fingers nervously twisting the strap on her bag. Gavin remembered the bag well, a Stella McCartney, bought two years ago for her birthday in the far-off days when everything had been right with their world. They'd had a routine that suited both of them: he played five-a-sides on Tuesday nights while she was at the gym. He'd never understood why a woman with a perfect size ten figure needed to exercise. She'd told him that *was* why. Afterwards they'd meet up and go for a curry, taking turns at choosing the restaurant. Monica usually favoured Mother India's Café on Argyle Street, across from the Art Gallery; or sometimes Chaakoo in the city centre. Though he'd heard it had closed, so she'd have to find somewhere new. Gavin stuck with the Shish Mahal in Park Road and always ordered biryani. On Fridays and Saturdays they'd take turns cooking, trying to impress with fancy chocolate desserts. Then Sunday – the best day of the week: breakfast in bed made by him; sex, unhurried and intense;

coffee; the papers and the often-heated discussion over what was in the news.

In the afternoon, they'd drive into the country. Scotland was beautiful, fantastic scenery in every direction and less than an hour from the city. Just being close to it refreshed them: breathing in the salty air on Pittenweem harbour with the Bass Rock in the distance, or trudging arm in arm into the winter wind over the sand dunes of Irvine beach.

A baby should have taken their happiness to a new level. Instead, they'd lost each other and the jokes his married male friends had made weren't jokes anymore. Monica was confused and in pain and however much he tried to help her it always ended the same. But he loved her and wanted to protect her, if he only knew how.

She spoke and his heart went out to her. 'Alice likes to take her time with her bottle. I should've told Mrs McLeod that...what if she chokes?'

He looked over at his wife, seeing the change in her. Monica was pale, uptight and distracted, her features sharpened by the evening light, her mind on search for something to fret about. When they met he'd found she'd been laid-back and unfussy, totally confident in who she was. That girl, the one he'd fallen in love with, had worn her good looks casually, comfortable in the knowledge she was desirable even in faded old jeans and a T-shirt. Where was that lady now?

He reassured her. 'That's not going to happen. Mrs McLeod has more experience with babies than most people I know. Alice is safer with her than both of us put together.' He took her hand. 'Switch off. You need to. *We* need to.'

She turned away. 'Easy for you to say, you're not her mother.'

The reply stung and he reacted. 'No, you're right. I'm her father, in case you've forgotten.'

As soon as the words were out of his mouth he regretted them. Gavin reached across and made another attempt to take

Monica's hand. 'Let's relax and enjoy ourselves. Catching up with everybody will be good.'

His wife's blank expression told him he was wasting his time trying to be positive. She changed the subject but not the tone. 'Mackenzie's only been to see Alice once. Once in three months. Not exactly interested, is she?'

Gavin sighed. 'Kids are a difficult subject for her. You know that.'

'Maybe it wouldn't be so difficult if she did something about her drinking. Just saying.'

Her husband gripped the wheel. 'Well, could you try not "just saying". It doesn't help, Monica.'

They drove on, lost in unspoken resentment.

This wasn't how it had been. This wasn't them. They'd loved being together in the car: discussing everything and anything; mooching around antique shops in Perth or Auchterarder; stopping for lunch at a village pub, sniggering at the horrified reaction of the locals when she kissed him.

Good times. Great times.

He ran a hand through his blond hair. Adele and Mackenzie – both brunette – kidded him he wasn't really their brother: the hospital had made a terrible mistake and given their parents the wrong baby. Maybe there was a grain of truth to it because he was very different. His sisters were more complicated: Adele, quick to judge and less apt to smile. And Mackenzie. What could he say about her? Ten years younger than him, eight younger than Adele: the baby of the family; a delightful child who'd grown into a rebellious teenager and then a confused adult.

He hadn't seen his young sister since the christening when she'd left directly after the service and hadn't come back to the house. Monica wasn't pleased. Mackenzie had seemed sullen and withdrawn that day and Gavin imagined her and Derek were rowing. It happened. Who knew it better than him?

At Charing Cross he took the M8 West towards Glasgow Airport over the Kingston Bridge where an hour earlier traffic would've been bumper-to-bumper.

'Listen. Families are hard work at times. What other people do or don't do isn't something we have any influence over. It can't come between us. The important thing is to stay close. Alice needs us, and we need each other. Let's do our best to have a nice night, okay?'

Monica mellowed and squeezed his hand. 'She will be fine, won't she?'

''Course she will. Tomorrow at the crack of dawn she'll tell us just how all right.'

His wife laughed. 'We should've called her Rooster.'

* * *

Blair and Adele Gardiner

The dull thud of loud music poured from the twins' bedrooms through the Gardiner house. Thirteen-year-old Adam and Richard were already showing signs they were not the children their mother had finally given birth to after a twelve-hour labour, but in fact, aliens scoping out Planet Earth in advance of an invasion. Both had the same blond hair as their uncle.

Since leaving primary and starting 'the big school' a habit had developed: they came home, raided the fridge, usually for cheese, and went to their rooms, reappearing only when they were called to the dinner table – the party had upset their routine.

Blair Gardiner stuck his head round the kitchen door and saw the look on his wife's face. 'What's wrong?'

Adele put the ramekins back in the fridge and pursed her lips. 'Panna cotta isn't set.'

Blair checked his watch. 'Plenty of time. Be ages before you serve them.'

'But what if they don't set?'

'Leave them as they are. None of them will know the difference. When it comes to food they're Philistines.'

'Gavin isn't. He's a great cook.'

Her husband said, 'He's the exception, I'll give you that. But it's your party. You should've let me book a table somewhere like I wanted to. Save all this work.' He nodded towards the beef browning in the oven.

'Well, it's why we spent so much money on the kitchen, isn't it? Besides, I don't mind. This is the first time any of them have seen the house. Two birds with one stone.'

Her husband shrugged. 'To hell with your family. No offence.'

'You don't mean that.'

'Try me. When was the last time Gavin or Mackenzie invited us to their places?'

'The christening.'

'The christening doesn't count. They couldn't avoid it and, if we're telling the truth, neither could we.'

'Mackenzie managed to.'

Blair hesitated. His sister-in-law was a subject best avoided. His reply was as neutral as he could make it. 'Mackenzie goes her own way. Always has.'

Adele wiped her hands on a dishcloth and turned her attention to chopping tomatoes for the salad. 'Didn't tell you, I called her last week.'

Her husband tried to sound casual. 'Oh yeah? How was she?'

'In a word: pissed. Swearing. Slurring her words. Couldn't make out half of what she was saying.'

'Where was Derek?'

'Working late, or so she said. Probably had as much of it as he could take. You wouldn't believe what she was saying about him. Terrible stuff. I think she hates him.'

'Well, he is old enough to be her father. And he certainly acts like it.'

Adele stopped what she was doing and put down the knife. Her voice took on a tone her husband was all too familiar with. 'What's that supposed to mean? Perhaps you've forgotten how Mackenzie was before she met him? I certainly haven't. As far as

I'm concerned my sister doesn't appreciate how lucky she is. Derek saved her.'

'But you have to admit he treats her like a child.'

'Maybe because she behaves like one.'

Blair held his tongue. Adele was a fan of Derek, he wasn't.

'She landed on her feet and can't see it.'

'But if she isn't happy…surely that matters more than money?'

Adele glared at him. He had blinkers on when it came to her sister. 'I wish you'd open your eyes. Nobody's attacking Mackenzie.'

'Doesn't sound like it.'

'I couldn't care less what it sounds like. She's a drama queen, always has been. Everybody gets it but you.' She scrutinised him. 'Why is that, Blair? Why're you always on her side?'

He rejected the suggestion. 'I'm not. I'm not on anybody's side. I look at her and I see an unhappy woman, that's all. Never been keen on Derek Crawford. Don't deny it.'

'Because in your opinion he's too old for her?'

'That's part of it, yes. But you have to admit he's very controlling. No wonder Mackenzie drinks.'

'Don't be ridiculous. Nobody *makes* anybody drink. My sister's an alcoholic, that's why she drinks. And yes, I'll admit Derek likes to be the boss, except somebody has to take the reins. Mackenzie doesn't.'

'Okay, fair point. But surely circumstances play a part?'

'You mean circumstance like that big house she lives in or the endless spending on clothes?'

Blair shook his head. 'You know what I'm saying.'

She gave ground, no more anxious than he was to row. 'Yes, I do but you're coming at it from the wrong angle. I've read a lot about alcoholism. It's an illness. If the person gets the help they need they start to understand how to deal with life without turning to drink.'

He was stubborn. 'Don't disagree with any of that. But it still can't be easy living with Derek Crawford.'

The corners of Adele's mouth drew back; the smile had a hard edge. 'Still defending her, eh? Really starting to think you fancy her.'

Blair felt colour rise in his cheeks and took a step towards the door – he should've stayed out of the kitchen and let her get on with it. An argument, especially this argument, was the last thing they needed. His reply sounded unconvincing even to him.

'Now you're being ridiculous.'

'Am I? Shall I tell you what she told me?'

Whatever it was, her husband didn't want to hear it. Adele didn't give him a choice.

'Apparently she's got herself a stalker.' She saw the confusion on his face. It pleased her. 'My sister claims somebody's following her. Makes a change from pink elephants, doesn't it? Trust Mackenzie to go one better with a drink problem than everybody else.'

'Maybe she's telling the truth.'

Adele snorted and went back to the salad. 'Get real, she's making it up. Or she's imagining it. Sad either way. Poor Derek – the guy you don't like – deserves a medal.'

The twins burst into the kitchen, too self-absorbed to notice the tension between their parents. Adam opened the fridge and studied what was there: a reflex action. His brother spoke for both of them. 'We're starving. When's dinner?'

Blair replied more sharply than he intended. 'Your mother's busy. I'll bring it up when it's ready.'

'What is it?'

'She hasn't decided yet.'

Adele said. 'I'll do pizza for you as soon as the roast comes out of the oven.'

Not what the boys wanted to hear. Adam screwed up his face, dissatisfied. 'How long will that be?'

'As soon as I can, darling.'

'But we're hungry now.'

Their father tried and failed to keep impatience out of his voice. 'How can you be hungry? You demolished a block of cheddar between you.'

His sons stared back at him until Adam – the eldest by twenty minutes – answered with logic of his own. 'That was an hour ago.'

Blair wasn't having any of it. He wasn't in the mood. 'Scat! Make yourselves scarce. Take some more cheese if you need to, then beat it. And keep the noise down.'

He turned to his wife. 'We better start getting ready.'

* * *

Blair was in the dining-room polishing glasses when he heard Adele's footsteps on the stairs. Dressing hadn't been an enjoyable experience, they'd ignored each other, and he'd left her putting on her makeup. He sensed his wife standing in the doorway and faced her. Adele's dark hair was twisted into ringlets and piled high on her head. She made a what-do-you-think gesture and waited for his reaction: the black dress, together with the pearl choker and high-heels, highlighted her slim figure. No doubt about it, she was still a looker.

He smiled; he couldn't help himself. 'Knockout. How do you do it?'

'I wonder that myself, sometimes.'

Blair pointed to the table-setting. 'Looks great, well done. And the panna cotta's beginning to set, I just checked.'

She nodded. 'Have you opened the wine?'

'All done.'

Adele ran her hand along the back of the chair nearest her, aware this was the closest they'd been in months. 'I want to say I'm sorry. I should've taken your suggestion and gone out, just the two of us. Instead I got us involved in this palaver. On top of that I haven't been sleeping well. It's Mackenzie. I get so stressed thinking about her.'

He steered the conversation to a better place. ''Course you're stressed. Isn't every day you're thirty-nine. I'm a year ahead, how do you think I feel?'

'No, really. Mackenzie's a touchy subject with me, always has been. She hasn't been an easy person to live with. I switch between wanting to mother her and having to stop myself strangling her with my bare hands. Suppose I haven't ever forgiven her for how she treated Mum and Dad. They couldn't understand her and blamed themselves.'

'That's not what you should be thinking tonight. I'm wrong, too. It's your birthday; your family's coming to share it with you. As it should be. Mackenzie has to work through her problems, same as the rest of us. And you're right. Derek isn't my idea of a husband for her. But what do I know?'

'I feel sorry for him. Her drinking's out of control again. I'm afraid she's losing the place. A stalker.' She laughed. 'Can you believe it?'

'Obviously she does.'

'Obviously, but you can't trust anything she says. Surely you haven't forgotten the fiasco over – '

'Forget that stuff. Forget it. Tonight's about you.'

For a moment they were together. Adele said, 'The boys are awful quiet.'

'Aren't they? I wonder why.'

She searched his face. 'What've you done, Blair Gardiner?'

'Hunted them to the new Star Wars movie. They're teenagers, bribery solves everything. Probably feeding their faces with junk as we speak. And don't worry, they've been warned to get themselves home as soon as the film ends.'

'Why didn't I think of that?

'So long as one of us did.'

Adele eyed her husband up and down, taking in his boyish face, a contrast to the grey at his temples. 'Looking pretty sharp yourself, by the way. Like a younger Michael Douglas.'

'Yeah? How much younger?'

'Young enough for me.'

She moved towards the door. 'And don't be too quick to top up Mackenzie's glass. She can't handle it.'

'I won't. But let's not kick the dog before it barks, eh?'

* * *

When Derek and Mackenzie Crawford arrived home, the scene they'd had in Buchanan Street was still very much alive. She ran upstairs to a bedroom and slammed the door leaving her husband to stomp around the lounge, furious and frustrated. At five o'clock he tiptoed in and stood for a moment, watching the rise and fall of her body under the clothes. Building his business from a dodgy second-hand outfit with only one employee – him – to two dozen dealerships had taken nearly thirty years. The journey hadn't been uneventful though nothing like as demanding as marriage. But he loved his wife.

He put a hand on her shoulder and shook her gently awake. 'Mackenzie. Mackenzie. Blair's asked us not to be late because Monica will want to get back to the baby.'

She pulled the clothes over her head without acknowledging him. Derek went downstairs; he'd give her ten minutes to come round. Drinking didn't agree with Mackenzie, especially lunchtime drinking. Was there anybody it did agree with? He listened for signs she was up. There were none. He tried the softly-softly approach again with no better result. Finally, he stormed into the room, dragged the clothes off the bed onto the floor, close to shouting. 'Always got to push it, haven't you? Enough of this fucking nonsense! Get yourself together or I'll throw a basin of cold water over you!'

Later, when he heard the shower hiss, he knew his threat had worked; she'd surfaced. But it was still forty minutes before she came downstairs, sullen and lethargic, her eyes hooded and heavy. Sleep hadn't helped; she was still affected, a mystery because she hadn't had that much. Derek thought he'd found them all but there had to be a bottle hidden somewhere. It didn't auger well. What state would she be in after a few more?

This was the wrong time to bring it up.

'Ready? Okay.'

On the drive from Whitecraigs he'd tried making conversation and got silence for his trouble. It couldn't go on – he wouldn't let it go on. Across from the Mount Florida Bowling Club, he pulled the silver Audi A5 into the kerb in front of a row of terraced houses, between Blair's blue Vectra and an emerald Peugeot SUV GT. The Peugeot was unfamiliar and he wondered if Blair and Adele had invited friends to the party.

Hampden Park wasn't far away. The national obsession with something the country was rubbish at these days was beyond him. Derek forced himself to play golf with his bank manager occasionally because it was useful and he was surprisingly good at it. Beyond that, sport didn't interest him.

He turned off the ignition and faced his wife. 'Before we go in here, remember it's Adele's birthday. Go easy on the booze, alright?'

Mackenzie gave a mock salute. 'Yes, sir.'

Derek felt like slapping her. 'Don't spoil it or there really will be trouble. Take a telling.'

'Sod off.'

He shook his head and got out. Three boys, about fourteen-years-old, were admiring the sleek lines of the Audi. Mackenzie dropped her bag and bent to pick it up. One of the lads said something which made his pals snigger. Derek had been brought up on the streets and didn't take shit from anybody. The look he gave warned them to back off.

Blair was waiting at the door, and inside after the usual hugs and kisses, he took their coats and clapped his hands together. 'Now, what can I get you two?'

Derek said, 'Sparkling water if you have any.' He mimed driving.

Mackenzie didn't hesitate. 'Dry white wine, please. And don't be mean.'

Derek shot her a look. She ignored him, walked into the lounge and spoke to her sister-in-law. 'So, Monica, how's the baby doing? How's Alison?'

'You mean, Alice. She's great. Can't imagine life without her now and it's only been three months. Didn't want to leave her with the sitter tonight. Gavin had to drag me here, didn't you, babe?'

His half-hearted smile said he was less happy with the new arrangement than she was.

From the side of his mouth, Derek said, 'Get the kid's name right, for God's sake.'

Gavin kissed his sister's cheek, catching alcohol on her breath. 'How you doing, sis?'

Mackenzie shook her head, her lip trembling, on the edge of tears. He patted her hand. 'We'll get a chance to talk. You can tell me all about it.'

Blair topped everyone up and made a toast. 'To Adele!'

They raised their glasses. Mackenzie drained hers faster than anybody else and Derek felt his chest tighten. She was off and running. No stopping her. Monica handed the birthday girl a present which was obviously perfume. Adele opened it, pretending to be surprised. Derek whispered to Mackenzie. 'Where's ours?'

'I…I forgot to bring it.'

'Oh, Jesus Christ. How could you forget?'

'I'm sorry. I'm sorry. It slipped my mind.'

'What did you get her?'

She didn't answer and he knew she was lying. It hadn't slipped her mind. There was no birthday gift. She hadn't bought anything. It was going to be another one of those nights.

The Gardiners had only been months living in the house. This was the first time Derek had been here. Adele said, 'Shall I give you the tuppenny tour or would you prefer to wait 'til later?'

'Now. Absolutely.'

They trailed around, listening to a blow-by-blow account of the decorating decisions – why they'd gone for this rather than that; how something had spoken to her and she'd known it was right; and even more boring tales about what they'd decided against. But it was nice. Expensive and understated. Mackenzie wasn't good at coordinating colours and fabrics and didn't have an eye for it, so most of the stuff in their house had been chosen by Derek. At the table, he weighed the heavy cutlery in his hands. The bottom of the dishes would be stamped Jasper Conran, or some such. And the wine hadn't come from a supermarket either, though by the way Mackenzie was knocking it back, it may as well.

It had to be said: they'd done all right. Not as all right as him, but still. He leaned across the dining table to Gavin. 'What're you driving these days?'

'Got myself a Peugeot this time.'

'Saw it when we came in. Smart.'

'It drives well and there's a lot more space for Alice and her caravan. Every time we go over the door it's like a full-blown military exercise. What about you? Still the BMW?'

'No, got rid. Doesn't make sense to hold on to them too long. Struggling to see past Audi at the minute, the A5 in particular.'

Gavin couldn't have cared less. Cars weren't a big thing with him. He had other priorities and besides, they were already stretched on the mortgage. In the past Derek had offered him a deal. He'd rather do without his help and didn't want to owe him anything, or feed his ego.

'Good, is it?'

'Better than good.'

'I'll take your word for it.'

Derek ignored the sarcasm. Gavin was a wanker. But at least his wife was sober.

Monica's question sounded innocent enough, except it wasn't. She knew exactly what she was doing, raising a subject Mackenzie and Derek Crawford were divided on: he wanted kids, she didn't.

'When're you going to start a family, Mackenzie?'

'Not everybody feels the need. Some people think using a baby to fill what's missing in their lives is selfish and irresponsible. Can't say I disagree.'

Monica started to reply and stopped. Mackenzie took a packet of cigarettes from her bag and felt Blair's hand on her shoulder.

'Sorry, new rules. Adele's idea. No smoking in the house, if you don't mind.'

Monica wasn't ready to give up. 'But isn't that what marriage is about at the end of the day?'

'Not for me.'

The new mother didn't hide her disapproval. 'All I can say is having my daughter has been the single most rewarding thing I've ever done.'

Mackenzie took a mouthful of wine. 'Good for you.'

'It's funny, suddenly life has more meaning.'

'Judging by his face I'm not convinced my brother agrees. You're not the first woman to have a baby, you know. Been done before.'

These days Monica was better at dishing it out than taking it. 'No need to be rude. I was just making conversation. Didn't mean to be – '

'Nosey. You're crowing about having a baby and fishing to find out why I'm not. I'll tell you why. You have to fuck to get pregnant. I hear it's part of the fun, though I can't swear to it.'

Everyone stopped talking at the same time. Mackenzie wasn't finished. 'I wonder who Gavin was thinking about the night he got you pregnant.'

Derek said, 'Mackenzie, stop it! Stop it now!'

His wife reached for her glass and knocked it over; wine stained the white tablecloth, some of it dripping off the edge onto the new beige carpet. Blair appeared with kitchen roll to wipe it up. 'No harm done.'

But he was wrong. The others realised what Derek already knew: Monica was being a tactless bitch. And Mackenzie was drunk. She struggled unsteadily to her feet.

Adele said, 'Where are you going? I'm just about to serve.'

'To the loo. If that's okay with everybody?'

When she left, Adele voiced what they were all thinking. 'She's my sister and I love her, but she's out of control. She needs help. We can all see she needs help.'

'I've tried, believe me I've tried. She won't listen.'

'How do you put up with it?'

Gavin rounded on his wife. 'Well done, Monica. Really well done. You just had to rub it in.'

Blair glanced guiltily at Adele – she'd warned him, hadn't she? 'It's my fault for not slowing the pace.'

Derek disagreed. 'No, it isn't. She got half-pissed at lunch today. Didn't take much. She wasn't straight to start with. We had a stand-up row in Buchanan Street. Almost came to blows. And there was a man waiting for her.'

Adele dropped her napkin. 'Not again!'

Blair couldn't keep irritation out of his voice. '*Again?* What do you mean, *again?*'

'You know. We all know. And I'd prefer we don't discuss it in front of Derek if you don't mind. He is her husband, after all.'

Derek said, 'It's no secret. She told me herself.'

Blair wouldn't be put off. 'She was seventeen – a kid – seduced by a married man. It was a mistake. People make them. Or hadn't you heard, Adele? Are you going to hold it over her head for the rest of her life? My God! No wonder she drinks.'

His wife dismissed the criticism. 'There was more to it than that, Blair. Sorry, Derek. You were saying.'

'Claims this one is following her.'

Adele sighed, 'She hadn't been in contact recently so last week I telephoned. Told me the same thing.'

'Didn't believe her, did you?'

'Of course not. What did he look like?'

Derek shrugged. 'Young. Younger than me, anyway. He was wearing a coat. It was black, that's all I remember. There wasn't time. Mackenzie was creating a scene. People were staring at us.'

'How awful.' Adele glared at her husband. 'Blair seems to have forgotten how often she had Mum and Dad at their wits end. Disappearing for days. Not coming home. And when she finally did, falling in the door looking like she'd been dragged through a hedge backwards with some dope-head in tow. Hoped that was behind her when she married you.'

'So did I.'

'That was ten years ago. Give her a break.'

Adele spoke to her brother. 'You remember don't you, Gavin?'

Gavin and Adele were born two years apart. Mackenzie was the 'baby' of the family. Growing up the girls had been close. Adele, especially, had been protective of her young sister. That changed when Mackenzie hit her middle-teens. By then, Gavin had left university and was working in London. Because he wasn't living at home, he'd tended to only hear about Mackenzie's misadventures later. And by all accounts she'd been a handful, enough for her father to nickname his daughter 'the enemy within'. Around then, the relationship between Adele and Mackenzie deteriorated and had never recovered. Things had got better in the three years since she married the much older Derek, though tonight it looked like Mackenzie was on a rocky road.

Her brother wondered why.

He answered, a note of undisguised censure in his voice. 'I do. And I also remember we weren't exactly angels at that age, either. Blair's right. Give her a break, that's ancient history.'

Adele wasn't surprised. Gavin was like Blair, always taking Mackenzie's side. Tonight was no different. She turned to Derek. 'But she was with you, why would he be there?'

'Think she intended to meet him. Me asking her to come to lunch got in the way. She was in a funny mood all morning. Started an argument over nothing. Threatened to leave me.' He toyed with his napkin. 'How many times have I heard that?'

Blair wasn't convinced. 'Wait a minute, let me understand this. A guy's waiting for her when she's out with you, her husband. She quarrels so she can walk away and join him? Mmmm. Bit far-fetched, isn't it? Buchanan Street's probably the busiest street in Glasgow. He could've just been – '

Derek cut him off. 'The cheeky bastard waved to her. He waved twice. The drinking's one thing, this is something else.

I'll tell you, I've had it. I'm past caring. As far as I'm concerned she can go wherever she likes with whoever she likes just as soon as she likes. I won't stop her.'

'But she was off the booze for a couple of months, wasn't she?'

'Yeah, Blair, she was. But there was a reason. That's when she started going out at night by herself. Took an age getting ready. When I asked where, she wouldn't tell me.'

Monica's lips tightened. 'How terrible for you, Derek.'

He shook his head, reluctant to say more. 'You don't know the half of it. One time I followed her and saw her getting into a guy's car.' He could've said 'just like yours, Blair'.

Adele was shocked. 'Right on your own doorstep?'

Blair questioned his brother-in-law. 'Why didn't you stop her?'

'It would've meant a scene. We've had enough of those. And I didn't want the neighbours to know what a fucking mess we are. Although they've probably sussed that.'

'You think it was the man you saw today?'

'What else is there to think?'

The way it was said Blair got the impression he was singling him out.

Adele lifted her wine, thought better of it, and set it down again. Alcohol was at the root of what they were discussing. 'I suspected she was going off the rails again when she stopped calling me. Should've spoken to the stupid bitch then.'

Derek said, 'It's the booze, the booze's to blame. Even when she isn't drinking it has a hold on her.'

Adele disagreed. 'Don't defend her. She's never grown up. Doesn't realise how lucky she is. You give her everything. We were so pleased when she found you. Until then – '

Footsteps on the stairs stopped her in mid-sentence. Monica glanced anxiously at Gavin. Her marriage had been settled and secure, very different from the Crawfords. Now it was in trouble and her stupid comment that had kicked the whole thing off hadn't helped. Why couldn't she just have played the game instead of having a dig? Then again, Mackenzie hadn't been slow to come back at her. But she had an excuse, she was drunk.

Mackenzie spoke from the hall without coming into the room. 'Don't stop talking on my account. In fact, I'll make it easy for you. Blair, would you call me a taxi, please? I'm going home.'

Blair took her arm and led her back into the lounge. 'Let's all calm down, shall we?'

'I don't want to calm down. I want to go.'

He smiled and put his arm round her waist. 'Of course you do but there's no need for that. Rows happen in every family. At the end of the day, we're all friends.'

Mackenzie leaned her head on his shoulder. 'You're my friend, Blair. Don't care if I never see the rest of them again.'

Jealousy got the better of Derek; he threw his napkin on the table. 'And they feel the same. I'll get your coat. I'm sure it would've been a lovely meal. Sorry it's been spoiled. Thanks for inviting us.'

Mackenzie snarled at him. 'Not with you. I'm not going anywhere with you.'

Adele tried to reason with her. 'What's Derek ever done except look after you?'

Crying had streaked Mackenzie's face with mascara. She glared hate at her husband. 'He knows.'

Blair said, 'Storm in a teacup. Put it behind you. Don't have any more to drink tonight and you'll be okay. C'mon.'

'I won't. I won't be okay. None of you believe anything I say.' She ran her hands though her hair. 'I'm being stalked for fuck's sake, while you sit discussing babies and cars and rubbish! None of you do anything. None of you!'

Monica spoke under her breath. 'Drama queen.'

Mackenzie heard her. 'You bitch. You total bitch. Know what? Forget it. You're right. He's my lover. Hear that, Derek. My lover.'

Adele spoke slowly, trying to calm her sister down. 'Mackenzie, we all want to help. It's just that… you and I need to talk more. You need – '

Mackenzie turned on her, tears brimming in her eyes. 'I need what? Rehab with a bunch of pathetic losers? No thank you. And as for talking to you, you've got a short memory.' She spoke to the others. 'Six months ago I phoned Adele and asked her to come and get me. And what did she do? She hung up.'

Adele pushed back. 'The next day you couldn't remember talking to me.'

'But I tried, and you wouldn't listen. I remember that well enough. You weren't there for me then and you're not there for me now. So you can take your concerned-big-sister-act and go fuck.'

It was kicking off again. Blair liked his sister-in-law more than her husband. He repeated what he'd said in the hall. 'Families are a nightmare. I'm on your side, Mackenzie.'

'You are, they're not. They're on his side.'

Gavin stepped in. 'That isn't true. We all love you. Look, sit down and we can talk it through. Adele, why don't you get everyone some coffee?'

Derek lost patience. 'You're wasting your time. Get her the taxi, Blair. Let her go.'

* * *

Adele walked Derek to the door. He pulled his coat round him. 'I warned her not to spoil your birthday. Tomorrow she'll have blacked out the whole mess. Wish I could do the same.'

She forced a laugh and kissed him on the cheek. 'Don't worry about it. I've had as many birthdays as I can handle. You look after yourself. We're here if you need us. I'll call and see if I can get through to her.'

'It'll take more than that. I think she hates me, Adele. Days go by without her saying a word. And as you heard, we don't sleep together.'

'Oh, Derek, I don't know how you stand it. At times she makes me so angry I want to slap her. But she isn't well. I get so frustrated

I forget alcoholism is an illness. It changes people. Keep trying to get her to accept she has a problem.'

'No chance. And as usual, I'll be a bastard. Honestly – whoever this guy is – he's welcome to her.'

'You don't mean that.'

'I bloody do.'

* * *

After Derek left, the mood in the dining-room was subdued. Monica went into the hall to call the sitter, leaving the others quietly toying with their drinks, asking themselves why families were so dysfunctional. Tonight's drama was the latest, not the first. The twenty-year age difference between Mackenzie and Derek had made them an unlikely pairing from the beginning. But they weren't the only couple with problems. Blair swirled the wine in his glass. 'Don't suppose anybody's hungry, are they?'

Adele snapped. 'Oh, for God's sake. How can you even ask that?'

His wife was angry because he'd sympathised with her sister. Lately, she found something to be upset about in almost everything he said or did.

'I only meant that there's a perfectly good meal in the kitchen. Seems a shame to let it go to waste.'

Gavin came in on his side. 'Actually, I haven't had anything since lunchtime. I'm starving.'

'Bowl of soup do?'

'Soup would be fine.'

Adele seemed to enjoy criticising their sister and Gavin thought he knew why – it was about Blair. Her husband was always ready to give Mackenzie the benefit of the doubt. Too ready, maybe. Perhaps because he was attracted to her or maybe he was just being kind to a woman he'd known more years than he cared to recall. Either way, Adele was jealous, and it showed. She said, 'Her behaviour is inexcusable. She's not a child anymore. We should stage an intervention when she's sober. Get her to face the truth about her drinking and the damage she's causing.'

Gavin wouldn't commit to the idea. 'Wouldn't be the first to have a problem, but an intervention?' He shook his head. 'Easy to guess how she'd react.'

'How? How would she react?'

He smiled a tight smile. 'The same way anybody would, she'd dig her heels in. Better if one of us has a quiet word with her.'

'You mean me. You mean it would be better if *I* had a quiet word with her. Well, I've already tried. It made no difference.'

'She's our sister, try again.'

Blair put a bowl of soup on the table in front of Gavin. 'And when you do, go easy on her.'

'What do you mean?'

'I mean, go easy on her. Don't lecture her, don't scold her. Don't make it about you. She's in trouble. Probably doesn't know how much. She looks up to you.'

'Mackenzie doesn't look up to anybody, that's part of the problem.'

He didn't mince his words. 'Well, you're obviously not in her corner.'

Adele's reply was tart. 'And you obviously are.'

Her husband ignored the implication; he'd heard it before and worse. 'All I'm saying is tread carefully. Judging somebody else's marriage is never a good idea. At the end of the day all we know is what we see in public. But there are two sides to every story.' Blair looked at his wife a moment longer than necessary. 'Derek's given us his. Doesn't anybody care about Mackenzie's?'

Before Gavin could answer, Monica came back. Her abruptness took everyone by surprise.

'You can eat at home. I want to go.'

'Is Alice all right?'

'She's fine. That's beside the point. Blair, could we have our coats?'

Gavin spoke sharply to her. 'Sit down, this is important.' He turned to Blair and Adele.

'Listen, there's no point in you two falling out over this. The most disturbing part of it is this stalker. What do you make of it, Blair?'

His brother-in-law drew a finger along the table. 'Hard to say. Derek's convinced the guy was waiting for her. And she knew him.'

Adele almost lost her temper. 'Of course she knew him. He waved to her.'

Monica weighed in. If she was being forced to stay she was determined to speak her mind – the men weren't getting it. 'I agree with Adele. Derek's right, he was waiting for her.'

This was exactly what Adele wanted to hear. 'Well said, Monica. Mackenzie was spoiled from the beginning and thinks she can do whatever she likes and to hell with everybody else. She's involved with this guy, whoever he is. Derek saw her getting into a car with him?'

Blair wasn't having that. 'We don't know who she got into a car with and neither does Derek.'

Adele threw her head back and laughed. 'Men, you're so gullible. She admitted it. We all heard her. No, I'm sorry but my sister's nothing but a selfish, self-centred bitch.'

Monica added her support. 'She hasn't come to see Alice in months. My sisters are round all the time, aren't they, Gavin?'

'They certainly are.'

The sarcasm was undisguised.

* * *

When Derek got home Mackenzie was waiting for him in the lounge, still drinking. Where the hell was she getting it? Not the right time to start down that road. Her expression was set hard, her fingers drumming against the glass, smoke rising from the cigarette in her hand. He couldn't avoid it. She wanted to fight and began where she'd left off earlier in the day. 'I'm leaving.'

'Oh, change the record, will you? We've heard it.'

'You can't stop me.'

'Why would I? I want you to be happy. Clearly you're not. Maybe it would be for the best.'

She sneered. 'As if you care about what's best for me.'

'I do, Mackenzie, I really do. I always have. Look, let's not get into it again. It'll keep 'til tomorrow.'

'No it won't. Why did you marry me?'

'I love you, you know that.'

'No, that's a lie. You've never loved me. Admit it, at least.'

Derek had come to the end. 'Know what, Mackenzie? This whole thing is a bloody smokescreen. You've met somebody. You admit that.'

Mackenzie goaded him. 'Yes! Yes, there's somebody else. Don't pretend you care.'

'Your friend from today I presume.'

Her face twisted. 'You're a pathetic excuse for a man. I loathe you.'

She threw her wine glass. It smashed against the wall. A shard rebounded and cut Derek underneath his left eye. Immediately, it started to bleed.

'You stupid bitch, you could've blinded me.'

She screamed 'I wish I had. I really wish I had' and threw herself at him. He caught hold of her wrists and held her. 'Oh grow up you silly woman. Just grow up.'

Mackenzie ran up the stairs with him shouting after her. 'Don't dare smoke in bed. I won't allow you to burn the house down.'

The door to one of the spare bedrooms slammed shut, a familiar sound these days. Derek touched his cheek, saw blood on his fingertips and fell into a chair, depressed. The fight had been the last straw. The marriage was over, anyone could see it.

Day Two

Abarking dog or a car backfiring had woken her – Mackenzie wasn't sure which – but part of her wished she'd died in her sleep. Her whole life was a mess.

Daylight poured into the bedroom, harsh and unwelcome, and with it flashes from the dinner party: postcards from hell – the stupid disagreement with Monica about children, spilling the wine, and the row with Adele. Somewhere in there, more disturbing than the rest was a vision of her screaming at Derek, attacking him. Mackenzie buried her head under the bedclothes feeling as bad as she'd ever felt in her life. The hangover was awful, the shame even worse.

All that mattered now was ending it.

She turned onto her side, trailing trembling fingers on the floor, searching for her bag and the mobile inside – unless she'd managed to lose the damned thing. The effort made her head spin and when her hand found the strap, she closed her eyes in relief and fell back, breathless and clammy and waited for the nausea to pass.

The number wasn't in the directory, she'd memorised it. After a few seconds, a man answered and she lowered her voice. 'Alec, it's me. I need to speak to you.'

Derek was standing outside the door. He'd assumed she would be sleeping it off. Suddenly, the two Paracetamol and the cup of coffee seemed foolish. The conversation – one-sided though it was – wasn't hard to understand. They were meeting in an hour. "Same place as last time."

He turned and went back downstairs.

In the room, Mackenzie's heart raced. What had she done? She wasn't a brave person. Already doubt was eating her; she wasn't sure she could go through with it. Sooner or later she'd have to face Derek. Be honest with him. Or settle for what she'd done so many times before – admit she was in the wrong and ask him to forgive her – promise it wouldn't happen again and endure the familiar lecture. He'd ignore her for days, she'd accept it as part of her punishment, and things would continue as they had. But in the deepest part of her Mackenzie knew it had gone beyond that.

Since she was a child, at bedtime she'd folded her clothes over the back of a chair. This morning they were scattered all over the floor, signs of how drunk she'd been though her aching head and the emptiness in her stomach were all the proof needed. In the bathroom she turned on the shower and stayed under longer than usual. Then she dressed slowly and went down to face her husband.

Derek didn't lift his eyes when she came into the lounge. Something was different. He spoke with an unexpected gentleness harder to bear than his anger.

'You should ring Adele and apologise.' Said without a trace of disapproval.

Mackenzie pulled on her coat. 'I will. Later.'

'Where're you going?' Asked casually, without interest.

'Out. And so you know, I've come to a decision.'

* * *

So now he knew his name: Alec.

However much she denied it, however much he wanted to disbelieve the evidence of his own eyes and ears, it was true. The day in town had never had the slightest chance of changing anything between them. Not while there was another man in the background.

This morning of all mornings, after the fiasco she'd caused last night, when she should've been begging him to forgive her, the first thing Mackenzie had done was call this man. Alec…the name was enough to fill Derek Crawford with hate. And he wondered: once Alec had had her, did they lie together, naked, talking about him?

Laughing at how easily she'd fooled him, asking questions about their sex life while his fingers casually played with her nipple?

Did she moan as it grew hard under his touch?

Derek pictured it and knew it would.

He balled his hand into a fist, put it to his mouth and bit down leaving bone-white indents on the knuckles. The images in his head tortured him, causing pain like he'd never known. Anger and jealousy were emotions any cuckolded husband would feel at a time like this. But he was shocked to discover another: lust. Like the day before in Buchanan Street: he'd wanted his wife, wanted to possess her, bring her to the climax of her life so she'd forget she'd ever seen her lover's face or heard his name.

Derek fought to get hold of himself. Forgiveness was out of the question. He'd never forgive what she'd done, he was certain of that much. The bitch had betrayed him, betrayed him with a man called Alec.

He pulled on his jacket and went after her.

Sixty yards ahead Mackenzie walked purposefully, her high-heels clacking on the pavement. Derek's longer stride closed the gap between them until he saw her get into the blue Vectra. Everything he'd felt drained out of him – there was no more anger, no more lust – only a desperate emptiness and a deep sense of loss as the car with his wife inside drew away. He turned and went back.

* * *

When he reached the house he was close to crying. Rage was the emotion now. He slammed the door hard enough to make the windows rattle, resentment spilling out of him. Who the fuck did she think she was? Had she forgotten how much he'd given her? The ungrateful bitch didn't remember he was the one who'd rescued her, saved her from herself, loved her when no one else – even her own family – gave a fuck about her. And this was the thanks he got.

Derek thought about pouring himself a large whisky. No chance. They didn't keep booze in the house. Mackenzie couldn't be trusted not to finish the bottle. Just another example of how considerate he'd been with her many shortcomings.

He shouted at the top of his voice. 'You bastard! You bastard, Mackenzie!'

So what if the neighbours heard? Fuck them as well. He lay on the couch, shaking with anger. After a while depression set in; he felt numb; useless. Looking round the lounge with its carefully-selected furniture he realised the house was too big and too quiet without her. His mind wandered, as it so often did now, to those early days – the good times – when everything had been wonderful.

The options were clear: cut her off without a coin and see how she survived without him, or win her back.

The shrill ring of the telephone brought him into the present. Reluctantly, he lifted the receiver and tried to sound his normal self. 'Hello.'

'Derek, it's Adele. How're things?'

'Not good.'

'She's not still drinking, is she?'

'I'm not sure. She's not here. She's gone out.'

'Didn't think she'd be in a fit state to go anywhere after her performance last night.'

He blew a frustrated breath down the line. 'Well, she has. She was fired-up and waiting for me when I got home. No idea where she's getting it. We had a huge bust-up. The worst ever. And she admitted the affair again. This morning I heard her on her mobile arranging to meet somebody called Alec.'

Mackenzie's sister hesitated. 'Is it him? Is it the man in Buchanan Street?'

'Must be. She was whispering.'

Derek stopped short of telling how he'd skulked on the street like a dog abandoned by its master, spying on the wife who'd chosen another over him, his sexual confusion and the impotence of rejection.

Adele was sympathetic. Unlike Blair, she liked her brother-in-law and considered him too good for Mackenzie. 'Oh, Derek, that's terrible. I'll speak to her. Get her to see sense. Time that lady heard a few home truths. Do you want me to come over?'

'Too late for that. Told me she'd made a decision.'

There was nothing to say and for a minute they didn't speak. Finally, Adele said, 'My sister's a silly bitch but she isn't well. Honestly, Derek, she isn't. Mackenzie loves you, even if she's got a funny way of showing it.'

'I'd like to believe that, I really would. But it's gone too far. Hoped I'd never have to say this: she isn't the only one who can make a decision.'

* * *

Alec ordered mugs of tea from the man behind the counter and they sat at a table in the café, away from the window. For two hours they talked, her speaking, him listening. Her hands shook, her stomach turned. Unhappiness poured from her, and when he described how much better the future would be, Mackenzie was in tears.

At the end of the conversation she was exhausted; saying it out loud had taken a toll on her. Before they went their separate ways he asked a question. 'So, are we on?'

She baulked. 'Don't know if I'm strong enough yet. I'd hate to disappoint you again.'

He smiled. 'I'll take my chances.'

She put her hand on his arm, trusting him. 'Just give me a little longer. I'll tell you when I'm ready. Let's keep things as they are.'

It wasn't what he wanted to hear. 'Okay, but we can't go on like this. Sooner or later you have to make a choice.'

Day Three

Since Adele's birthday party the atmosphere between them was worse than ever. Derek refused to even look at Mackenzie, blaming her and her alone for the breakdown of their marriage, not accepting they'd tried and failed to make each other happy. Getting out of the house was the right thing to do.

When she put on her coat he'd pretended to read a newspaper. She knew he was dying to quiz her about where she was going. Not knowing would drive him crazy.

In the fresh air with the sun on her face she felt free for the first time in years. For a moment Mackenzie considered calling Alec to let him know she was all right, then thought better of it – she'd see him soon enough. Besides, she needed time to adjust to the changes ahead of her, changes so huge that when she thought about them she felt faint.

There was guilt, of course there was, because in many ways Derek was a good husband. She'd wanted for nothing – at least, nothing money could buy. When she wakened on her birthday there was always an expensive surprise waiting for her; a watch, a fur coat; one time a double-string of real pearls she'd admired in a shop window in Bond Street on a weekend in London. Mackenzie only had to show interest in something, and before she could stop him, Derek would have bought it.

Plenty of women would trade places with her, happy to be treated like royalty. She was a queen, no question about it. But a queen to his king.

Now she'd stopped drinking – the notion made her laugh. It had only been a day but it was the one thing Alec insisted on – so many things were clearer: alcohol had cut her off from her true

41

self, become such a part of her life it was impossible to think of getting through a day without the stuff. Derek believed it was a habit, and like all habits – good or bad – with self-discipline it could be broken. Mackenzie had to account for every penny spent at the supermarket while he controlled how many glasses of wine she was allowed at dinner. For a time – a few weeks – it appeared he'd been successful. Then one evening he'd arrived home, found her unconscious on the couch and came face-to-face with an unacceptable fact: his wife was a drunk.

How difficult that must have been for him.

Mackenzie walked on the grass at the side of the road. Behind her buried in the traffic noise she heard male voices, though she wasn't able to make out what they were saying. Thirty yards further on they were closer. Surely their bigger stride would take them past? She slowed to let them. When they didn't, she quickened her step. It didn't make sense. They should've overtaken her by now. Maybe they felt as uncomfortable as she did.

But the voices were still there. Indistinct. Louder. In the middle of the afternoon there was no one around. She was alone.

Suddenly, a pleasant walk had become something else, something scary and sinister, and she was afraid. Her heart pounded in her chest. Her throat was dry. She broke into a run.

A mocking laugh died in the air.

Or did she imagine it?

When she couldn't run any further she stopped, panting and exhausted, too spooked to look round. At first, there was nothing. No footsteps. No conversation. She breathed a sigh of relief, glad Adele wasn't there to witness her overreaction to what was probably the wind in the trees. The explanation was obvious and she almost blushed. She'd underestimated the effect of coming off booze. Added to the strain of her marriage her nerves were stretched to breaking point. That was it. A smile tugged the corners of her mouth. Christ, what an idiot.

Then she heard it again. Closer.

Mackenzie screwed up her courage and spun round. It wasn't two men, it was one man, the one in the black coat from the supermarket, talking to himself.

She stepped back and stumbled on the verge, almost falling under a passing car. The startled driver pulled into the middle of the road, nearly crashing into a van in the other lane. Both vehicles blasted their horns and raced on. She felt faint. For a moment she thought she was going to pass out. Nobody had believed her but they were wrong. It was him.

He was real.

He tilted his head and smiled. Mackenzie got to her feet and faced him. 'Who are you? What do you want?'

The man in the black coat stared unblinking and didn't answer.

Mackenzie screamed at him. 'Who the hell are you?'

Nothing except a slow smile.

'Get away from me, d'you hear?'

He didn't move.

She tried to hail a passing car. Then another. When that didn't work, Mackenzie Crawford did the only thing left: she ran. And this time she didn't stop.

Day Four

Derek Crawford had no idea what was on the TV screen; he couldn't concentrate, his mind wouldn't let him. He hadn't been to work in days. Crawford Cars would have to survive without him until he got his head sorted. He'd lost control of his life.

From the bedroom, the depressing sound of his wife getting ready to meet another man slipped between the floorboards and drifted down.

He imagined her fixing her hair, adding the finishing touches to her makeup, checking how she looked in the mirror they'd bought in a dusty antique shop in Auchterarder on a sunny Sunday afternoon. And earlier – carefully selecting underwear, drawing the stockings over her slim legs, putting on high-heels. Derek forced himself not to think about what she was doing and why. He wanted to rush upstairs, throw her on the bed and make love to her so hard that leaving him would be forgotten. Except it had gone beyond that. She was lost to him, and it would take a complete transformation to win her back.

Mackenzie turned to the side and studied her reflection in the mirror, not unhappy with what she was seeing: the figure was good – even if she said so herself – and the face was still *her* face. Though the smoking would have to go. Derek ranted and raved every time she lit up. It was a filthy habit, he said. Nothing aged a woman more. And he was right. So far she'd got away with it, her skin was clear and the tell-tale downturn at the corners of the mouth hadn't arrived. But they would, eventually. So she'd quit.

When she wanted to. When she was ready. Her decision.

The days of striving to please were over, especially when she could count the number of times she'd succeeded on one hand.

She leaned closer to the glass, wondering if the lipstick made her look like a tart. And the heels – were they too high? Shag-me shoes Adele once called them and Mackenzie had laughed. The person she was meeting didn't judge. Alec accepted her for who she was and didn't insist she be somebody she wasn't.

Very different from Derek.

She shouldn't feel guilty. From the beginning she'd been honest with him about her previous life, freely admitting she hadn't always made the smartest choices, especially with alcohol. It didn't matter because by then he was already in love with her.

Derek blamed himself: the signs had all been there. He just hadn't recognised them.

After twelve months of bliss, the lies started about what she'd done that day or money spent with nothing to show for it. He'd demand an explanation, she wouldn't have one, and quarrels – often public, sometimes vicious – became a feature of their relationship. His response was to retreat into silence while his wife took refuge in drink.

They hadn't spoken since the morning after the party. Derek realised he preferred arguing to what they'd become. Ships that passed. People living together apart.

Not so long ago, their differences were minor irritations, no more than blemishes on an otherwise perfect relationship. Ironically, he couldn't remember what those differences had been. How sad was that?

The previous night, when she left the house, he'd followed her again, using the shadows of the trees lining the avenue to hide. At the end of the road, the car sat with the engine idling, grey smoke sputtering from the exhaust. From where he was it was difficult to recognise the make. He got closer. It was the blue Vectra. Like Blair Gardiner's. He'd watched her get in and the driver pull away, leaving him alone on the street, close to despair. Phoning Adele to see if Blair was home crossed his mind. He dismissed it, not ready to have his fear confirmed.

Tonight – like last night and the one before – pretence at fidelity was abandoned because it was no longer necessary. Footsteps on the stairs and the latch closing on the front door told him she'd gone. Derek went to the kitchen and filled the kettle, his hands shaking. The clock on the wall said seven-fifteen.

He would be waiting for her.

* * *

Mackenzie thought about yesterday. The guy in the black coat had freaked her out. She hadn't told Derek. What was the point? She'd intended to talk to Alec about it and changed her mind. It had been such a wonderful evening she hadn't wanted to spoil it with something that would probably turn out to be about nothing. When she got home she'd gone on the Internet and researched stalkers, surprised to discover how common they were. Most reports were about men stalking women although – occasionally – it was the other way round. She took comfort from the fact that thousands of people – male and female – had had the same experience as her. Occasionally the stalker turned out to be some jilted lover or former husband. Often the culprit was a mentally unstable stranger; sad and pathetic and harmless.

Mackenzie made a decision to focus on the positive: this was the third day she hadn't had any alcohol. The miracle was she didn't crave it. The first twenty-four hours had been rough – her head ached, she felt ill and whenever she remembered the show she'd made of herself – of both of them – at Adele's, she thought she was going to be sick. Her sister was due an apology, no doubt about that, except Mackenzie wasn't ready to face her. Not yet.

The second day was better, only shame remained. Even in such a short time clarity had replaced confusion and she was certain she was doing the right thing. Derek couldn't possibly be happy. God knows she wasn't. Hurting him wasn't what she wanted but he needed to accept the marriage was over, that she didn't love him.

Opposites attracted and so it was with them. The attention of a man, older, wiser, and more worldly than she could ever hope to be, had been flattering. Being with him made her feel special and protected in a way she'd never known. Other men were immature boys in comparison. Derek had been places and done things. Had adventures. For Christ's sake, even Adele liked him.

One morning Mackenzie woke up and knew she'd fallen for him. Within months they were engaged. She would've married right away, he'd insisted they slow down. If there were second thoughts, he'd said, now was the time. Once they'd taken their vows she would be his and it would be too late. His one condition – that they hold back physically until after they were married – had taken her aback. She'd promised to respect his wish, a promise she'd broken on the couch in his living-room one night after they'd shared a second bottle of wine, most of it drunk by her.

Slowly, completely, he'd dominated her until she was afraid she might suffocate with the intensity of it. Afterwards, Derek held her in his arms and told stories of how wonderful it would be when she was his wife. Those stories came true and lasted a year before Mackenzie realised the mistake she'd made.

It began with disagreements over inconsequential things which grew heated, difficult to put behind them. And the sex, so fabulous in the beginning, became infrequent, brief and unfulfilling. Derek found fault with her to the extent she couldn't please him even with the simplest tasks. It was obvious he was as disappointed in her as she was with him. The generosity he'd shown in the beginning dissipated, replaced by accusations she didn't understand.

Mackenzie had managed to keep her drinking to acceptable levels when she met Derek. For a long time he didn't see her drunk. But as their relationship deteriorated, she found herself reaching for her old friend. And her alcoholism was where she'd left it; it hadn't gone anywhere. Giving in to it was easier than confronting the truth.

* * *

The avenue was deserted except for a group of young girls in the distance, playing a game. It had been a sunny day and, on most windows, the blinds were drawn against the glare. Who knew what went on behind them? Mackenzie was leaving a sham marriage. It wouldn't be the only one in this respectable suburb. She dismissed the thought. Other people's relationships were their business. There was nothing to be gained by speculating. She was headed for a new life and freedom and, in case she forgot, hardly in a position to cast the first stone.

Her step quickened when she saw the tail-end of the car at the corner. Without meaning to, she smiled. Some women might disapprove of what she was doing. Others would support her, call her brave. Bravery had nothing to do with it. She had no choice, and, for the first time in a long time, Mackenzie was happy.

She didn't pay attention to the white van at the kerb or register the sound of someone behind her. When she did, it was too late. A hand closed over her face and a sweet smell filled her nostrils. She felt herself being dragged backwards before she sank into unconsciousness. The back doors of the van closed. The driver got in and drove away.

No one saw. Like a leaf falling to the ground, it went unnoticed. Mackenzie Crawford's new life would have to wait.

* * *

Alec drummed his fingers impatiently on the steering wheel. If Mackenzie was coming she should have been here by now. The last time they'd spoken she'd seemed so sure, so certain, and he'd believed her because he'd wanted to believe her. Of course what he was asking her to do wasn't easy. No matter how miserable she was, choosing to remain unhappy meant not having to burn bridges.

On the radio a band was playing live and the balance wasn't right; the bass guitar was louder than it should have been and the singer was out of tune. He dialled it down and checked his watch. A few more minutes and he'd go. The only thing to have happened in the last half-hour was a white van racing along the street, its diesel engine growling as it passed. Probably some young idiot trying to impress himself. Fine, as long as he was the only one he killed with his recklessness.

So this was it. This was the chance. Take it or leave it. From here on he was out of it. The days of dropping everything and running whenever she called, frantic and distraught, were over. Life was too short. He wasn't prepared to allow her to use him.

Alec took a final look in the mirror; no sign of her.

He sighed, turned on the ignition and pulled away.

* * *

The Baxter House
Lowther Hills

Mackenzie tried to open her eyes and couldn't; she was blindfolded. The last thing she remembered was footsteps on the pavement behind her then a rough hand across her face and a strange smell.

Now, cold metal pressed against her cheek and diesel fumes filled her nostrils. She heard the grumble of changing gears and knew she was on the floor in the back of a van – the white van she'd noticed in the street? She struggled against the bonds tying her wrists behind her and tried to call out. The gag bit into her. No words came. Panic overwhelmed her as the horror of her situation hit home: she'd been abducted.

Alec had been there, she'd seen his car. Her new life had been waiting. He'd assume she'd changed her mind – again – and decided not to show up.

He wouldn't know where she was. Nobody would know.

She writhed, kicking and struggling to free herself, driven by fear, almost choking on it, sobbing like a child. In the end, she curled into a ball and lay still. After what seemed like a long time she sensed the road rise and the van bump over uneven ground. Finally, it came to a stop. Mackenzie's terror rose to new heights.

The back doors opened and she was hauled into the cool night air. Her unseen kidnapper gripped her arm, ignoring her muffled cries. She dropped to her knees, resisting with everything she had. He pulled her upright and the gag came loose. Mackenzie's screams amused him. He laughed, slapped her face and pressed it against a wall, grazing her cheek while he struggled to get her inside.

'Scream all you want. No one will hear you.'

A musty smell and an echo told her they were in an old building. He forced her forward. Mackenzie dug her heels into the rotten floorboards as hard as she could, only managing to make him angry. He swore, grabbed her by the hair and dragged her dead weight across the floor, then pushed her, still struggling, down steps. Without warning, he let go. She fell into space and landed heavily on the ground, kicking out blindly, finding her mark, hearing him curse. 'Bitch! You bitch!'

He punched her. She tasted blood. Her abductor struck her again and she passed out.

When she came to, the gag and blindfold had been removed, her head hurt and the room spun out of control. From behind the damp walls and decaying plaster she heard scratching: rats. Mackenzie was terrified of rats.

She retched, unable to prevent it, and emptied the contents of her stomach on the flagstone floor. Bile seared her throat, leaving a foul taste in her mouth and she shivered, terrified. In the silence the sounds of her ragged breathing and her beating heart were deafening. Scared to move in case she wasn't alone, she forced herself to look at the awful place she'd been brought to, thankful he wasn't there.

Mackenzie tried to get up and found she was chained to a bed. Round her wrist a cold bracelet chaffed her skin, its dull rattle a terrible reminder of what had been done to her, and for a moment she couldn't breathe. She pulled on it with all of her strength, desperately trying to free herself. It stretched as far as a chemical toilet and no further. She tried dragging the bed but it was bolted to the floor and wouldn't move. Fear overwhelmed her. The mattress was tossed aside as she searched for a loose spring – anything she could use. There was nothing. Hope of escape died.

Someone had planned this carefully. She was trapped.

Mackenzie screamed again – over and over and over. Eventually, hoarse and exhausted, her cries faded to a whimper. Soon, even that stopped.

Day Five

Mackenzie woke up to the nightmare her life had become. How could anybody sleep at a time like this? She forced herself to take stock: she was in a cellar, shackled to a bed, with no idea why. A battery light hanging from the handrail cast a yellow shadow across her prison and Mackenzie saw a cane chair and a gas heater at the other end of the windowless room. Fungus grew on the grey walls and the smell of damp and sour earth made her vomit a second time. Mucus ran from her nose and her eyes watered. Closing them brought no relief. Vague recollections swam behind them like fragments of a terrible dream, dark distant shapes on the margin of memory.

Her mind wanted to deny the terrible reality. It was impossible: she'd been taken, sixty yards from her home, in broad daylight.

None of her family had believed her. Derek had accused her of having a lover, Adele thought she was a drunk, making it up to hurt her husband, and Gavin and Monica saw her as a needy woman looking for attention. Even Blair, who was a friend, doubted her.

Bastards. All of them bastards. Because she hadn't imagined it. The stalker had been real. But the people who were supposed to love her had treated her like a difficult child. If it had been Adele or Monica they would have closed ranks and kept them safe.

Not for her. They were to blame, they'd done this to her. And Mackenzie hated them for it. Why hadn't she told Alec about the stalker? He would have believed her and known what to do. But she hadn't and now it was too late. He'd be disappointed, though from the beginning he'd made it clear he'd respect her decision and wouldn't try to contact her. Mackenzie was as alone as she'd ever been in her life.

Hours – or maybe it was days later – a car door slammed and she tensed, more afraid than ever, aware she was completely at this stranger's mercy.

Heavy steps sounded on the floor above. A thin stream of fine earth fell like mist from the rafters. Mackenzie backed against the corner of the bed and drew her knees tight against her body.

She shuddered. He was coming.

* * *

The door opened and the man in the black coat edged down the stairs carrying a cardboard box under his arm. He was wearing a balaclava. If it was meant to intimidate her it succeeded – although she could scarcely be more frightened than she already was.

He knelt on the floor, opened the box and unpacked a carton of soup, three pre-prepared sandwiches and a coffee cup with Costa written on the side. From the bottom he took out a bottle of water, a bowl, toothpaste and a toothbrush.

Mackenzie's terror shot to a new level. He intended to keep her here. The shaking started, so bad she couldn't stop it. She spoke, fighting tears, close to hysterical. 'You…you can't keep me here, you can't.'

Her abductor went on with what he was doing. Mackenzie shouted and tore at the air. 'Let me go! Let me go! Just let me go!'

He threw a packet of sandwiches onto the bed. She ran at him until the chain hauled her back. The stalker didn't flinch. He'd known how far it would play.

Mascara ran in black rivulets down her face. The makeup, so carefully applied, was smudged and ruined. Mackenzie fell to the floor, distraught. She whispered. 'What do you want? What the hell do you want? Speak to me. Please.'

He got on his knees and used paper towels to clean up the mess she'd made being sick. Then he sat on the chair, his head tilted, observing her like a specimen in a jar. When he came towards her, she cowered like a beaten dog and drew away. His finger ran over the graze on her cheek, barely touching it. The gentleness of the gesture repelled her, degraded her in a way she couldn't explain.

There was one last item in the box. He tossed it into her lap and unlocked the padlock, releasing the chain. Mackenzie considered attacking him but realised it was doomed to fail. She was emotionally and physically exhausted: the energy to resist wasn't there.

Her dress was torn and dirty. She stepped out of it and into the grey tracksuit bottoms while the stalker devoured her with his eyes. When she was dressed he refastened the chain around her wrist. Mackenzie made a final attempt to understand why he was doing this. 'How much longer will I be kept here?'

Again, he ignored her.

'What have I done to you? Why won't you talk to me?' She screamed. 'Talk to me, you bastard! Talk to me!' She begged. 'Please, tell me why I'm here.'

Her abductor didn't reply. Before he climbed the stairs he bent to turn up the gas heater, leaving Mackenzie afraid and confused. The food and the toiletries meant he didn't intend to let her go. He'd come back. And when he did, what then?

* * *

Derek was lying on the couch in the lounge listening to the rain batter against the window when the telephone rang; he let it. An hour later, it rang again. This time he reached over to answer it and heard his sister-in-law's voice on the other end of the line.

'Derek. I called earlier. You must've been out. Can I speak to Mackenzie, please?'

She would know sooner or later. There was no easy way of breaking the news.

'Afraid not, Adele. She isn't here.'

'Oh, when will she be back?'

'I've no idea.'

'Gavin's right. I need to talk to her, get her to call me as soon as she gets home.'

He sounded resigned. 'Too late for that, she's gone off with him. Threatened she would, and now she has.'

'Derek, I'm so sorry. Is there anything I can do?'

Derek answered quietly, without emotion. 'I'm fine. I'm fine.'

'You can't be fine.'

'But I am. It's like a weight's been lifted. The last couple of years…I've been living a nightmare. Now she's finally out of my life I feel free.'

'But you love her. You love Mackenzie.'

He laughed a grim laugh. 'Once maybe, not anymore. To tell the truth I'm glad. So much wasted time. Wish she'd done it sooner.'

'When was this?'

'Last night. I had to go out to get something to eat. Can you believe it? The latest fuck-off fridge, yet it only has milk and butter in it. Came home. The house was empty.'

'Has she contacted you?'

'Not a word. Don't expect she will. And even if she did, what is there to say that hasn't been said a hundred times?'

'Do you want me to come round?'

He rejected the offer out of hand: Adele was all right, but only in small doses. Having her fuss and fawn would irritate him. 'It isn't necessary and in this weather it would be madness. I really am okay. Actually, I'm surprised just how okay.'

She wasn't listening. 'It hasn't sunk in yet. When it does you shouldn't be alone. I'll be there in thirty minutes.'

The conversation ended abruptly and Derek was left staring at the telephone.

Half an hour later the doorbell announced Adele's arrival. When he opened the door she threw her arms round him and gushed regret. Derek put his hands on her shoulders and forced a smile. 'Did you expect my hair to have fallen out? Be a gibbering idiot? Believe me, I'm okay.'

A brave try, but the bleary bloodshot eyes and the whisky on his breath gave away the pain he was in. Over his wife's shoulder a solemn Blair held a red umbrella. Blair nodded to him and they made their way into the lounge. The TV was on with the sound turned down. A bottle of Johnnie Walker Black Label with no more than a couple of shots left in it sat on the coffee table beside a glass and a can of some foreign beer. Others lay on the carpet.

Adele fired an anxious glance at her husband – it was just as she'd feared. Since the first night when Mackenzie introduced the older man as her boyfriend, Adele had never known Derek Crawford be anything other than moderate. He didn't smoke, didn't gamble; she'd never seen him affected by alcohol. Now he was drinking by himself. And who could blame him? Her sister had done this.

'You shouldn't have driven in this weather. There's a big storm coming. It's already started.'

Thunder rumbled in the sky to prove him right. He waved at the room. 'Sorry about the mess. Wasn't expecting company. Haven't so much as dried a cup in the last twenty-four hours. Can't face it.'

Adele eyed the almost empty whisky bottle and the beer cans; cups hadn't been needed. 'You have a cleaner, don't you?'

Derek drew a finger over his unshaven chin. 'Cancelled her for a few days. You know how it is. Not much point. Can I get you something? Tea? Coffee? What would you like?'

'We're fine.'

He disappeared into the kitchen. Blair shouted after him. 'Take a beer if you have one.' Adele glared at him. 'For God's sake Blair, couldn't you have asked for coffee? The last thing he needs right now is a boozing buddy.'

'You can drive, can't you? I'm trying not to overreact. He's in a bad place.'

'Of course he is. How could he be anything else? Mackenzie's a selfish bitch.'

Blair whispered an irritated reply. 'You don't know that. All you've got to go on is Derek's version.' He stared hard at his wife. 'Said it before, it takes *two*, Adele. To make it or to break it.'

Derek brought Blair a beer and another for himself before she could reply. For the first time she noticed how crushed her brother-in-law's clothes were and guessed he hadn't been to bed. 'So what happened?'

He rested his arms on his knees and shook his head. 'Like I told you on the phone. I came home, she wasn't here.'

'Did she leave a note?'

'Didn't need to. The message was loud and clear.'

'Was she still drinking?'

'That's the strange thing. As far as I could tell she hasn't had a drink since the night of your party. Made no difference, she was still determined to leave. She hates me.'

Adele was reluctant to ask specifics. Most marriages went through the odd rocky patch, like the one her and Blair were having. If it could be worked through, it was worth fighting for.

'Are you sure she's gone off with this guy? She's not just trying to scare you, being a drama queen as usual?'

Blair said, 'Doesn't it strike you as odd she just left like that?'

'Everything Mackenzie does these days is odd. She's been threatening me with it for months, heard her yourself. I should have told her to go. Instead I put up with it. What kind of man would stand for that nonsense? What does that say about me?'

Adele defended him. 'Only that you're a loving husband trying to save his marriage.'

He lifted the bottle and sloshed the last of the whisky into the glass. 'Well, I've failed spectacularly, haven't I?'

Blair said, 'I keep thinking about the guy from Buchanan Street. I mean, are you sure he wasn't stalking her?'

Derek lost his temper. 'Oh, for fuck's sake. There isn't a stalker. There never was a stalker.' He turned to his sister-in-law. 'You don't believe all that rubbish, do you?'

'No, but it's not impossible. There are a lot of crazy people in the world.'

Derek cracked. 'And your sister's one of them! Nobody understands that better than me. I told you, I followed her. She got into a car. Same again the other night. Should've challenged them, of course I should. Dragged the bastard out and beat him to a pulp. Not a minute passes when I don't curse myself for being a bloody coward. I didn't have the guts, didn't want to know who was taking her away from me. Can you understand that?'

'I can.'

Blair pushed the point. 'But was it the guy from Buchanan Street?'

Adele's expression said 'leave it.'

'Couldn't tell for sure. It was a blue Vectra.' He eyed Blair accusingly. 'Same as yours.'

He shifted uncomfortably and avoided looking at his wife.

'Three hours later she came home and went straight to bed. So don't talk to me about stalkers. The word we're bending over backwards to avoid here is *lover*. Mackenzie's left me for her lover.'

He put his head in his hands and sobbed. Adele wanted to go to him before a look from her husband stopped her. 'Let him get it out. In the long run, it'll be better for him.'

They watched his shoulders heave silently. When Derek was cried-out, Blair sat down beside him. 'When was the last time you slept?' Derek didn't answer. Blair saw he was exhausted and lifted the empties. 'Let me get rid of these dead-men for you.'

He threw them in the bin under the sink. Nobody could fault Derek's taste, though alcohol wasn't the solution to anything. He'd read somewhere that seventy percent of prisoners in Barlinnie were there on drink-related offences. For many it was a pleasure, for others – like his sister-in-law – it was an addiction, one he believed that with the right care and enough love, could be overcome. Derek had problems, no doubt about that. His wife had left him. He was depressed and hammering the whisky. But for him it wasn't a problem, it was a crutch. Useful in the moment, nothing more.

Back in the lounge, conversation had ground to a halt. Everything had been said. Derek slumped on the couch, tired and dejected. Further discussion would keep for another time. Blair took hold of his brother-in-law's arm. 'Come on,' he said, as gently as he knew how, 'Let's get you to bed, old son.'

* * *

Adele sat in the passenger seat, gazing straight ahead, thinking of her brother-in-law, fingers toying with a button on her coat. Derek was distraught, almost destroyed, and Blair realised his own wife wasn't far behind. Mackenzie was her young sister, after all. He could only imagine what they were feeling – anger, guilt and every emotion in between. Perversely, a part of him was pleased. When she was so obviously crying out for help they'd preferred to criticise.

The first words Adele spoke told him he was wrong. 'I'm not sure he'll survive. To see him so low and know my bloody sister is responsible. She has a sin to answer for. When she comes back after she's had her fun I won't miss her and hit the wall.' She turned to face him. 'You shouldn't be driving.'

'I only took it to keep him company. And I didn't drink it in case you didn't notice.'

She ignored him and went on. 'How could she? How could she hurt him like this?'

Blair kept his eyes on the road, navigating a path through the flooded streets.

'How many times? There are two sides to every story. We should wait for Mackenzie to tell us hers. Show a bit of loyalty and don't be so quick to judge her.'

The suggestion didn't go down well. 'Oh, change the record. There isn't another side. She's drinking – bad enough, in case you've forgotten – because she can't handle the pressure of cheating on her husband. Poor Derek's been getting the worst of both worlds. Living with an unfaithful drunk. No wonder he's on the floor. I could strangle her.'

He disagreed. 'We aren't sure what's happened. We don't know why she left. We can't until we speak to her.'

'Yeah,' Adele was skeptical, 'and how long will that be?'

Her husband ignored her. 'He says she hasn't been drinking.'

'Look, Mackenzie's crazy. You saw her at my party. She was drunk and vicious. Remember how she spoke to Monica.'

'Monica was being a bitch and you know it. Picked the wrong time and got what she deserved.'

She shot him a suspicious look. 'I'm beginning to wonder about you.'

'What're you talking about?'

'You've got a soft spot for her. Strange considering nobody else has. Whatever she does, it's always down to somebody else: Monica's a bitch…'

'Monica *was* being a bitch, said it yourself.'

'…I'm not being fair to her. One excuse after another. Admit it, you've always fancied her.'

'Don't be ridiculous. I've known her since she was a gawky kid with acne. Some people struggle to find their place in the world. Mackenzie's one of them.'

'Not sure I believe you.'

'Doesn't matter what you believe. She made a stupid mistake and has never got over it. Her own family won't let her. Of course I'm going to pitch-in on her side. Who else is there?'

'You're forgetting she's a married woman with a husband who's on her side. And this is how she treats him. Doesn't Derek merit some sympathy? Or is it only Mackenzie?'

A flash of lightning, then another, lit up affluent suburban Giffnock and Blair answered, his voice steady and calm. 'Your sister has had a rougher time than any of you are prepared to acknowledge. Her drinking's a symptom. What's at the root of it is more complicated.'

'*Dr* Blair is it now?'

'I'm serious. You can see she isn't happy. Hasn't been for a while.'

'And you're blaming Derek?'

'I'm not blaming anybody. All I'm saying is she isn't happy.'

Adele scoffed and mimicked him. '"She isn't happy". Mackenzie isn't happy? For Christ's sake who is? I'm not, that's for sure. But I don't get pissed and run off with another man, do I?'

Not the worst suggestion Blair had ever heard; he kept his opinion to himself.

'All I'm saying is the girl's in trouble. She needs help. Criticising her only drives her further away. She's had enough of that to last a lifetime. As far as I'm concerned if she's found a man who makes her happy, then good luck to her.'

His speech hadn't impressed his wife. She stared through the rain-spattered window, nursing her resentment. 'What if she doesn't come back? What're we supposed to do then?'

'I have no idea.'

'As for this stalker nonsense – don't know where to even begin with it.'

A drain unable to cope had overflowed, forcing Blair to slow to a crawl. He edged the car through inches of water before he replied. 'If Mackenzie says somebody was following her then somebody was.'

Adele sneered. 'She's really got you fooled, hasn't she?'

'Stranger things happen, said so yourself.'

'They do. But not because some pitiful attention-seeking woman says so. Derek doesn't believe it even though it might be easier than thinking his wife has left him for another man.'

'You're too quick to dismiss it. Right now she could be dead in a ditch somewhere.'

His wife pressed her lips together; here it was again. 'If my sister's in harm's way, nobody put her there except herself. Seems to me you're prepared to go with any explanation other than the obvious one: that she's a wild irresponsible person who selfishly hurts her family with her behaviour and always has. Dead in a ditch is too dramatic. More likely she's in a cheap hotel shagging her brains out with a man she hardly knows. And it sounds like you wouldn't mind trading places with him. Maybe you already have. You leave the house without telling me where you're going and don't get back to all hours.'

He reacted angrily. 'That's uncalled for.'

'Is it? You haven't shown a moment's concern for Derek. Or me for that matter. Instead it's poor misunderstood Mackenzie. What about the rest of us?'

He pulled the car into the kerb and turned the ignition off. 'You can look after yourselves and you do. I feel sorry for Derek, of course but, if you want the truth, I think marrying him was a mistake.'

'Really?'

'Yes, really. He's too old for her. It's a husband she needs, not a father.'

'Are you volunteering for the job?'

'Oh, for fuck's sake, Adele, give it a rest.'

She wouldn't let it go. 'Except in your case you wish I'd do you a favour and run away with somebody.'

Blair pushed the car door open and got out without bothering with the umbrella: it was only rain. 'Right now we need to keep our minds on Mackenzie. Though now you mention it, it's not the worst idea you've had tonight. If there's anything I can do to make it happen, just say the word.'

Day Six

The Baxter House
Lowther Hills

It had been the longest night of her life. Or was it day? She lay awake, afraid to close her eyes in case the rats got bold enough to show themselves. Sometimes, the scratching behind the walls seemed like it would never end. Stamping her feet and clapping her hands had worked for a while. The scratching stopped. When it started again Mackenzie realised there were too many of the filthy creatures and put her hands over her ears to block out the hellish sound. She'd never seen a rat but just thinking about them made her skin crawl.

And all the time her tortured mind demanded answers to two questions: who had kidnapped her and why? She was sure it was the man who'd followed her. But the balaclava was strange because she'd already seen his face.

The why was simple: Crawford Cars was well-known in Scotland. Abducting her was about money: Derek's money.

The victims of kidnapping were usually famous – Frank Sinatra Jnr or John Paul Getty III, not ordinary people like her. Both those crimes happened before her time but Mackenzie had read about Getty – just sixteen years old when he was abducted in Rome. The kidnappers asked for seventeen million dollars which his grandfather refused to pay, arguing his fourteen other children and grandchildren might be kidnapped. An envelope delivered to a newspaper containing a lock of hair and an ear changed his mind.

Not the best thoughts to be thinking right now. She turned her mind back to her own situation. Kidnap seemed too outrageous to be true, but it had to be. If she was right, Derek may have already received a demand for money and Mackenzie was certain about how he'd react: he'd pay whatever was asked, she was sure of it. A new terror seized her. She'd told him she was leaving. What if he'd refused to pay? The stalker would abandon her. Nobody would come and she'd die in this place.

Mackenzie jumped to her feet, pacing as far as the chain would allow, talking to herself, on the edge of madness, her fingers tearing at the tracksuit. She fought to get a hold on her fear. Pins and needles shot through her hands. She clenched and unclenched her fists to keep the cramps starting in them at bay, wanting a drink. Wanting alcohol.

'Stop it! Stop it! Don't think like that. Derek loves me. He loves me.'

The marriage was over – in time he'd accept it – yet, in spite of everything, she didn't doubt he'd do whatever she needed him to do.

That thought banished the unnamed demons in her darkest imaginings and gave her hope. Nothing terrible was going to happen. She wasn't going to be tortured, wasn't going to be raped. The stalker wasn't some crazed monster. He'd treated her roughly to shut her up. It was about money, only money. Derek was a persistent man who wouldn't give up until she was home again, safe and well. Adele's face rose up in front of her eyes, her apology already on her lips. 'I'm sorry for not believing you. Can you ever forgive me?'

Mackenzie laughed an unnatural laugh. Her reply to no one was harsh.

'No, I can't and I never will.'

She tore the sandwich open and started to eat.

* * *

Calling each other wasn't something Adele and her brother did very often. As soon as he heard her voice on the other end of the line, Gavin knew it wasn't good news. He was still pissed-off with her for being so critical of Mackenzie at the party. Their sister was obviously unhappy, maybe even unwell. She deserved support. Adele sensed his mood and began cautiously.

'Hope I didn't wake the baby.'

'No, you're all right. They're both sound. What's up?'

'It's Mackenzie, as if you hadn't guessed.'

'What about her?'

'She's only gone and run away.'

'You're joking. When?'

'Wish I was, brother. Derek came home two days ago and she wasn't there. I went to see him yesterday.'

'How is he?'

'Confused. Distraught. Just what you'd expect. Doesn't understand it. She threatened to leave him, we all heard her.'

'Yeah, but that was the booze talking.'

'Gavin, open your eyes, will you? How would we know the difference? It's always the booze talking with Mackenzie. She certainly has the men fooled.'

He snapped back. 'And she brings out the claws in the women.'

Adele wasn't looking for an argument; it wasn't why she'd called. 'Listen, I apologise for the other night.'

He said, 'No problem' and almost meant it.

'As you probably noticed I was a bit on edge. Blair and I haven't been getting along. Still aren't as a matter of fact.'

Gavin remembered his own relationship and threw out the standard line. 'Wouldn't worry. Marriages go through bad patches. It'll settle down again.'

Adele was unconvinced. 'Not sure that's how I'd describe it. Anything about Mackenzie sets him off. If I ask him where he's been he gets defensive. The rest of the time he's distracted, like his mind is somewhere else thinking things he doesn't want to share. Even when he's with me he isn't.' She laughed, embarrassed. 'Considered hiring a private detective to follow him. How crazy is that?'

Her brother didn't comment. She noted his silence and continued. 'Derek said something he didn't mention before: the car he saw Mackenzie getting into was the same as Blair's.'

'And you've put two and two together and come up with five?'

She paused, irritated to have her concern described so flippantly. 'Something like that, yes.'

'Blair's always had a soft spot for Mackenzie, he wouldn't deny it. But what you're suggesting is hard to believe. You're letting your paranoia get the better of you. Blair's a good guy. He's been a friend to our sister from the beginning. End of story.'

Adele gave ground. 'I expect you're right.'

'I know I am. So where's she gone? Any idea?'

'None.'

'Then there must've been more going on than we guessed.'

She disagreed. 'About what exactly? Derek adores her. She's lucky to have him. Who else would put up with her carry-on?'

'You're assuming it's all Mackenzie's fault. Maybe it isn't. Nobody knows what goes on in a marriage. Any marriage. And to tell the truth, Derek does try to be the boss.'

'You sound just like Blair. You've never fancied him, admit it.'

'Not true. I think he's too old for her, always have.'

'She's thirty-one.'

'And he's fifty-one. Could be her father, for Christ's sake. What do they have in common?'

'You're forgetting how mixed-up she was. Derek's helped her. He's the only one who has.'

'No I haven't forgotten, but what kind of a life do they have? They don't go anywhere, don't do anything. I mean, when's the last time they went out for something other than a meal? Any friends she had, she's lost. That isn't healthy.'

'Friends? You mean those losers she used to hang around with?'

He didn't get into it with her. Mackenzie's crowd had been kids, doing the crazy shit everybody did at that age. The lady he'd married would have been the first to appreciate their energy – where had that girl gone?

This wasn't getting them anywhere. She said, 'He's depressed and drinking. His wife's gone off with her lover. It must hurt like hell.'

Gavin mellowed. 'I feel for the guy. Though how much of a surprise can it be to him? They live quieter than we do, and we've got a baby.'

'Will you speak to him, he'd appreciate it.'

Gavin very much doubted it. 'I'll give it a day or two. He'll be feeling rough, who wouldn't be? Mackenzie might have contacted one of us by then. We'll know a bit more about what's going on.' He tried to encourage her. 'And don't fret too much about Blair. You two will be fine.'

* * *

Adele hung the phone up and stared at the wall. Far from reassuring her, the conversation had stirred old resentments she'd thought were dead. Just like Blair, Gavin had always had blinkers on when it came to Mackenzie. She was his favourite, understandable given she was the youngest by ten years. All her life Adele had been the sensible one, the responsible one: a girl who'd never given her parents a moment's worry. Mackenzie had been a tomboy at twelve, a tearaway at sixteen, and the black sheep of the family until she met Derek Crawford and straightened out. But she was loved. Adele didn't feel loved, or even appreciated.

This latest drama had come at the wrong time for her. Describing her husband as distracted wasn't accurate, he was more than distracted, he was distant. In recent weeks evasive and secretive. They hadn't had sex in two months. Neither had complained which said a lot about where the relationship was.

She glanced at the clock above the fireplace: seven-thirty and Blair still wasn't home. If someone asked where her husband was, she wouldn't have an answer for them because she didn't know where he was or what he was doing. She was tired of making up lies about their father for the boys although they were in a world of their own and didn't notice.

What kind of marriage was that?

* * *

Monica was standing in the doorway, pale and drawn, dark smudges at the corners of her eyes. She yawned, pulled her dressing-gown round her shoulders and came into the room.

'You woke me. Who was on the phone?'

He paused on the point of telling a lie – the news wouldn't go down well with his wife – and changed his mind. She'd have to know sooner or later.

'It was Adele.'

'What did she want?'

He cleared his throat. 'To tell me about Mackenzie.'

'Mackenzie?'

'Yes, she's left Derek. He believes she's with another man.'

Monica almost laughed and stopped herself. 'Why am I not surprised? Poor Derek.'

The women had never been friends and it was the reaction he expected. But the smug certainty that the fault must lie on his sister's side annoyed him.

'Who is he, do we know?'

'No. Derek came home and she wasn't there. He hasn't heard from her.'

Monica settled into the armchair opposite. 'Well, he's better off without her if you ask me.'

'I didn't.'

'You didn't...what, Gavin?'

'I didn't ask you. I guessed what your reaction would be.'

'Can you blame me? Mackenzie was a selfish brat when I met her. She hasn't changed. You all thought an older man would have a good influence on her.'

'Me and Blair didn't, though I admit for a while it looked as if he'd helped her find herself.'

Monica snorted. 'How do the rest of us find ourselves, I wonder? As for changing her, I was never convinced.'

'Because you don't like her. You don't understand her and don't want to understand her.'

Monica pushed herself out of the chair and headed back to bed; she was too tired to quarrel.

'Understanding her has nothing to do with it. And it isn't a question of liking her. Your sister doesn't care about anybody other than herself. Derek Crawford's only the latest in a long line to find that out.'

* * *

Gavin put his jacket on and headed for the door; Byres Road was a fair old hike but the walk would do him good and he needed to think.

His wife wasn't the woman he'd married. She was sad, at times suddenly overwhelmed, and – despite what she'd said at Adele's party about motherhood being the most fulfilling thing she'd ever done – Monica wasn't bonding with Alice in the way she'd expected. Mackenzie had been an easy target to help her overcome the feelings of inadequacy she was drowning in. Some of the guys at work had told him it could last as long as a year. Christ Almighty!

Adele's call came back to him and Gavin had to admit Monica was right. Mackenzie had always been hard to handle. The spirited little girl adored by her parents became a rebellious teenager then a troubled adult, who crashed through their lives like a whirlwind, so different from their other children. They blamed themselves and wondered where they'd gone wrong.

The affair with the married man was the low-point and, like so many of these things, doomed from the start. After six months, inevitably, he'd gone back to his wife, leaving Mackenzie confused and rejected. That was when her drinking took off in earnest. And if it had been a worry before, it quickly grew to be a serious concern. An anxiety that evaporated when Derek Crawford arrived on the scene.

The first time Mackenzie introduced the man in his late forties as her boyfriend, Gavin had found him uncomfortably self-assured. The meeting only lasted minutes. All through it, Mackenzie held on to his arm, clearly happy. He didn't want to spoil it for her and kept his reservation about the twenty-year age difference to himself for the time being. His sister was still fragile, the last thing she needed was disapproval. Especially from him.

Obviously things had changed.

Gavin recalled the drunken scene at the party. Guilt rolled over him: he should've stepped in. Adele wasn't the only one to let her down that night.

Day Seven

The Baxter House
Lowther Hills

How long had she been here? Was it a day, two days; two days and two nights? The dusty light was always on and she'd slept some of the time, so it wasn't possible to tell. Mackenzie guessed he'd check on her probably every twenty-four hours while he waited for the ransom to be paid. He'd been twice, the second time bringing the tracksuit, the food and the other stuff.

She looked down at the tracksuit, a relic from a charity shop, and bit her lip; the dress had been so pretty. Derek would ask for proof she was still alive. Maybe they'd sent it to him to persuade him not to call the police. The kidnappers – for some reason she assumed there was more than one – would've warned him not to involve them. Didn't they always do that? But what if he had? What if he'd called the police? Her husband was a man used to giving orders, not taking them. Then the kidnappers would know and abandon her? Maybe they already had?

She muttered questions without answers, her frantic voice echoing in the basement, searching for reassurance and finding only confusion.

'Derek's smart, he wouldn't do anything stupid.'

Her mind raced backwards and forwards over the same ground.

'But he's stubborn. He might.'

Mackenzie felt as if her brain was about to explode. She put her hands to her head and shouted. 'Stop it! Stop it! Stop it!'

The sound of a car door slamming snapped her out of it. She crawled onto the bed and waited, watching clouds of dust fall from the rafters. The door opened and the man in the black coat came down the stairs. He placed a coffee, a carton of soup and more sandwiches on the floor near her and turned to go. She scrambled towards him. 'Wait. Please wait. Has my husband given you the money? He's getting it for you, isn't he?'

Her jailer eyed her coldly.

'When will he come for me? When can I go home?'

For the first time the stalker spoke. And behind the balaclava Mackenzie Crawford knew he was smiling. 'You crazy bitch. What the fuck are you talking about?'

* * *

The bedside clock showed two-fifteen when the baby cried out. Her father wasn't asleep. The conversation with Adele had left him tossing and turning and worrying.

Gavin went to his daughter and held her against his shoulder, feeling the warmth of her tiny body through the Babygro, sensing her big eyes watching him in the dark while her mother snored gently. He padded through to the kitchen and put on the light. The feed was in the fridge. He reheated it and sat on the couch cradling Alice in the crook of his arm, holding the bottle to her mouth with the other.

His thoughts returned to his sisters. They may have come from the same gene pool but the girls were very different. Mackenzie had been a late baby, a 'surprise' his mother called her. And from the day she'd brought her home, Adele had been jealous of the new addition to the family. Of course she wouldn't admit it, probably wasn't even aware of it.

Marrying a man with a soft spot for the young teenager Mackenzie had been when Blair first met her hadn't helped and Derek's claim to have seen Mackenzie getting into a blue Vectra like her husband's had driven her over the edge. But they'd be fine, he didn't doubt it. Blair Gardiner was one of the good guys.

Derek and Mackenzie were another story; their troubles had deeper roots. What was going on with them was more complicated.

Adele liked Derek and came down firmly on his side. Maybe she was right, though from what Gavin had seen there was more to it than that. Mackenzie's outburst at the party was revealing, as if she'd wanted to humiliate her husband in front of them.

And something more, beyond the booze talking – despair.

Alice had stopped taking the milk and gone back to sleep. Her father kissed her forehead noticing the long blonde eyelashes she'd got from him. He didn't have Derek Crawford's cash. Then again, he didn't have his problems either. Swings and roundabouts, although not exactly. Money couldn't buy what he was holding in his hands.

He lay Alice in her cot and pulled the single sheet over her. She kicked it off and her father smiled. Gratitude washed through him. Unlike his brother-in-law, he was a lucky man. Derek had to be feeling low right now. He'd visit him after work and try to find out what was at the heart of it. Maybe he could help.

* * *

Gavin joined the motorway at Charing Cross. From the Kingston Bridge the silver skin of the Armadillo sparkled in the afternoon sunshine like the giant ant-eater it resembled. In the distance, a jet was making its descent into Glasgow Airport.

He'd called his brother-in-law late-morning and got the impression he'd caught him off guard; there was a wariness which could be embarrassment. After all, his wife had just left him for another man. From what Adele said, he'd half-expected Derek to be maudlin drunk. He wasn't. Perhaps he'd have been more friendly if he had.

'Derek? It's Gavin. How're you doing?'

The reply was thick with resentment. 'How do you think I'm doing? What do you want?'

He ignored the hostility in Crawford's voice and went on. 'To tell you how sorry Monica and I are about what's happened.'

'Really? Thought you'd be pleased.'

'Of course I'm not pleased. Why would I be pleased?'

'Because you were against her marrying me in the first place?'

'I wasn't against it.'

'You tried to talk her out of it. She told me.'

'Not true. I'm her brother. I was concerned about the age difference. This is something else. Everybody thinks she's made a terrible mistake.'

Derek spoke in a monotone. 'Nice to hear.'

'Look, why don't I come over, say around six? We can talk.'

'Don't see what it'll achieve. You're Mackenzie's brother. When the chips are down you'll side with her. That's how it works, isn't it?'

'Not with me. It isn't a question of sides. You're part of the family.'

The response was tinged with impatience and disbelief. 'I appreciate what you're doing but I prefer to work through this my own way, if you don't mind. No need to put yourself out.'

'I won't be putting myself out.'

Derek breathed heavily on the other end of the line. Reluctantly, he agreed.

'So six it is. See you then.'

Derek and Mackenzie never entertained. Gavin had only been to the house once before, shortly after the new Mr and Mrs Crawford returned from honeymoon, three years ago. Seeing where they lived again took him by surprise; it had to be on the far side of a couple of million. By all accounts Derek Crawford had been a rough diamond. Success had smoothed the edges; he'd worked hard: this was the reward.

The Audi A5 he'd confessed at Adele's birthday party to not being able to see past, sat in the drive. Gavin pulled alongside it, got out and walked up a wide path bordering a perfect lawn with gravel crunching underneath his feet. Before he reached the front door it opened. Derek wore a cardigan over a shirt and tie and grey trousers. Even in the few days since the party, he'd aged: his eyes were bloodshot and there were bags under them; his skin was dry and flaking and his breath was sour. Without offering to shake hands they went inside. Derek stood in the middle of the lounge. Judging by the number of empty beer cans lying around, Crawford wasn't holding it together very well. Gavin saw the cut on his cheek. He didn't ask – he could guess how he'd come by it.

Derek restated his position in case his brother-in-law had missed it. 'I'll be frank with you, Gavin. As much as I appreciate the support, your sister isn't a subject I'm keen to discuss. In fact, I'd rather not talk about her at all. She was the one who decided to leave, so that's that as far as I'm concerned.'

'I understand.'

'Do you? I doubt it. Whose idea was this, anyway? Adele's?' He shook his head. 'Why don't people mind their own business?'

'She means well.'

'And that's the most disturbing bit of it.' He set his frustration aside. 'Let me put my cards on the table and save us both some time. I realise this may sound harsh: I've no idea where she is, or who she's with. The saddest part is…I don't care.'

'Are you sure she's gone for good? Could be hiding out for a few days to teach you a lesson.'

'Yes, I'm sure.'

'How can you be, she's never done this before?'

'Would you know if it was Monica?'

Gavin didn't reply. He said, 'At the party she seemed desperately unhappy.'

Derek's hands balled at his sides. 'Unhappy! Of course she was unhappy. And she wasn't the only one. Mackenzie was ruining our lives – mine as well as her own – with drink. You saw the state she was in. I wouldn't allow it, so I was the bad guy.' He looked at the floor and shook his head.

'You can't imagine what living with an alcoholic is like. Not knowing what you're coming home to.'

Gavin remembered the anxiety in his mother's voice when he'd phoned home.

'Alcohol was a problem for her in the past.'

'She blamed her childhood.'

Gavin reacted. 'Mackenzie had a great childhood. I know. I was there.'

'Not how she remembers it. You and Adele were the original family. She was the 'surprise' – the outsider. She felt left out... the kid nobody wanted.'

'That just isn't true. Mum and Dad doted on her. If anything they gave her too much.'

'Try telling her. If you're looking to justify your behaviour I suppose it's as good an excuse as any.'

The conversation had taken an uncomfortable turn. They didn't speak until Gavin said, 'I assume there hasn't been any contact?'

'None. Didn't expect any.'

'Have you tried phoning her?'

'No. And I won't. Absolutely not.'

'Did she take much with her?'

'Nothing.'

'What do you mean, nothing? What about money and credit cards?'

Derek shrugged, irritated. 'Look, I really haven't given it much thought, although, you're right. I should put a stop on them. Fucked if I'm paying for her fun. But what she took isn't important. It doesn't matter.'

Suddenly he looked even older and Gavin didn't believe him. Derek said, 'Listen, I appreciate what you're both trying to do though, not to put too fine a point on, it I don't give a flying-fuck any more. I've other things on my mind.'

He sat down and quickly stood up again. 'I'm having another drink. Want one?'

'I won't, thanks. Zero tolerance and all that.'

'Suit yourself.'

He went to the kitchen, leaving Gavin alone. The lounge was as big as most people's homes. Money had been spent and it showed: tastefully decorated, leaning towards minimalist – a lot to leave behind.

Derek came back with a cut-glass tumbler of whisky. 'Sure you won't change your mind.'

'No. I better get going. I just thought it was important you know we're here for you.'

* * *

A box of Black Magic sat open on the coffee table. Monica lay on the couch, dressed for bed, working her way through it when Gavin came through the door. She spoke through a mouthful of chocolate. 'How did it go?'

He made a face and fell into the armchair opposite. 'Derek says he's past caring but you should see him, Mo. He's aged ten years.'

'Has he heard from her?'

'Not a word. Doesn't even know how much cash she's taken, credit cards, or anything.'

Monica put a hazelnut swirl in her mouth. 'The benefit of being well-off, I suppose.'

'"Well-off" doesn't describe it. The bloody house is three times the size of this.'

'I remember. Have to be crazy to turn your back on it.'

Gavin reached over and picked up a chocolate. 'Looks like that's exactly what she's done. Hasn't even taken her clothes.'

Monica sat up. 'What? None of them?'

He shook his head. 'I asked. He's not sure. He's not sure about anything at the moment, poor bastard.'

Monica didn't want to panic her husband. She searched for the right words and didn't find them. 'He must have that wrong. There isn't a woman on the planet who would leave without her clothes.'

He hadn't grasped the significance of what his wife was saying. 'Maybe she didn't take them because Derek bought them. Maybe she didn't have time.'

'How? What was the rush? Could've been packing stuff for days. I would've been.'

'Good to know. If things start disappearing from the wardrobe I'll prepare myself for the worst.'

She didn't smile. 'What I'm saying is she would've taken them unless…she left in a hurry.'

Gavin took his phone out of his pocket. 'I'm going to call Mackenzie. She'll accuse me of interfering in her life, but too bad.'

He tapped his sister's number into his phone and heard the continuous hum of a dead line.

'Unobtainable, how can that be?'

'Could be she's changed her number?'

'Adele might know.'

Adele Gardiner was sitting in the kitchen, watching the clock. Blair should've been home two hours ago and she had no idea where he was. When her mobile rang she assumed it was him.

'Where the hell are you?'

Gavin said, 'Is this the wrong time?'

'Oh sorry. Didn't realise it was you.'

'No problem. Wanted to give you an update. I saw Derek today.'

'How is he?'

'About as well as you'd expect a guy to be when his wife runs away with her lover.'

'Has the stupid bitch contacted him?'

'No, she hasn't, why I'm calling you. Her number's unobtainable. Has she changed it, do you know?'

'I tried yesterday and couldn't get through. Suppose she must have.'

'And I discovered something Monica thinks is disturbing. It seems Mackenzie left without taking her clothes.'

'Mmmm… that is odd.'

'Derek isn't sure but he thinks she didn't take anything.'

'Nothing at all? She'd have to be out of her mind. Then again, as we saw at the party, the silly idiot isn't thinking straight, is she? Get him to have a proper look and call me back. Blair isn't home yet. Something came up at work.'

The untruth fell awkwardly between them. Gavin let it go. Derek answered on the first ring and couldn't keep his disappointment hidden when he heard his brother-in-law's voice. 'Oh, it's you. Thought that might be Mackenzie.'

'Yeah, sorry about that, mate. Monica and Adele don't like the sound of her leaving without at least some of her clothes. As women, it feels off. Could you have another look and see what's gone?'

'Hold on.'

Five minutes later, Derek was back. 'I'm not the best judge. Your sister has more shoes than Imelda Marcos, let alone clothes.'

'So what's missing?'

The pause lasted a long time. Derek seemed to be struggling to get the words out.

'If I had to guess…I'd say nothing's missing. They're all there.'

Not good news. 'What about her mobile, has she changed her number?'

'I'd be the last to know, wouldn't I?'

'Well, it's likely she has. Nobody can reach her. I've tried. Adele's tried.'

Maybe Gavin was mistaken but when Derek spoke he imagined a trace of something in his voice that, on another day, he'd call smug satisfaction.

'Then it's not just me. Mackenzie doesn't want anything to do with any of us.'

* * *

The conversation had ended on a disquieting note. Mackenzie leaving, taking nothing, was disturbing enough without hearing his young sister resented her siblings and had done all her life. It hardly seemed possible the cherished late baby, the cute tomboy they'd all adored, was in reality a mass of insecurity who'd misunderstood her place in the family. They'd lived under the same roof – albeit only for a short time before Gavin went off to university – joking round the dinner table, in different ways winding their parents up; laughing about it together: the gang of three. To be told Mackenzie remembered herself as invisible concerned her brother because it wasn't true.

Behind those big brown eyes, demons had been hiding, telling her lies, slowly poisoning her mind. Given that, what had come later wasn't a surprise.

He didn't discuss it with Monica; her reaction was predictable. After she'd gone to bed he remembered Adele had asked him to ring her back. He took out his mobile and checked the time: ten forty-five. A bit late, except he'd promised and Adele was a worrier. She'd worry even more if she didn't hear from him. Gavin imagined her turning the news about Mackenzie not taking her clothes over in her mind and fretting. She'd turned the blue Vectra Derek had seen into proof her husband was having an affair with her sister. Crazy stuff.

She answered on the first ring, her voice heavy with sleep. He said, 'It's me. Sorry about the time. I completely forgot.'

For a moment, his sister seemed not to understand what he was saying. 'What? Oh, oh yes, the clothes.'

'Derek's as sure as he can be Mackenzie hasn't taken anything with her.'

'He must have that wrong. She's got so many clothes, how could he tell? How could anyone tell?'

'I agree, but that's what he thinks.'

'So what do we do?'

'Until she contacts one of us, there's nothing we can do.'

They'd reached an impasse. On instinct Gavin said, 'Did Blair sort out his work problem?'

Seconds passed. When Adele replied, her tone was stiff, defensive, and he realised he'd asked the wrong question. 'I really couldn't say. I haven't seen him. He hasn't come home.'

Day Eight

S he hadn't slept, not even for a second. The moment he'd uttered those words the hope she'd been clinging to died.

If he didn't know what she was talking about, then it wasn't about money. So what did that leave? Mackenzie remembered stories – horror stories – about women who'd been held against their will for decades before they'd been freed.

Not months, not even years: decades.

After he'd gone, she'd lain on the bed shaking with fear as the fantasy she'd told herself dissolved. In the aftermath, no one was spared: superior insecure Adele, jealous of her from childhood, and pathetic Blair, who'd fancied her for years but had never had the guts to do anything about it; Gavin her big brother – *big brother*, that was a laugh – and his bitch-faced wife. Too absorbed in their own little world to see how badly she'd needed them. And last but by no means least, Derek: demanding and controlling – a public saint and a private tyrant. She hated all of them.

Mackenzie made a decision: she'd starve herself to death rather than let this bastard win. She ripped the sandwich cartons open and poured soup and the cold coffee over the contents, grinding them with her heel, feeling strength return because she'd taken back control. Her concentration had been so intense she hadn't heard him arrive.

'Well, well, well,' he said, mocking her. 'You won't need this, then.'

He turned and climbed the stairs. Mackenzie screamed defiantly after him. 'That's right, bastard! Take it away. I'd rather die. Do you hear? I'd rather die.'

Sitting on the bed, the consequences of what she'd done crashed in. The spoiled food was already attracting the rats. She heard them scurrying behind the damp walls, gnawing the concrete; excited. Mackenzie had learned about the Black Death in school. The seemingly harmless nursery rhyme *Ring a Ring O' Roses* was written about the symptoms: people who were healthy when they went to bed could be dead the next morning. Rats had caused it. Centuries ago, but the fear in her survived. How could she sleep knowing they might be crawling over her, at first biting out of curiosity before one of them drew blood, and the frenzy began?

Many believed the plague was a divine punishment for sins against God – greed, heresy and fornication – and the only way to survive was to win the Almighty's forgiveness. On another day, Mackenzie would've laughed at the nonsense from an unenlightened past. Not today. Today she didn't laugh. Instead she sang, absently playing with her hair:

Ring a ring o' roses,
a pocket full of posies;
atishoo, atishoo,
We all fall down.'

Eventually, with nothing to hold on to, she took sanctuary in denial, telling herself it wasn't true. It couldn't be true. He was toying with her. Fucking with her head for fun. Playing games because he could. Cruel games. Like wearing the balaclava when she'd already seen his face.

* * *

It was morning and Blair was sleeping beside her. Adele had waited until one o'clock before crawling off the couch and going to bed, so had no idea when he'd finally come home. She stared at the bedroom window, angry and hurt and close to tears. Marriage was difficult to make work over the long haul. Counting the number of truly successful relationships she knew could be done on one hand; the excitement faded, familiarity brought discontent, the inevitable infidelity and the predictably acrimonious split. Adele had never been unfaithful, never even considered it, and, until recently, believed Blair could say the same. Most of their friends were divorced, a fortunate few tolerating the needed compromises of living together with a new partner.

If that was happiness, then she guessed they were happy.

Her and Blair were different, at least, so she'd told herself. But not anymore. Somewhere along the way they'd lost each other. The marriage was on the rocks. Blair stirred and Adele lay still. A row would wake the twins asleep next door. They weren't stupid, they'd already sussed things weren't right between their parents. The truth was, she was past caring. He rolled onto his back and rubbed his eyes. His wife's question set the agenda. 'Who is she? Who is she, Blair?'

He groaned, got out of bed without answering and staggered to the bathroom. The sound of the shower came through the wall. Adele pulled on her dressing gown and went to the kitchen. But ordinary familiar things brought no comfort. The coffee machine, the toaster, the blue and white cups they'd drank from a thousand times, were no match for betrayal. It couldn't be helped if the boys heard them arguing. Putting a brave face on it for their sake wasn't protecting them, it was dishonest – they'd learn sooner or later.

She sipped her cappuccino, wishing it was something stronger, and waited for her husband to come down. When he did, she started where she'd left off. 'Who is she? And don't insult me with a lie.'

Blair kept his voice low. 'This isn't the time.'

'Really? I disagree. It's as good a time as any as far as I'm concerned.'

'We'll talk later. I'm not prepared to have this discussion now.'

His arrogance astonished her. 'Oh! *You're* not prepared. Well, screw you, Blair Gardiner. It's happening. Where the hell were you last night?'

He wouldn't be drawn. 'When the boys have had breakfast I'll run them to school.'

'You'll be late for work.'

'I'm not going in.'

The phone rang in the lounge. Adele screamed, 'Who the hell is that?' and brushed past her husband to get to it. Before Gavin could speak his sister cut him off. 'Not now. Bad timing. Call you in half an hour.'

They ate breakfast in silence, the twins subdued, sensing something wasn't right and, for once, didn't noise each other up. Their father finished his coffee and rose from the table.

'Soon as you're ready I'll be in the car.'

Alone in the house with her world falling around her, Adele cried. Blair wasn't the only one who wasn't going to work today. She showered, felt a little better, then returned Gavin's call. He immediately noticed the strain in her voice. 'Everything alright?'

'Since you ask, not really.'

'Want to talk about it?'

She ignored the question and answered with one of her own. 'Any news about Mackenzie? Has she contacted Derek?'

'No, she hasn't and that's why you're hearing from me when you obviously would prefer not to. I'm beginning to feel uneasy about this. I think Mackenzie's in trouble.'

'What kind of trouble?'

'Don't know, but something's not right I suggested to Derek her disappearing act might not be what it seems. Maybe she's trying to scare him, staying at a friend's house. He didn't think so, though I want to follow up on it anyway. Do you have phone numbers for any of the crowd she used to hang out with?'

'That was years ago. But Karen's the receptionist at our dentist. See her whenever I take the boys for a check-up.'

'The redhead?'

'That's her.'

'Where is your dentist?'

'Battlefield Road.'

'Good, it's a place to start. Now, what's going on with you?'

Adele wasn't keen to talk about it. 'Oh, you know. Stuff.'

'Kind of stuff?'

She put a hand over her mouth; tears weren't far away. 'What I told you the other night? I was right. Blair's having an affair.'

Gavin gave himself a moment before he replied. 'I don't believe it.'

'It's true.' The next part was harder to say. 'With Mackenzie. I'm sure of it.'

'Now you've lost me. How can it be with Mackenzie? She's disappeared.'

'He didn't come home last night. This morning when I challenged him, he refused to discuss it. And another thing – he always charged his phone in the kitchen. Hasn't done that for weeks. Never lets it out of his sight. Keeps it beside him on the arm of the chair when we're watching television, as if he's expecting it to ring. Why would anyone suddenly act like that?'

'Even if he's having an affair, what makes you think Mackenzie's involved?'

'Blair's always had a soft spot for her. Admits it. What does that mean, exactly? He fancies her. You must've seen how he defends her. He's been distant for weeks. Got so bad even the boys have noticed.'

'Okay. I agree with some of that, but your conclusion's way out.'

'Is it? Sure about that, Gavin? She's left her husband and Blair's skulking around.'

'So why is he still here? Why haven't they run away?'

Adele had her answer ready. 'Adam and Richard. He loves them.'

'Sounds a bit thin to me. Think for a minute. This is Blair Gardiner we're talking about, the straightest guy I know.'

She pulled herself together. 'That's what I thought. Will you help me?'

'Want me to have a word with him?'

'No, I want you to follow him.'

He pursed his lips. 'A bit melodramatic, isn't it?'

'Maybe. Except I can't go on like this. I have to know. So, will you? Or is Mackenzie the only sister you care about?'

* * *

It was blackmail. Emotional blackmail. No others words for it. Adele knew he loved his sisters equally; he'd never given her reason to doubt it. Apart from anything else they were friends. Suggesting otherwise was twisting his arm to get him to do what she wanted. And though it didn't sit well, he'd recognised the anxiety building in her and agreed. Asking him to follow Blair – a euphemism for spying on him – was a sign of how little trust she had in her husband. Of course an affair might be possible; it happened. But with Mackenzie? No, the Gardiners were just in a rut. Adele was imagining things, taking Blair's fondness for their sister and making it into something it wasn't.

The same might be true of Derek. In the aftermath of the man in Buchanan Street and the ugly scene at the party, he'd come home, found his wife wasn't there and allowed his darkest fears to take over. Adele wasn't alone in believing Mackenzie was at fault. Monica hadn't been slow to criticise either. As far as the women were concerned, being Mrs Derek Crawford wasn't the worst deal in the world. Almost every time they met, Monica commented – with a trace of envy – on the new outfit Mackenzie was wearing; the perks of marrying a guy with too much money who was happy to spend it on the lady he loved.

Crawford was his brother-in-law but, in truth, apart from Mackenzie they had little in common. Derek was a stranger he bumped into now and again. All any of them knew about him was what he'd told them across dinner tables at family gatherings – he sold cars and he was good at it, witness the house in Whitecraigs.

In the beginning, Gavin wasn't convinced the relationship was good for his sister and not just because of the age difference. Perhaps because he was a self-made man used to making decisions, Crawford seemed determined to be in control, albeit in an attempt to save Mackenzie from her excesses. His life before Mackenzie was rarely mentioned, as if there had been no life. He admitted to being a workaholic and left it there.

Gavin hadn't responded to his question.

would you know if it was Monica?

He didn't have an answer.

A parking space opened up for him in Battlefield Avenue, close to the monument commemorating the Battle of Langside in 1586. Mary, Queen of Scots had come away with nothing that day. Gavin hoped he'd have better luck.

At the end of the street he stopped. Left or right, he wasn't sure? On a whim he turned right. Fifty yards along, he saw a sign saying DONALDSON AND DREW, DENTAL PRACTICE; he'd found it. The woman behind the reception desk looked up and smiled. The Karen that Gavin recalled was in her early twenties, wore too much makeup and stared at him whenever he came into the room. This wasn't her. The hair was darker, swept up in a bun; there was a ring on her finger and even sitting down he could tell she was pregnant.

'Can I help you?'

'Don't remember me, do you?'

Her eyes narrowed, studying him. 'Should I?'

He held out his hand. 'Gavin Darroch, Mackenzie's brother.'

Karen smiled. 'Of course. How are you?'

The accent was east coast: Kirkcaldy, Pittenweem, somewhere like that.

'Fine. I'm fine.'

'And Mackenzie? Haven't seen her for ages.'

His question had been answered before he'd asked it.

'You haven't seen her?'

'Not since she started going out with that guy…what was his name?'

'You mean Derek?'

'That's him. Hope she ditched him.'

'As a matter of fact she didn't. They got married.'

Her expression soured. 'Don't tell me that, though I'm not surprised. She thought she'd discovered Mr Right. Mr Always-Got-To-Be-Right we called him.'

'I take it you didn't like him.'

'None of us did. Sounds bitchy but the feeling was mutual, I assure you."

'How do you mean?'

She thought about it. 'Well, for starters he was too old for her. More like her father than her boyfriend. After she met him we saw less and less of her.'

'Yeah, but that's normal when people get serious about each other, isn't it?'

She shook her head and absently rearranged papers on the desk. 'He turned her against us.'

'Why would he do that?'

'We were a "bad influence".'

'And were you?'

She took the question seriously. 'We were young and stupid, so I suppose sometimes maybe we were. But that wasn't why he put the mix in.'

'Why did he?'

'Didn't like her having friends. Saw us as a threat.'

'A threat? What kind of a threat?'

'He wanted her all to himself.'

Gavin offered an alternative view. 'Did anybody consider the poor guy felt embarrassed? That the age difference was easier for him to deal with without a bunch of young women around?'

Before Karen could reply a man with a swollen jaw asked for an emergency appointment. She entered his details in the computer, told him to take a seat and picked up the conversation again. 'Has something happened to Mackenzie?'

The directness fazed him and he was momentarily flustered. 'No, of course not.'

But it wasn't the truth and a knot of anxiety balled in his stomach.

'Then why're you asking about this?'

If a lie had come to his lips he would've told it. It didn't, so he settled for the truth.

'Mackenzie's left Derek. We're trying to find her. I'd an idea she might be with a friend.'

Karen was clearly delighted. 'She's left him? Good girl. Everybody'll be pleased to hear that.'

'Are the others still around?'

'Sure, we hook up all the time.'

'Is there a chance she's with one them.'

'No, I'd have heard. We would've had a party for her.'

Karen took a card, wrote her phone number on it and handed it to him.

'When she turns up give her this. If she needs somewhere to stay we've got a spare room.' She ran a hand over her swollen belly. 'Though tell her to be quick, the offer closes in four months.'

* * *

On his way to the car it started to rain and he quickened his step. Derek had a habit of winding people up. Mr Always-Got-To-Be-Right: the nickname suited him. But he deserved credit. Their sister could be a heavy number to handle; they'd seen it at the party. Karen didn't like him any better than he'd liked her or her friends and when Mackenzie dropped out of their tight little circle, they'd resented it. Hearing the relationship hadn't worked out confirmed her opinion that Mackenzie had made a mistake.

But they hadn't seen her. She hadn't gone to them, leaving him back where he started.

By the time he got to the Peugeot the rain was heavy. Gavin got behind the wheel, switched on the wipers and eased away. Adele's idea of hiring a private detective to follow Blair had sounded crazy. Maybe that's what it would take to find Mackenzie.

At the junction, he joined the traffic on Battlefield Road and headed towards the city. Karen had been a long shot. No surprise it hadn't paid off. Okay, so what did that leave? Going to the police crossed his mind except this was Mackenzie they were dealing with; impulsive and unpredictable. Irrational might be a better word. It would be just like her to show up tomorrow, hungover and full of apologies, begging for another chance the same as she'd done most of her life.

On Pollokshaws Road a Skoda cut in front of him. He blasted the horn and swore. The driver blasted back and gave him the finger and Gavin realised he hadn't been concentrating. Frustration boiled in him. He hammered his fist on the steering wheel. 'Fucking hell, Mackenzie! You should've spoken to me, why the hell didn't you?'

Not all the anger was directed at his sister. Some of it, most of it maybe, was about himself. He'd known how upset she'd been at Adele's stupid bloody party and still let her leave alone. Blair was the only one who'd seen the pain she was in. The only one of them with a shred of decency.

Blair! The guy Adele wanted him to spy on.

Gavin was ashamed.

Cathcart Police Station appeared on Aikenhead Road and the decision about what to do now was taken for him. He bumped the SUV onto the pavement and went inside. The desk sergeant was grey and balding with hooded eyes that had seen everything there was to see and disapproved of most of it. Gavin cleared his throat. 'I want to report a missing person.'

The sergeant lifted a pen, ready to take down the details when a voice behind him said, 'It's all right, Harry. I'll handle this one.'

The face was familiar. For a moment, Gavin couldn't place it. Then he realised it was a guy from the five-a-sides. 'Andrew! Haven't seen you in ages.'

They shook hands.

'Given up the football?'

DS Andrew Geddes grimaced. 'Gave it up before it gave me up. Got sick of teenagers running rings round me.'

Gavin was at that stage himself. 'Depressing, isn't it?'

Geddes spoke over his shoulder. 'Harry's old school. Needs a dozen forms filled in before he'll answer the phone. Hates it when I stick my neb in. Winding him up's a perk of the job. Not many of those, trust me.'

'Didn't realise you were a policeman. You never said.'

'Like to keep it dark. Be surprised how it changes peoples' opinion. Going for a fifty-fifty ball it's better they know sod all about me. C'mon, let's find somewhere to talk.'

They walked down a corridor and into a room. Apart from a table and two chairs it was empty. Geddes said, 'I overheard "missing person". Tell me about it.'

'Don't honestly know if I should even be here.'

'Let's hear it and we'll see.'

'My sister disappeared more than four days ago. Her husband came home and she wasn't there.'

Geddes interrupted. 'First question: why're you here instead of him?'

'Derek doesn't want to know. Says he's done with her.'

'Is there another man?'

'Yes. Somebody called Alec.'

The DS nodded. 'In the bad old days women stuck it out. No choice, they'd made their bed. Happy didn't come into it. Not now. But, if the husband – Derek, is that right? – if he's correct, it isn't a police matter. Running out on a marriage isn't a crime, otherwise we'd all be in jail.'

'Then there's nothing you can do?'

'We'll see. When someone's reported missing they're put into a category – high, medium or low, depending on the circumstances. Okay. Start at the beginning.'

Gavin took a deep breath. 'Eight days ago, at my sister's birthday party, Mackenzie caused a scene and stormed out. She's got a problem with drink. The family thinks she's an alcoholic.'

'Somebody you don't like who drinks as much as you do, or the real thing?'

'It's real, all right. Mackenzie's thirty-one. She's been in trouble with booze since she was a teenager. Derek helped her through it. Adele knows more about it than me. Every other week Mackenzie phoned her smashed out of her head, crying, coming out with all kinds of stories. The next day she couldn't remember speaking to her.'

'Called a blackout. Not a good sign.'

'I know. Mackenzie left the party early. When Derek got home she went for him. Had a huge row. The worst ever. The next morning he heard her arranging to meet this Alec character. Naturally, he was ready to call it quits. Mackenzie beat him to it. Three days later, she was gone.'

Geddes wasn't hearing anything to persuade him the police had a role to play. Other peoples' relationships were a foreign country. A bloody mystery. Experience had soured him. His marriage to Elspeth had been a disaster he still hadn't recovered from, financially or emotionally.

'And he's heard nothing since?'

'Not a word. I called her mobile. It's unobtainable. Guess she isn't ready to talk to anybody.'

'Does he know the guy?'

'No. Mackenzie stopped drinking and started going out at night by herself. Not the first time she'd done that, apparently. Refused to tell him where or who she was meeting. He followed her and saw her getting into a car.'

The policeman was blunt: this was a waste of time. 'Of course you're concerned, this is your sister were talking about, though it's hard not to think he's better shot of her.'

Hearing the DS say it out loud it sounded like that to Gavin, too.

Geddes took a notebook from his inside pocket. 'Give me her full name and I'll add her to the register. Can't justify making it a high category. Even medium's pushing it. Have to be low.'

He clicked a pen into action. Gavin gave the information he'd asked for. 'Mackenzie Crawford. Her husband's Derek Crawford. Crawford Cars?'

The policeman leaned back in his chair. 'Really? Bought a Passat from them fifteen years ago.'

'And?'

'And nothing. Most reliable car I ever had. Where do they live?'

'Whitecraigs'

Geddes raised an eyebrow. 'Nice neighbourhood.' He remembered Elspeth and her vampire lawyer and smiled at some private joke. 'Clean him out, did she?'

'No, as a matter of fact she didn't take anything.'

The policeman hesitated. 'When you say she didn't take anything...'

'I mean *anything*, Andrew. Her clothes are in the wardrobes. Credit cards haven't been used.'

Geddes' expression hardened. No football jokes now. 'And you've waited this long to report it?'

Gavin defended the delay. 'We were expecting her to contact us. You don't know Mackenzie like we do. My wife calls her a drama queen. She reacts first and thinks later, always has. When she's drinking every other word that comes out of her mouth is a lie. She invented a stalker to cover up her affair.'

DS Geddes sat forward. 'Stalker?'

'Yes. They were in town. A man waved to her in Buchanan Street. Derek saw him. Mackenzie claimed he been following her. He didn't believe her.'

'And was this the only time she talked about being stalked?'

'She told Adele as well.'

'What was her reaction?'

'She didn't believe her, either.'

'So none of you thought she was telling the truth?'

'It was difficult. She was drunk. And she admitted the man was her lover.'

'When was this?'

Suddenly, Gavin's throat was dry. 'Not sure when she spoke to Adele but the rest of it happened the day of the party. A week ago.'

Geddes eyes bored into him.

'Are you saying…she might've been telling the truth?'

The detective stood. 'I'm saying your sister just moved up a couple of categories.'

Day Nine

The Baxter House
Lowther Hills

The decision to fight back wasn't born out of courage. It came from the need to keep believing Derek would rescue her. Otherwise –

Mackenzie didn't pursue the thought; she'd been there, it wouldn't take her anywhere good. But so long as there was breath in her body she wouldn't let the stalker win. He imagined he was the master of the situation, expecting her to cower before him, begging for her life.

She wouldn't oblige.

The bottled water and the few toiletries he'd brought were against the wall. Mackenzie washed her hands and face and brushed her teeth, hearing the chain rattle with every movement. Her hair was a mess – not that it mattered. She ran a hand through it then lifted the coffee cups and sandwich wrappers, stripped the bed and re-made it, shaking her head at the insanity of the prisoner tidying the dungeon. Lastly, she used her hands to scoop up the trampled food and put it down the toilet. Ridiculous though it was, the effort made her feel better and her will to survive returned.

The car door slamming had become the only sound from the world outside. He came down the stairs carrying two plastic bags with Tesco printed on the side. Letting her starve wasn't the plan. She got to her feet and stood in the centre of the room, ready, determined to have the first of it, speaking with a confidence that wasn't real. 'I know this is about money. I demand you tell me what's going on. When is my husband coming for me? He'll pay you.'

His eyes swept the cellar, taking in the changes, finally settling on her. Did she detect a trace of confusion in them?

'Tell me!'

He ignored her and started to unpack the food. Mackenzie spoke again. 'You can't keep me here forever. When this is over they'll hunt you down. Your fingerprints are all over everything, they'll put you away for life.'

The stalker stopped what he was doing. His head turned slowly towards her and she knew she was getting to him. That knowledge made her bold. She sneered. 'What a pathetic excuse for a human being. Hiding behind your stupid mask. Don't you remember? I know who you are.'

'Shut your mouth.'

Mackenzie taunted him. 'Take it off. Be a man for once in your life!'

She lunged at him, teeth bared. He drew back but wasn't fast enough, she caught him and ripped the balaclava away. His reaction was beyond anything she'd expected. His fingers closed round her throat, his face inches from hers, distorted in hate.

'Bitch! You silly fucking bitch! You've no idea what's going on. Forget about your husband, he won't be coming for you. And after I'm finished, he won't want you. Nobody will want you.'

Mackenzie smelled stale cigarette smoke. Light flashed behind her eyes, the room started to fade and his voice seemed far away, cursing her.

'Bitch! Bitch! Bitch!'

Unless she could break his hold her life would end in this dungeon. Instinctively she brought her knee up hard; he howled and staggered away.

The victory was short-lived. He recovered and they circled each other in the middle of the cellar, moving one way and then the other with the chain dragging on the flagstones. Mackenzie searched for something to defend herself with, but there was nothing. The stalker read her mind, took off his belt and tightened it between his hands, grinning like a maniac, certain he was going to win.

She jumped on the bed and gathered the length of chain, turning it into a weapon. It cut through the air with a swooshing sound. Her first attempt to hit him fell short; he stepped out of range and she missed. Her second attempt failed, too.

He laughed. 'You little fool. I could strangle you right here and now. Be years before anybody finds you. What's left of you, that is, after the rats are done.'

The belt snapped taut and struck her face. She screamed in pain. For a second her courage failed her as she realised how, inevitably, it would end.

The punch caught her hard across the mouth, knocking her to the floor. He towered over her and kicked her in the ribs. Something cracked. The pain was unbearable as he kicked her again. She struck out wildly with her legs, not knowing where the next blow would fall. He grabbed the chain, dragging her like a dog across the room and back to the bed, panting like an animal. The tracksuit and her underwear were torn from her and thrown away like rags and his mouth found her breasts, biting so hard they bled, making her cry out. He ran his hands over her smooth skin, and grinned as the belt struck her flesh. Then he pinned her under him and forced her thighs apart. Through tears she saw the cold look in his eyes. He hit her once more and Mackenzie's mind closed down as she retreated to another place.

Ring a ring o' roses…
a pocketful…
atish…

* * *

The cellar was in darkness. Every bone, every muscle in her body ached. Her face was sore and swollen, her lip was cut and her breasts so bruised and tender that just breathing brought pain bad enough to make her call out. Dark memories crowded on the margins of her mind, terrors old and new, ready to overwhelm her. Mackenzie didn't want to think but couldn't help herself.

The assault had been vicious and degrading. Goading him brought it sooner rather than later. Her naive assumption he'd keep his side of the deal and set her free must have amused him. Her fingers searched for the flimsy sheet, pulled it over her naked body and she lay still, despising herself for being foolish enough to imagine he'd ever meant to return her to her family.

That had never been his intention even if the money was paid, because she'd seen his face – the first time in the supermarket, the day she'd run from him, Buchanan Street, and now here – she could identify him. Her fate had been sealed when they hadn't believed the stalker was real.

Mackenzie closed her eyes and sought the oblivion of sleep. She didn't cry; there were no more tears.

* * *

The alarm went off at six forty-five and, for the first time in a week, Derek was hungry. He showered, shaved and went downstairs to make scrambled eggs. Mackenzie had rarely cooked, and anytime she'd made an attempt at it, managed to burn the arse out of the pan.

Before he left, he cleared away the last of the bottles and dropped them into a black bin bag in the kitchen. The drinking wouldn't go on. The previous afternoon he'd put a stop to it. It was time to get his life back.

Derek had made two calls the night before, the first to the woman who cleaned for them informing her she could resume her duties the next morning, the second to the gardener.

Rose Hawthorne was delighted to hear from him: the house was beautiful, she liked working there and was happy to go back; she'd missed the money, too. So she didn't ask questions. Mr Crawford wasn't a man who explained himself. He'd given no reason when he put her twice-weekly visits on hold – though she had her suspicions his wife was giving him trouble. More than once she hadn't been able to vacuum or change the bed because Mrs Crawford was still in it. On those days, she tiptoed into the room and opened a window to let some air in: the figure in the bed didn't move. Sad to watch a young woman ruin her health with alcohol.

Rose didn't drink. She'd seen the damage it could do, with her father and after that her husband before he went to AA and got help. They'd been married thirty-two years now, had three children and seven grandchildren, but in the early years they were headed for divorce. She wanted to give Mrs Crawford a hug, sit her down, and convince her that, whatever was at the root of it, it would be all right.

But it wasn't her place and she kept her opinions to herself.

Archie Campbell's reaction was more measured. The gardener had learned that, despite what they said, people didn't appreciate you if you were too available. He promised to fit Derek in later in the week if it didn't rain – the best he could do.

At ten-to-nine, Derek pulled the Audi on to the showroom forecourt in Hamilton Road, Mount Vernon, and went to his office. It amused him to see the panic on the salesmens' faces, stubbing out their cigarettes and hurriedly finishing their coffee because the boss was back. Around eleven o'clock he got a call telling him someone was here to see him.

'Who is it?'

'A policeman.'

'What does he want?'

'Wouldn't say. Needs to speak to you.'

'Keep him waiting then send him in.'

Ten minutes later, Geddes came through the door, flashed his ID and introduced himself.

'Detective Sergeant Geddes.'

Crawford stood, offered his hand then gestured to the chair across from him.

The detective looked round. 'This takes me back.'

'Really?'

'Bought a car from you, must be fifteen years ago, maybe longer.'

Crawford smiled. 'Hope you haven't come to ask for your money back.'

'Not at all. Got 200,000 miles out of it before it gave up the ghost. Traded it in to Arnold Clark.'

'Glad to hear we didn't get landed with it.'

Crawford scrutinised the officer: stocky, short dark hair, bulldog jowls, and an undisguised intelligence behind tired eyes. 'Are you after another motor?'

'Not exactly.'

'Then what can we do for you, Detective?'

'We've had a missing person report. Your wife.'

Crawford's bonhomie fell away. 'That's ridiculous. This is between me and Mackenzie. Not a police matter, surely? Understood it was your policy to avoid getting involved in domestic upsets.'

'In the normal scheme of things, you'd be right. Except we're duty-bound to follow up on some of them.'

Crawford was barely able to contain his anger. 'Who? Who reported her? She isn't *missing*, as you put it. How the hell did anybody get that idea?'

The detective's tone didn't change. 'Do you know where she is?'

'I'm not supposed to know. That's the bloody point.'

Geddes knew from experience Crawford had to be hurting. Few husbands would be keen to talk about their wife dumping them. He'd been caught unawares and it showed in his blustery response: the man was embarrassed.

'Has she contacted you?'

'Of course she hasn't. With respect, I don't think you're getting this, Detective. My wife's left me for another man.'

'Yes, so I believe.'

Crawford sat up straight. 'You're well informed.'

The policeman leaned across the table. 'I apologise, Mr Crawford, this can't be easy for you.'

'What do you want me to tell you?'

'Everything.'

'All right. Although you've obviously been told already. Mackenzie has a serious drink problem. She didn't appreciate me trying to help her, so she's found somebody who doesn't mind that she's pissed all the time.'

'Just how bad is her drinking?'

Crawford turned his cheek to show the fading marks of the cut. 'She hid bottles in the garden, all over the house. I'd get home, she'd be out of it, and I expect you've been told about her fiasco at the party.'

'I assume you suggested she needed help.'

'A hundred times. First you need to admit there's a problem.'

'And she didn't?'

'No, no. She admitted it easily enough. Swore she'd do something about it. But she never did.'

'Did you consider divorce?'

'Absolutely not.'

'Even at its worst?'

'I don't believe in it. You don't understand, do you? I love Mackenzie and, even if she doesn't act like it, she loves me. We belong to each other.' Crawford paused. 'At least I thought we did. The woman who drank wasn't her. So no, I never thought about divorce. All I wanted was my beautiful wife back.'

'When did she tell you about being stalked?'

Derek lost it. 'Ah, please, please. Can't we drop this fantasy once and for all? For the last time. Yes, there was a man in Buchanan Street, and no, he wasn't stalking anybody. Unless you mean waiting for Mackenzie to cause a scene and walk out on me.'

Geddes repeated the question. '*When*, Mr Crawford?'

'The first time was after I caught her drinking again. She tried to convince me a guy was following her in the supermarket.'

'How did you react?'

'I wanted to go to the police. She backtracked, said she'd probably imagined it. The next time was in Buchanan Street. I'd suggested a day in town. Mackenzie agreed – reluctantly – then deliberately started a row so she could leave me and meet him.'

'You think she was having an affair with him?'

'Wouldn't you if some bastard waved at your wife?'

'He waved? What did Mackenzie say?'

'Claimed he was following her but I'm not that stupid. He was waiting for her. She tried to cover it up, of course. But believe me it was her he was there for. She'd picked a fight so she could go to him.'

'Describe him.'

'He looked like…a man. Just a man.'

'How old would you say he was?'

'Oh for fuck's sake, the age thing again. Yes, he was younger than me. Is that what you're asking? Look, this is a bloody waste of time.'

'Her family don't know where she is. They want to be certain she's safe.'

Crawford sneered. 'Whatever else my wife is, she's safe.'

'And after that?'

'The last time was at the party. Mackenzie admitted in front of the whole family that he was her lover. We didn't talk about it after that and she started going out on her own at night.'

'Had she done that before?'

'Yes, that was the pattern. Whenever she stopped drinking she went out by herself. Wouldn't tell me where or who she was meeting.'

Talking about it had upset him. He rubbed his hands together, agitated. Geddes gave him a moment to pull himself together.

'How did you deal with that?'

'I didn't. She's a grown woman. Short of chaining her to the radiator I couldn't stop her.'

'You seem very sure she was meeting someone.'

'Sure? Of course I'm sure, I followed her twice and saw her get into a car at the end of the street.'

'Who was driving?'

'A man.'

'The man from Buchanan Street?'

Crawford shook his head. 'Couldn't get close enough.'

'What about the car?'

'Too far away to see the number plate but it was a blue Vectra, the same as my brother-in-law's.'

Geddes raised an eyebrow. 'Gavin?'

Crawford's lips met in a thin line. 'So it was him that reported it. Cheers, Gavin, I owe you one. No, not him. Blair, Adele's husband.'

'Isn't it possible he was just running her to her sister's?'

'I spoke to them about it. Adele didn't know what I was talking about.'

'And Blair?'

'He didn't say anything. Looked uncomfortable. Probably because I said the car was the same as his.'

'Both times?'

'Yes.'

'Yet you can't identify the driver?'

Crawford heard the implied criticism; his reply was terse. 'I can't or I'd have said so, wouldn't I?'

Geddes let it go. 'And that's as much as you can tell me?'

''Fraid so. I was concentrating on Mackenzie. Besides, this is where we live.' He corrected himself. '*I* live. Didn't want the neighbours to know the mess we were in.'

'What did she take with her?'

Crawford moved in his seat. 'It's difficult to guess. My wife had a lot of clothes, could've filled two suitcases without making a dent in her wardrobe.'

'Are there suitcases missing?'

'We have more suitcases than you can count, so again, sorry but I don't know.'

'Did she drive?'

'Not a chance. Last thing I need is Crawford Cars on the front page of the *Daily Record* when she ploughed into some poor buggers standing at a bus stop.'

'How much money did she have?'

'Whatever was in her purse.'

'Have you checked the bank?'

'No need. It wasn't a joint account. Mackenzie was irresponsible. Her behaviour forced me to keep a tight grip on her spending.'

'Credit cards?'

'I've cancelled them.'

'Then she hasn't run off with a bundle of cash?'

Bitterness salted Crawford's reply. 'Maybe her boyfriend's got a few bob?'

Geddes stood. 'Okay. Thanks for your time. Seems straightforward enough. Though I still need to interview the family and I'll need to get a look at the house.'

Crawford relaxed. 'I've been out of the business because of this. As you can imagine, I'm up to my elbows in it. But the cleaner's there this morning. I'll tell her to expect you.'

'That would be helpful.' Geddes dropped his card on the table. 'If your wife contacts you, let me know.'

Crawford's final words revealed his resentment. 'And if you do find her, please tell her I don't want her back. Under any circumstances.'

* * *

Geddes glanced out of the car window at Derek Crawford's house. Some people really did have it made. If he gave up eating and drinking and saved every penny he'd earn in a couple of lifetimes he still wouldn't be able to live like this. Maybe just as well. It would've been sore to see his ex-wife's Rottweiler lawyer persuade the judge her lazy bastard client was entitled to half of it.

A curtain rustled. Someone was watching. Before he reached the front door it opened. A woman wiped her hands on the blue overall she was wearing and brushed back her fair hair.

'Rose Hawthorne. Mr Crawford told me you were coming.'

He showed his warrant card. 'DS Geddes.'

'Is something wrong?'

If the cleaner wasn't aware her boss was missing, it could only be because Derek Crawford hadn't told her, which spoke volumes about their relationship.

'Just need a quick look round.'

The hall was bigger than Geddes' lounge, expensively furnished with floral designs reminding him of the 1980s, for his taste, twee then and twee now. Nothing was out of place and the detective had the impression of a show house rather than a home.

Rose saw his expression, remembered the first time she'd seen inside, and misjudged his reaction. 'Impressive, isn't it.' Said with pride.

Geddes played the game. 'Very. Is it hard to keep clean?'

'Not really, there's only the two of them. Different if there were kids. Not what I tell them, of course.'

'How long have you been here?'

'Best part of two years.'

'Do the wages match the house?'

The cleaner laughed. 'Joking, aren't you? Folk with money like to hold onto it. How most of them got it in the first place. Thought you'd know that.'

'I do, but I live in hope there's always the exception.'

'Well, when you find them, put in a good word for an honest working woman, will you? I'll be in the kitchen if you need me.'

Geddes strolled into the lounge. Giant orchids towered above swirly pink leaves against a beige background, and a neat pile of books, meant to impress rather than be read, sat on a glass-topped coffee table: Renaissance Florence; Napoleon's Commentaries on Julius Caesar; The History of Olive Oil. Geddes sensed he was witnessing somebody's notion of perfect. People would spoil it. Whatever he was looking for wouldn't be here.

He climbed a broad mahogany staircase to the top floor and went into the first bedroom he came to. Like the lounge below, it was decorated with the same excess, as if waiting for Alice to scramble back up the rabbit hole.

Next door was every woman's dream: full-length angled mirrors, shoe racks, bag racks and a hairdressing station. The best was to come. Off to the side, a walk-in wardrobe caught the detective's attention: hundreds of garments – some on hangers, some folded on custom-built shelves, others with the price tag still on them – dared him to guess what might be missing.

could've filled two suitcases without making a dent

Derek Crawford had told the truth. Only the lady who wore these clothes could know. Or perhaps her cleaner. In the master bedroom overlooking the front of the property, the *Day of the Triffids* theme was back on the walls. Geddes went downstairs. Mrs Hawthorne met him at the bottom. 'Find what you were after?'

'Could you look at something?'

She hesitated and stepped back, suddenly wary. 'What's all this about?'

'If you could just come upstairs a minute. I'd like you to take a look at Mrs Crawford's wardrobe. See if you notice anything she might've taken with her.'

'Don't know anything about Mackenzie's clothes. She sent her laundry out. Mr Crawford insisted. Liked a professional finish. But what's going on? Why're you really here? Where's she gone?'

'Sorry to put you on the spot. Mrs Crawford's been reported missing.'

Rose reacted to the shocking news. 'Oh my God! I knew there was something up when it was him who phoned me.'

'Her family's worried about her. We need to be satisfied she's safe. It may be she's just left her husband and nothing to do with the police. But we can't be sure until we have all the facts. Whatever you can add is valuable. You're here every week. That puts you in an ideal position to help.'

Geddes could see she was upset and softened his approach. He held up his hand. 'Scouts' honour. Everything you say is between us.'

The cleaner's obvious uncertainty made him add 'Promise.'

She smiled. 'Doubt you were ever in the Scouts.'

'You're right, I wasn't. It was the Cubs.'

'And how long did that last?'

'Not long. Got drummed out.'

'What for?'

'Childishness.'

Despite herself, Rose Hawthorne laughed and Geddes was in.

* * *

The tea was strong and sweet like his mother had made it. Geddes sat on a barstool at the marble-topped island in the middle of the kitchen and ate the digestive Rose offered him.

'The biscuits are mine, by the way. Bring them with me. Don't want you to think I'm stealing.'

Geddes answered honestly. 'Never occurred to me.' He waved at their surroundings: the outsized fridge, double-oven and the copper-bottomed pans hanging from a rack on the ceiling.

'Surely your employers can afford a couple of McVities?'

Rose saw it differently. 'Doesn't matter whether they can or can't. Bring my own. Teabags, too. Avoids misunderstandings, if you know what I mean.'

'Are the Crawfords difficult to work for?'

'No. Mrs Crawford's a lovely woman. When she's at herself she'll make coffee for both of us. We sit here and chat. Some days nothing would get done if I didn't call a halt to it.'

'Sounds like she's lonely.'

Rose realised where the conversation was headed. 'Aren't we all?'

'Why doesn't she do what you did, get a job?'

The cleaner glanced down at the blue overall and laughed. 'What? Like mine, you mean? Sticking her head down somebody else's lavatory pan? Can't see it. Besides, she had a job.'

'Where?'

'Garden centre near the Ayr Road.'

'Had?'

'She packed it in. Shame really, it was good for her.'

'When was this?'

'A month, maybe six weeks ago.'

'Did her drinking have anything to do with it?'

The cleaner lifted her cup and the plate of biscuits and took them to the sink. She came back wiping her hands and avoided looking at the detective. She'd closed down. Geddes guessed he'd crossed an invisible line. Gossip was okay – up to a point – betraying a confidence was something else. Mackenzie Crawford had been lucky. Rose Hawthorne was a friend.

She brushed imaginary crumbs off the table. 'You're asking the wrong person. I only work here.'

'The family say their sister has a problem with alcohol.' Geddes paused. 'What do you say?'

'That it's none of my business.' Rose Hawthorne changed the subject. 'Doesn't surprise me though.'

'What?'

'That she left him.'

'Why doesn't it?'

She pulled on pink rubber gloves. 'Chalk and cheese.'

'You mean the age difference?'

'No. My husband was older than me, it wasn't a problem.'

'Then what?'

'Mrs Crawford's a person who lights up a room when she comes into it. At least she was.'

'What changed?'

'That I can't tell you. As I say, I only work here.'

'Yes, but she talked to you.' Geddes pressed for an answer. 'What happened? Was it the drinking?'

'The drinking came later. Mackenzie drank because she was unhappy.'

'In her marriage?' He wanted to add 'who isn't?' and stopped himself.

Rose sat down. 'This is a beautiful house and the money's pretty good. I like it here, don't ruin it for me.'

'Finding out where she's gone is all I'm interested in. 'Why' seems like a good place to start. Maybe you can tell me.'

The cleaner sighed and stripped the gloves off. 'You have to understand, Mr Geddes, all I got was one side of the story: Mackenzie's side. He'll have a different tale to tell.'

'You reckon?'

'Of course. Mackenzie's nice, but she's complicated. Must've been hell coming home and discovering your wife in the states she got into. Sympathise with him.'

Geddes said, 'Don't like him, do you?'

The reply was frank. For Rose Hawthorne the jury was back and the verdict was in.

'Not much, no.'

'Because of what Mackenzie said or is there another reason?'

She thought about it and frowned. 'Because of what I saw. He treated her like a child. Kept her locked up in this ivory tower. Gilded cage, more like. You'd imagine a successful businessman would entertain, have dinner parties…yet, in all the time I've been cleaning here, there's been no socialising at all. And to my knowledge nobody ever comes to the house. Mr Crawford won't have it. Doesn't that strike you as strange?'

Geddes nodded.

'One afternoon she came downstairs crying.'

'Was she drunk?'

'Not at this stage, just very unhappy. Told me that before they got married he'd stopped her from meeting her friends. She'd wanted to start seeing them again but he refused.' She snorted. 'Apparently, he didn't approve of them. Imagine marrying a woman young enough to be your daughter and insisting she can't have company her own age. Bloody old fogey.'

'When was this?'

'I'd only been here a few weeks so, yes, about two years ago. After that she changed completely, started drinking. Bottles hidden all over the place. The gardener would find them in the hedges; empties mostly. I'd take them away and put them in my bin.

It was sad. On the surface she had everything. In reality she was shrivelling away'

'Did Mackenzie ever mention she was seeing somebody else?'

The question surprised her. 'No. No, she didn't, though I did hear her on the phone to somebody a couple of times.'

'What about a man following her, did she say anything about that?'

Rose sat straight in the chair, obviously shocked. 'Has something bad happened to her?' She put her hand to her mouth. 'My God! Poor girl.'

* * *

The woman behind the counter at the garden centre had the whitest teeth Geddes had ever seen. He asked if he could speak to the manager and saw her brow furrow.

'Certainly. I'll get Mr Morrison for you.'

While he waited he looked around. He wasn't a gardener and would rather poke himself in the eye with a fork than come there. It said retirement, surplus to requirements – the thing Andrew Geddes dreaded most. Colleagues counting the days, sticking it out until they could take the pension, had persuaded him there wasn't anything good down that road. The job could be a bastard, no argument there, but it was better than spending the morning in the bookies and the afternoon in the boozer. Or worse. Cutting the grass, pruning the roses, worrying whether an overnight frost would damage the marrows and mooching around places like this. Too often, death arrived early. Geddes complained about the brass as much as the next man but they'd have to drag him out, screaming and kicking, or carry him in a box.

A tall man wearing a short-sleeved shirt and the company tie introduced himself. The DS flashed his warrant card. 'I'd like to speak to you about an employee: Mackenzie Crawford.'

'You mean, former employee.'

It was going to be one of those conversations.

'How long did she work here?'

'Off the top of my head I'd say nine or ten months.'

'Why did you let her go?'

The manager rubbed his hands together. 'No choice I'm afraid. Mackenzie was a good worker and I liked her. The customers liked her. Knew her stuff, too.'

'So what was the problem?'

He glanced round, afraid of being overheard. 'Maybe we'd be better off in my office.'

Geddes followed him to a door and watched him tap a code into a keypad. Inside the room was tiny, the desk awash with paper. They sat down. The policeman took up where he'd left off.

'You were going to tell me about the problem. Was she drinking?'

Morrison toyed with a pen. 'I spoke to her more than once about turning up smelling of alcohol. She'd apologise and promise it wouldn't happen again.'

'But it did.'

He nodded. 'After the third complaint I took her aside and said I was letting her go.'

'How did she react?'

'Not well. Broke down. In the end I ran her home.' He looked at me. 'Have you seen the house? Most people who work here, and I include myself, need the money. Obviously that wasn't the case with Mackenzie. Yet she wasn't happy. Never understand that, do you?'

Geddes didn't reply. 'Who were her friends?'

The manager shook his head. 'Didn't seem to want them.' He corrected himself. 'Well, that's not strictly true. She got on well with everybody but it stayed on the shop floor. Any time the girls invited her on a night out she always turned them down. Maybe they didn't fit in with her social scene, or maybe she was shy and that's where the drinking came in. Mackenzie just did her job and left.'

'To your knowledge did anyone ever meet her from work?'

'Something at the back of my mind says yes. You'd need to ask the staff.'

'I will.'

'Were there any incidents?'

Morrison's brow furrowed. 'Not sure what you mean.'

'Did Mackenzie complain about somebody making her feel uncomfortable, maybe watching her?'

'Not to me, but again that's probably something she'd say to the girls.'

Geddes called it quits. Morrison couldn't tell him anything. He got up to go. 'I'll speak to a couple of her colleagues if that's all right.'

'Of course. Try Sylvia and Angela. They were closer to her than the others.'

His curiosity got the better of him. 'Mind if I ask what this is about?'

The DS fielded the question. 'Just a routine enquiry at this point. Mrs Crawford left home rather suddenly and naturally her family are worried.'

'Right. I hope she sorts herself out. She's a nice person.'

At the door the detective sprung perhaps the most telling question of all. 'Would you take her back?'

The manager found something interesting to watch over the policeman's shoulder.

'Honestly? Because I liked her, I let the drinking go on longer than I should.'

'Is that a yes or a no?'

He grimaced. 'Sorry. I'd have to think about it.'

* * *

Gavin Darroch stood in the middle of his lounge. What he was about to say wouldn't be popular and he was nervous. Adele, Blair and Monica waited for him to begin. He cleared his throat. 'You're wondering why I asked you to come. Okay, long story short, I've contacted the police about Mackenzie.'

The bombshell exploded in silence.

Adele's face was taut with anger. When she found her voice, she said, 'How dare you. How dare you, Gavin! We know what's happened. Mackenzie bloody well told us, or have you forgotten? She admitted she had a lover and screamed she was leaving Derek. Who, by the way, is her husband.'

He tried to justify himself. 'Fine, except she didn't take anything with...'

His sister cut him off. 'I don't care what she took and what she didn't take. It doesn't matter She's gone off with another man. Derek's the one who should decide if the police need to be called. Derek. Otherwise known as the injured party. Can't believe you did that without talking to the rest of us. She's my sister too.'

Monica said, 'Wouldn't have imagined domestic upheavals were much of a priority unless violence is involved. Not a crime otherwise. Did they take it seriously?'

'Serious enough to put her name on the Missing Persons Register.'

Adele wasn't impressed. 'Don't they have better things to do?' She made a dismissive noise. 'For years you ignored her existence. Now you suddenly morph into Superbrother.'

'Not true. And unlike you I've never been jealous of her. It's staring out of you.'

'That's a bloody lie. She's spoiled and selfish, and because you don't like Derek you don't want to admit it.' Adele let it all out. 'A sorry excuse for a brother you turned out to be. Mackenzie isn't here to tell you, so I'll say it for both of us. But what's new? When Mum and Dad needed you, you were missing. Now you're riding to the rescue like a bloody knight in bloody shining armour.' She dropped to one knee and held out her arms. 'My hero! Don't make me laugh.'

Monica defended him. 'That's not fair. Gavin's always been there for you and Mackenzie. He was doing what he thought was right. You're convinced there's nothing to worry about, what if there is?' She spoke to her husband. 'What did they say?'

'I met a detective sergeant I know from playing five-a-sides. His attitude was the same as Monica's, not much interested until I told him she'd left everything behind. Changed pretty sharp when he heard that.'

Blair said, 'And where is it now?'

'Already questioned me. He'll want to interview all of you.'

Adele mocked Blair. 'No use asking what you think, is there darling? I'll bet the idea of Mackenzie with a lover makes you sick. Well, get used to it, because that's the reality.'

He didn't respond and kept to the purpose of the meeting. 'For what it's worth, I support Gavin. It's been five days. Mackenzie hasn't contacted any of us. That feels wrong. Getting the police in on it makes sense.' He glanced at his wife. 'Adele could be spot-on, but why take a chance? We've waited long enough. As for Derek, from what he told us when we visited him, he doesn't care if he never saw Mackenzie again. Good riddance, so far as he's concerned.' Blair ran a hand through his hair. 'I agree Gavin should've discussed it though maybe that wouldn't have been the best thing. I mean, listen to us. He took the action he thought was justified. We'll live with the consequences. The question is: is Mackenzie okay? If the answer is yes, it won't bother me where she is or who she's with.'

His wife applauded sarcastically. 'Nice speech. Pity I don't believe it.'

Monica tried to change the subject. 'What's this policeman friend called?'

'Andrew Geddes. And he's not a policeman, he's a CID detective. A good guy. Imagine he's good at his job, too. Bloody awful at football.'

Nobody laughed.

Monica got up. 'Anybody for coffee, I'm having some?'

Before they could reply, the kitchen door opened and Derek Crawford barged in. His eyes ran over the group and settled on Gavin. None of them had ever seen Derek out of control. His eyes were wild and he was breathing heavily.

'Who the hell do you think you are, Darroch? Do you realise what you've done? Do you have the slightest notion?'

'What's wrong, Derek?'

'Had a visitor this morning, thanks to your brother. A copper. Everybody in the fucking showroom saw him.'

Gavin tried to apologise. 'I understand how you feel. Adele thinks I overstepped the mark. If so, I'm sorry. But Mackenzie's my sister and you said you were out of it. Somebody has to look out for her. No offence was intended, honestly.'

Adele said. 'No wonder you're upset, it's a bloody disgrace. Must be sorry you ever met this family!'

Blair butted in, 'Gavin was concerned. Surely we can all understand that?'

Derek directed his anger at him. 'What about you? You're the one the police should be talking to. You bastard!'

'Me?'

'Yeah! The car Mackenzie got into was the same as yours. I saw it.'

Blair reacted. 'The same as mine. But not mine. There's a big difference.'

Derek's fists balled at his sides. 'Of course you deny it. Wouldn't expect anything else, especially in front of your wife.'

Adele's cheeks burned. Having their marital problems publicly discussed by someone else mortified her, but it was what she already believed.

Blair said, 'Leave Adele out of this. It isn't true and I object to you claiming it is. If you thought the car was mine why wait 'til now to challenge me about it? Wasn't the guy in Buchanan Street supposed to be Mackenzie's lover? They're queuing round the block according to you.'

Derek grabbed his brother-in-law by the throat, threw him to the floor and started hitting him. 'You bastard! You barefaced lying bastard. She got into your car. I saw her! Where is she?'

Gavin prised his hands free, one finger at a time, forcing him to release his grip. In the middle of the room Derek snarled and panted, eyes blazing. 'We all know how you feel about her. She's with you. Tell the truth, Adele deserves that much.'

Blair got to his feet; there was blood on his shirt. 'What the hell's got into you, Crawford? Mackenzie's left you. And not before time. I don't blame her. Try asking yourself why. You saw her getting into a car? Well it wasn't *my* car.' He shot an angry look at his wife. 'I should be so lucky.'

Adele burst into tears, in the next room Alice started crying too, and Gavin realised his family had taken dysfunction to a new level. There was no way they could recover from this.

He said, 'Fighting amongst ourselves won't get us anywhere. Let's all calm down and figure this thing out.' He appealed to his brother-in-law. 'Blair, please, we're worried sick. If you know where Mackenzie is, for God's sake tell us.'

Blair rubbed the bruise already forming on his throat, scanning the faces waiting for his answer. These people were his family yet their minds were made up: Monica, frank blue eyes fixed on him; Derek, tense, poised to attack again; and Adele – his wife – refusing to look at him, convinced he was involved in her sister's disappearance.

He lifted his jacket. 'Even you, Gavin. Even you.'

Day Ten

Eventually she had to sleep, she couldn't help herself. And in her dreams Mackenzie saw the little girl she'd been, smiling and carefree. Her parents were there, forever young, her mother laughing, her father holding her hand, lending her his strength. He spoke but the words were lost. They didn't matter; he was close and she was safe.

Something touched her breast – once, then again. Reluctantly, she felt herself lifted through the subterranean plateaus to the surface.

The rat on her chest didn't run away. It wasn't afraid. Unfamiliarity made it bold enough to explore her through the tracksuit top, sniffing the flesh beneath. For half a second they stared at each other and she saw the rodent's pink ears and black eyes. Mackenzie screamed and felt the claws dig into the cloth before it leapt from the bed and disappeared behind the wall with the others.

The dream was over but the nightmare was still going on.

When the shaking finally stopped she stared at the ceiling. Apart from her ragged breathing, the silence in the cellar was absolute. But they were there. Waiting for her to become weak. Then it would take more than screaming to make them run away.

Ring a ring o' roses
a pocket full of posies

Coughing was agony and already a fever was taking hold. Mackenzie accepted her situation was hopeless – nobody was coming to rescue her. She'd been a fool to believe otherwise and an even bigger fool to blame everybody else for the mess she'd made of her life. Derek and Gavin and Adele weren't responsible. She was the one who'd refused to face the facts. And the facts were undeniable.

She was an alcoholic, had always been an alcoholic; would always be an alcoholic.

She'd been angry at Derek for trying to control her drinking. And yes, he'd taken decisions which could only be made by her, but she'd allowed it. Her agreement was intended to placate him and, more importantly, it meant she wouldn't have to give up completely. Two glasses were better than none. Except, of course, they weren't and never would be, she could see that now. All they'd done was feed the craving, keeping alive a need that couldn't be satisfied. Her illness had progressed to the point where she lived for the next drink and the one after that. Everything and everyone came second. Mackenzie was addicted.

Her behaviour had estranged the people who loved her. She'd lost their trust. Adele, especially in the early days, had encouraged her to get help, even offered to take her to an AA meeting. Mackenzie was appalled at the suggestion and wouldn't consider it. She liked to drink and occasionally took too much. Didn't most people? She didn't have a problem. Or if she did, so did half the world.

Adele didn't raise the subject again.

Gavin had never pressured her, apart from once when he'd taken her for coffee and a 'chat'. "Did she know she could come to him any time?" Well-meant but naïve. Would Monica welcome him bringing his sister's problems into their lives? Like hell! Not a chance. And it would end in a lecture, these things always did. Why couldn't they just leave her alone?

One by one, as the promises to quit were broken, Adele had given up. Her drunken performance at the birthday party – stupidly claiming the man following her was her lover and screaming she was leaving Derek – had shocked and embarrassed them. Now they'd assume their little sister had carried out her threat and go on with their lives. What else was there for them to do?

It had taken being abducted to reveal the truth.

Thank God her parents weren't alive to see how far their youngest child had fallen; she'd hurt them enough.

Derek would survive. In time he'd marry again, someone better suited to him, a partner who didn't disappoint him like she had, who lived up to his expectations. Maybe the new woman would make him happy. Maybe there would be children. Derek had wanted a family, she was the one who'd been against it. Now, in this dank dungeon, she understood why – she'd been afraid to commit to the marriage. Somewhere deep inside she'd known she wasn't fit to be a wife, let alone a mother.

So many amends to be made. So much to apologise for.

None of it would happen because she was going to die in this awful place. They would never learn what had become of her. Mackenzie sobbed herself to sleep, crying for the new life Alec had talked about, for the people she'd hurt and the child she would never know.

A noise startled her and she imagined the rats were coming back. She was wrong: it was the cane chair scraping on the flagstones. He was there. In its own way worse than anything. Mackenzie had no idea how long he'd been in the basement and braced herself for another attack.

But it didn't come. He just sat there in his black coat, staring at her for the longest time. After a while he got up and left.

* * *

DS Geddes spoke to the women the manager had identified as knowing Mackenzie Crawford best. They were around the same age and both agreed Mackenzie had been lovely to work with. 'So cheery. You'd never guess she had money. Not a bit flash and didn't mind mucking in.'

The detective asked about outside of work. Sylvia said, 'No, she didn't come out with us. I reckon it was because of her husband. We were sure she wanted to but she always seemed to have a previous arrangement.'

The next question was delicate. Geddes met it head-on. 'What about her drinking? Did it cause problems?'

Angela answered. 'Not really, though you could understand why Mr Morrison had to let her go. I got the impression things weren't great at home.'

'Did she ever mention anybody watching her?'

'She was a good-looking girl. Lots of men tried to chat her up. She'd have none of it.'

'So she didn't complain about being harassed?'

'Not to me. How about you, Sylvia?'

Sylvia shook her head. 'Mind you, we do get some creeps in here. Is she okay? Why are you asking these questions?'

Geddes stuck to his line. 'Routine enquiry.'

Ten minutes later, he was done. Mackenzie's former colleagues had added little to what the manager had told him. She'd been as much of an enigma to them as she was to her family. Except, unlike her family, they didn't disapprove. The consensus: she'd been pleasant enough but for reasons she hadn't shared wasn't interested in being friends and politely turned down their social overtures, coming and going without giving herself away. They were pressed to say anything more illuminating than that she'd been '" – lovely to work with – "'.

Whatever that meant.

A picture was coming together of a woman who hadn't kept in contact with old friends and avoided making new ones. Geddes had hoped he'd hear something he hadn't as yet been told and was disappointed.

Back in the city he picked up PC Emily Lawson from the station. Lawson was delighted. She'd been a fan of DS Andrew Geddes long before she ever met him. His reputation in the CID was well-known. He'd put away serial child-killer Richard Hill and helped bring down Jimmy Rafferty, the head of the infamous East End gangster family. Why he was still a DS was a mystery.

The constable had worked with him once before, when Glasgow councillor Tony Daly was found hanging from a bridge in Kelvinside. They'd visited the dead man's sister and Lawson was impressed by the detective's empathy. Behind the sometimes gruff exterior was a decent guy.

In the car, he explained where they were going. 'Could be a wild goose chase. Probably is. Derek Crawford's wife has dropped out of sight. The family hasn't heard from her and they're worried.'

The name rang no bells for the PC. 'Crawford. Should I know him?'

'Know of him, maybe. Crawford Cars. Showrooms all over the place. More likely than not she's done a runner with another man. Signs are there. Even admitted there was someone else.'

'So, with respect Sir, what's that got to do with us?'

Geddes cursed at the driver dawdling in front, keeping within the speed limit. 'Come on, come on. Hurry up or get out and fucking walk.' Lawson stopped herself from laughing out loud.

He shook his head. 'Makes you wonder what some of these people are smoking.'

She repeated her question. Geddes answered. 'Didn't take anything with her.'

'Nothing?'

'Far as her husband can tell, not a stitch. And in the weeks leading up to her disappearing Mrs Crawford claimed she was being followed.'

'I see.'

'Wish I did. But throw in a drink problem and a history of attention-seeking and you'll understand why nobody believed her. Nevertheless, it deserves looking into.' He flashed a grim smile at the passenger seat. 'Alkies are people too, eh?'

There was no answer to that.

'We'll see what her sister makes of it. That's why you're here.'

They turned off Great Western Road, parked and got out. Gavin Darroch's wife would be expecting them. The first thing the detective noticed was the contrast between the grass here and at Crawford's house – these people didn't spend their Sunday afternoons in garden centres. Geddes liked them already.

The DS knocked the door and waited. It opened and a dark-haired woman cradling a baby in her arms stared at him with tired eyes. The detective didn't have kids, not something he regretted; he doubted he'd have enjoyed the experience.

'Mrs Darroch. DS Geddes – Andrew. This is PC Lawson.'

'Monica.'

Inside, the living-room smelled of 'baby'. Apart from a pile of nappies on the couch it was neat. Monica said, 'Alice's almost asleep. She'll go down in a minute and we can talk, though I'm not sure what I can tell you. Would you like tea?'

Geddes declined. 'Gavin's told you why we're here?'

'Yes. How do you two know each other again?'

'From the five-a-sides.' He grinned the grin Lawson had seen in the car. 'Last time I played against him he tried to break my leg.'

Monica smiled and Geddes said, 'Just a few questions, if that's okay?'

'He's worried and I think it's my fault.'

'Why?'

'Hold on.' She left the room and came back a minute later without the baby. 'Best time of the day. I sleep when Alice sleeps.' She made an exasperated face. 'At least, that's the plan. Doesn't always work out.'

'Sorry. We'll make it quick. You were telling me why Gavin was worried.'

'It started when Derek told him he was as sure as he could be Mackenzie hadn't taken anything with her. That just didn't ring true to me. Mackenzie loved clothes, especially if they had designer labels. Everything she wore had a designer label.'

'I've seen her wardrobe.'

'More than I have. We've only been in their house once, three years ago when they came back from honeymoon.'

'So you weren't close?'

Monica directed her reply to the constable as if she would understand. 'They're not the kind of couple you can get close to.'

'Why's that?'

'A few reasons. We don't fit Derek's idea of socially acceptable – not upwardly mobile enough for him, and Mackenzie's drinking got in the way. But, and this is where I disagree with Gavin, he believes something bad has happened to her. And while I was the first to say that leaving without taking her clothes was odd, I absolutely don't.'

'Why so sure?'

Monica got up and started folding the nappies. 'Gavin has a selective memory when it comes to his younger sister.' She paused. 'Mackenzie's a drama queen and always has been. I suppose she discovered creating a scene got her what she wanted when she was a child.'

'And what did she want?'

Monica didn't have to think about it. 'What all drama queens want. Attention.'

Geddes made no comment. 'Tell me about her drinking. In your view does she have a problem?'

'Derek and Adele are best placed to answer that one. We don't see much of them. Anytime we do she overdoes it. Everybody in the family's convinced Mackenzie has a problem with alcohol. Although, now and then when she stops, she's a completely different girl. All I know is she's too fond of the bottle.'

'Gavin said the birthday party was a disaster.'

Monica frowned. 'One way to put it. Don't feel great about my part in it. All I seem to be able to talk about these days is babies. Drives Gavin mad.'

'What's wrong with that?'

'It's a sore point with Mackenzie and I went over-the-top. Deliberately.'

'Why?'

Her reply was frank. 'Derek and Mackenzie left the christening after the service. Couldn't get away quick enough. You'd expect an aunt to show some interest in her only niece, wouldn't you? Mackenzie's been to see Alice once, in the hospital.'

'You resented that?'

'I did, yes. I wish I'd kept my mouth shut because that's what set her off. Gavin wasn't pleased with me.'

'What did she say?'

'Christ! What didn't she say? Derek was telling us about the row they'd had in Buchanan Street. She'd announced she was leaving him. Apparently, that's a regular thing. A guy waved at her. Derek saw him. Mackenzie claimed he was following her.'

'And?'

'Mackenzie overheard and went mental. Lost it completely. Screamed the bloody house down and admitted he was her lover.'

DS Geddes clarified the point. 'She definitely said he was her lover?'

'Oh, yes, she said it all right. Added some comment about having to fuck to get a baby, like she wanted to hurt Derek.' Monica shook her head. 'It was vicious and humiliating. Everybody felt for him.'

'Could've been the booze talking?'

'Pretty convincing, though.'

'Sounds like a marriage made in hell.'

'Does, doesn't it?'

Geddes had a final question. 'Why did Derek put up with it?'

She shrugged. 'Loves her, God help him. Mackenzie only has to mention she's interested in something and he buys it. Gavin thinks he's too old for her, too set in his ways, and it's true he likes things the way he likes them. But her carry-on...doubt a younger man would stand for it.'

Geddes gave her his card. 'Still got her sister and her husband to speak to.'

'That should be interesting.'

'Why?'

'Adele's very much in Derek's camp and Blair...'

'What about him?'

She hesitated. 'Let's just say, he isn't.'

* * *

DS Andrew Geddes had been on the force for more than twenty years. He liked being a policeman. Catching criminals wasn't difficult, more often than not they caught themselves. Even the smartest eventually made a mistake. His job was to be there when they did.

'Domestics' were something else again, complicated and unpredictable, married couples especially. On Friday night a wife accuses her husband of assault, calls 999 and has him arrested. By Monday morning she remembers the whole thing differently, claims it was all a misunderstanding, blaming her black-eye on falling over the cat. Geddes had seen people who'd been tearing the face off each other three days earlier leave court hand-in-hand, like young lovers reunited.

Blood was thicker than water, even when it was running down the wall.

Geddes turned the ignition off. 'You've got brothers and sisters, Lawson, if I remember right.'

'Two of each.'

'How do you get on with them?'

'Fine. I'm the runt of the litter. They all feel responsible for me.'

Geddes nodded. 'Hear about the Irish girl who couldn't understand why her brother had three sisters and she only had two? Never mind.'

The gold nameplate read B GARDINER. He knocked the door and waited. Across the road, grey clouds gathered in the sky above the Mount Florida Bowling Club; they'd be lucky to get a game in today. Apparently, Adele and Mackenzie had been at odds with each other most of their lives, in Geddes' experience, par for the course. He wondered how that would influence what he was about to hear.

A minute later he had his answer. Adele Gardiner bristled with hostility, her opening statement summing her feelings up. 'This is a piece of bloody nonsense. I'm sorry police time is being wasted on it.'

Geddes introduced PC Lawson and morphed into diplomatic mode. 'You know your sister better than almost anybody. I'm sure you're right. Just a few questions if you don't mind, Mrs Gardiner.'

It would take more than that to mollify her. 'Gavin had no right to involve you. It wasn't his place.'

'He was concerned.'

Adele folded her arms and glanced anxiously at her watch. 'Mackenzie specialises in worrying folk. Always has. As for Gavin, he can shove his concern. Where was he while she was breaking our mother's heart?' She answered her own question. 'Messing around in London. Before that, Edinburgh. Never there when she was acting-out. He doesn't realise this is who Mackenzie is.'

Geddes let her get it out before he tried to have a conversation – she was going to anyway.

'There was an incident at your birthday party.'

'An incident?' She scoffed. 'Fiasco would be a better word.'

'What happened?'

'Nothing we haven't seen before. She showed up the worse for wear and – thanks to my husband – drank three times faster than anybody else.'

'Is he here?'

'Not yet.' Adele flushed and the detective realised her antagonism wasn't about him. At least, not only about him. 'He should be but he isn't.'

'We were hoping to interview both of you. Are you expecting him?'

The tone revealed her contempt. 'I really haven't the slightest notion where Blair is. Much as it pains me to say it, I really don't care.'

She was wound-up and defensive. Geddes didn't believe her. Adele flashed a humourless smile, there and gone in a second. 'You'll have to make do with me, I'm afraid.' Her lip quivered; the mask slipped. 'What must you think of us?'

Geddes coughed into his hand and brought out his notebook. He hadn't written much in it.

'Maybe he'll arrive before we're finished, failing that we'll catch up with him.' He opened the book. 'As I said just a few details to confirm. You were going to tell me about the party.'

Adele thought out loud. 'The party. The bloody party. Wish I'd never bothered. By the time Mackenzie was finished causing a scene, nobody was in the mood to eat. She was looking for a fight the minute she came in the door. Monica said something stupid.'

'What about?'

'Babies, of all things. Mackenzie reacted and it went downhill from there. Gave us a pretty graphic description of her and Derek's sex life we could've done without, then made insinuations about Monica and Gavin. It was ugly and unnecessary. On her way to the toilet she spilled her drink.'

'Did her husband say or do anything to stop her?'

'Derek tried. She ignored him. It was embarrassing. I asked him how he put up with it and he told us about the row they'd had in Buchanan Street. Sounded awful. I felt for him. We all did.'

She glanced at her watch again and rubbed her hands together, agitated.

Geddes said, 'According to Derek she claimed the man he saw was stalking her.'

'Oh, that. It's a cock-and-bull story.'

'You seem very sure.'

'A hundred percent. Only lasted two minutes before the truth came out he was her lover.'

'Then you didn't believe it?'

'Not for a second.'

'Why not?'

'Mackenzie's an attention-seeker.'

'Really?'

'Absolutely. Not happy unless she's the centre of everything. Part of the problem. Mum and Dad were great parents but instead of nipping it in the bud, as they should have, they encouraged it. Derek's paying the price.'

'Was this the first time Mackenzie had claimed she was being followed?'

'No. She told me one night when she was drunk.'

'What was your reaction?'

'Called her the next day. She couldn't remember even speaking to me, so I let it go.'

'Gavin says the family thinks alcohol is at the root of the problem. Is that your opinion, too?'

'My sister needs help. It hurts me to say this, but she's unstable.'

Geddes didn't respond. 'Can I ask your opinion of her leaving her clothes behind?'

'Well, she'd got so many bloody clothes we can't be sure she did. Maybe she just wants to draw a line. I mean, she hasn't contacted a single one of us. And she's changed her mobile number so we can't contact her.' Adele didn't hold back. 'Swanning off with the next fool while we're left to clean up her mess. I'm furious with her.'

Geddes glanced across at Lawson, remembering the conversation outside.

'And what about the car Derek Crawford saw her get into? I believe it's the same make as your husband's.'

Adele stiffened. The bristling came back. 'So I'm told.'

'It occurred to me he might be bringing her to visit you.'

She dismissed any notion of sisterly togetherness. 'Don't know where she was going. I can assure you, it wasn't here.'

'Can you confirm if it was your husband's car?'

'You'd have to speak to him about that. I'd be the last to know.'

Geddes realised he'd touched a nerve. He stood and handed her a card. 'Tell him to give me a call. I need to speak to him urgently.'

'*Urgently?* Surely you aren't taking this seriously? It's a private matter. Nothing to do with the police. And I'd appreciate if we were allowed to sort this out by ourselves.'

Geddes ignored the plea; it wasn't happening. 'As I say, if you ask your husband to contact me so we can eliminate him from our enquiries.'

She walked them to the door. 'Should charge her with wasting police time.'

It was starting to rain. Geddes turned up his collar. 'Thanks, Mrs Gardiner. We'll be in touch.'

The women they'd spoken to were agreed Mackenzie Crawford was troubled. And it was obvious the missing woman – if indeed she was missing – had caused serious division in her family. In the car, Geddes fastened his seatbelt. 'What did you think?'

Lawson said, 'I'm luckier than I realised.'

* * *

Gavin Darroch saw the caller ID on his mobile and guessed what was coming. He wasn't wrong. Anger poured down the line. His sister didn't hold back. 'You must be pleased with yourself, you really must.'

' What's happened?'

'Your policeman pal came round. *Andrew.* Nice man.' The sarcasm was bitter and leaden. 'Asking about the party and the nonexistent stalker.'

'Told you he was coming. He spoke to Monica, too. What's the problem?'

Her brother's naivete inflamed Adele. 'Thanks to you this family's being dragged through the mud on the strength of a drunken fairytale.'

Gavin dismissed the assessment. 'You're overreacting. Nobody's being dragged through anything.'

Not clever. He'd lived long enough to have learned that telling a female she was overreacting wasn't a great idea. He ignored the sharp intake of breath at the other end of the phone and ploughed on, digging the hole deeper. 'Not getting along with your partner's one thing. But this! It's not rational.'

Adele seized on the statement and beat him with it. '"Not rational". Exactly what I've been saying. We're dealing with a child in a woman's body. Normal goes out the window. We don't know what state she was in when she left.'

Gavin spoke calmly. 'Then shouldn't we find out? Don't we owe her that much? Doesn't it make sense to do whatever we have to, to be sure Mackenzie's all right? What's Blair's thinking?'

The white heat in Adele's voice turned to ice. 'I haven't a clue.'

'What did he say to Andrew Geddes?'

Silence.

'He did speak to him, didn't he?'

She faltered. 'That's why I'm phoning. You caused this mess so you can bloody well clean it up. Blair hasn't been home and *your policeman* needs to eliminate him from his bloody enquiries.'

She burst into tears.

'I'm sorry. I'm only trying to do the right thing.'

'The right thing!' She almost choked on her anger. 'The right thing for Mackenzie, maybe, *not* for me, Gavin. Never for me. But why am I surprised? It's always been that way.'

'That's just not true…'

She interrupted. 'Not true! I asked you to find out what Blair was up to. You said you would, but you haven't.'

'I will. I promise I will.'

Her voice cracked. 'Don't bother, it doesn't matter. Nothing matters.'

'Adele…'

'Don't "Adele" me. You'd listen if it was Mackenzie. She's got you all fooled with her candle in the wind routine.'

'So where is Blair?'

'I don't give a damn where he is.'

'Have you contacted his office?'

The anger returned. 'I haven't, and I don't intend to. I told you it was your mess. You find him. Blair Gardiner isn't the "good old Blair" you think he is and it's about time you realised it.'

* * *

The men walked into a deserted Cathcart police station and approached the officer on the desk. One of them, the one carrying a briefcase, told him why they were there. The policeman wrote down their names and asked them to take a seat.

An hour earlier Gavin had called Blair. The conversation was fresh in Blair Gardiner's mind, though 'conversation' wasn't an accurate description. His brother-in-law had made his point and rung off.

'The police want to speak to you. Need to eliminate you from their enquiries.'

The expression had sounded unreal, something he'd never imagined someone would ever say to him. Gavin had been curt. 'I'm texting you the number. Call it. Call it now. And whatever's going on with you and Adele, for Christ's sake, sort it out. There's still no word from Mackenzie.'

DS Geddes deliberately raised an eyebrow, looking at Finnegan, then at Gardiner. Nobody had accused him of anything, why bring a lawyer?

Blair remembered the policeman was an acquaintance Gavin had met at five-a-sides. If it was an advantage it certainly didn't feel like it. The phrase 'eliminate you from their enquiries' had convinced him he needed to defend himself. He'd caught Finnegan at home and got him to agree to 'accompany him to the station'. Another expression straight out of crime fiction. At such short notice, God knows what he'd charge him for that.

Not important. He'd seen the family's reaction, their opinion written on their faces. Turning up with a lawyer had altered the dynamic, that wasn't important either. The DS looked like a guy who didn't play much football, or any other sport for that matter. He offered Blair his hand. 'I was hoping to talk to you earlier.'

The disguised accusation hung in the air. 'Something came up at work.'

The detective empathised. 'Happens all the time in this job, one of the reasons the divorce rate's so high. Get it sorted, did you?'

Blair didn't reply and introduced his companion. 'This is Gerald Finnegan.'

Geddes barely glanced at the bald-headed man in a three-piece suit before giving his attention to Gardiner. 'Just a few questions. Shouldn't take long.'

They made their way to the room Gavin Darroch had been in two days earlier. Geddes closed the door behind them and they sat round the table. Finnegan opened the briefcase and readied to make notes.

Blair said, 'Doubt anything I tell you will help much.'

The lawyer placed a restraining hand on his arm, its message clear: say nothing.

The detective noticed the gesture, flashed a smile and cut it off. 'People often think they know less than they do. It may be your sister-in-law has decided to quit her marriage and drop out of sight. It happens and it isn't against the law. I've spoken with her husband as well as Adele and Monica. They're pretty much agreed Mackenzie Crawford was erratic and had a drink problem. There's also reason to suspect she was having an affair and may have run off with her lover.'

He paused. 'On the other hand, her brother's worried that isn't the case. I'd like to hear what you think.'

Geddes could've spun it out with questions about the birthday party and listened to speculation about the lover/stalker. Instead, he chose a more provocative approach, guaranteed to have the lawyer jumping up and down. 'Where were you earlier, Mr Gardiner? Your wife seemed upset you hadn't come home. What was the "something" that "came up" at work?'

Finnegan whispered in his client's ear then answered for him. 'Detective, do you have reason to suspect Mr Gardiner's whereabouts earlier this evening is relevant to Mrs Crawford's disappearance?'

'That's what we're here to find out, isn't it?'

'In that case, not relevant. He was with me.'

Lawyers, you had to love them. Geddes coughed and got straight to the point.

'Mr Crawford stated that, on more than one occasion, the car he saw his wife get into was a blue Vectra, the same as Mr Gardiner's. I simply want Mr Gardiner to confirm if it was, indeed, his car.'

Finnegan slowly shook his head. 'My client has already assured all parties concerned that, despite similarities, it was not, in fact, his car.'

Geddes stared directly at Blair. 'Well, now I'd like him to assure me. Was Mackenzie Crawford, at any time in the last three months, in your car?'

The lawyer nodded his permission for him to respond. 'Absolutely not. She's never – '

Finnegan's hand was back on his client's arm. 'If that's all, Detective?'

'For the time being.'

'Good.' He closed the briefcase and slid a card across the table. Geddes ignored it and kept his eyes on Blair. The interview had been short and sweet and unsatisfactory.

* * *

Outside in Aikenhead Road, Gavin Darroch sat in the darkened car, listening to a DJ in love with the sound of his own voice prattle away between tracks from artists he hadn't heard of. Monica had been less than happy to be told he was going out. It wasn't a choice. When he'd called Andrew Geddes to let him know he'd spoken to Blair, he was pleased to hear his brother-in-law had made an appointment to see the detective.

What the policeman added changed his mood. 'He's bringing his lawyer.'

'Why on earth does he need a lawyer?'

'Why indeed?'

More than anything, else the mention of a lawyer convinced Gavin to do as Adele had asked and follow her husband. He'd watched the men enter the police station and come out again twenty minutes later. Did that mean it had gone well or badly?

They disappeared behind the building and appeared again when the lawyer's car nosed into the traffic. Blair looked out from the passenger seat as they headed into the night, towards the city. Gavin edged onto the road, keeping two vehicles behind. At the traffic lights in St Vincent Street, they stopped, animatedly discussing what had just happened. Planning the next move?

They pulled up outside the Lorne Hotel in Sauchiehall Street and Blair got out and the car drove off. He stood on the pavement checking one way then the other before going inside. Gavin was forced to drive on by so he wouldn't be seen. His world was rocking. He'd known Blair Gardiner for fifteen years and liked him, but with the Spanish baroque silhouette of Kelvingrove Museum and Art Gallery etched against the midnight blue sky, he wondered if he'd ever really known him at all.

He took the next left and left again into Argyle Street. A third left turn brought him to the side of the hotel near Mother India. In the Lorne's almost empty foyer, a couple sat at either end of a dark leather couch, drinking coffee and reading magazines – in the middle of an argument or killing time? But they weren't Blair and Mackenzie. He tried the bar and saw a group of business-types lounged in the corner – diehards from a meeting earlier in the day – loudly drinking their expenses, too busy laughing to notice him.

The last possibility was the restaurant: The Bukharah. He stood at the door scanning the tables without seeing a familiar face. Blair must have gone up to one of the rooms. Gavin approached the reception desk and went into his act.

'Has Mr Gardiner come back yet?'

A serious girl behind the counter peered over her spectacles at the online register and shook her head. 'Can't find a Mr Gardiner. Are you sure he's staying with us?'

He glanced round and saw the couple on the couch holding hands. If they'd been having a row, peace had broken out. His family could do with some of the same.

'Sorry,' he said. 'I must have the wrong hotel.'

* * *

Monica's eyes had sleep in them but she wasn't in bed, she was waiting for him, her iPad discarded on the arm of the chair. Gavin hadn't told her where he was going and, for once, she hadn't asked. She'd realised that wherever he'd gone it was to do with Mackenzie and wished she'd contact her brother to let him know she was all right. If something had happened to her it would devastate him.

She spoke softly. 'Alice wanted to know where her daddy's been all night.'

He smiled. 'What did you tell her?'

Her hand stroked his cheek. 'That he was worried about his sister and, like a good brother, he was trying to help her.'

'And what did she say?'

'She says she loves you.'

Gavin bent to kiss his wife's upturned face. 'Next time you see her, tell her he loves her, too.'

He sat down across from her. 'I'm lost, Mo, I really am.'

She reached over and squeezed his hand. 'Do you want to talk about it?'

Her husband yawned. 'It's a long story. Where would I begin?'

'I'm not going anywhere.'

'Adele thinks Blair's having an affair with Mackenzie.'

'Well, I gathered that much.'

'You reckon there's something to it?'

She considered lying and changed her mind. 'Honestly, I don't know. He obviously likes her. Then again, this is Blair we're talking about. He likes everybody; he's a nice guy.'

'So why does a nice guy need a lawyer?'

'Now you've lost me.'

Gavin collected his thoughts. 'Andrew Geddes spoke to Adele earlier. Blair didn't show – he ducked out. She called me and was pretty upset. Apparently, he didn't come home last night, either. I phoned him and told him to get his arse in gear and contact Geddes.'

'And did he?'

'He certainly did. Only showed up with a bloody lawyer.'

'You're joking. Why bring a lawyer?'

'Good question. Wish I knew the answer. But it doesn't look great, does it?'

'Does Adele know?'

'Not yet.'

'Don't you think you should tell her?'

'Tell her what? Nothing I could say will make her feel any better. I'll wait 'til I know more.'

'Poor Adele. Those boys of theirs aren't children, they'll know something's wrong. Bound to.'

'Christ. I forgot all about the kids. What a mess.'

For a minute they didn't speak; what was there to say? Monica brought them into the present.

'So what about the interview then?'

'No idea. Haven't spoken to Andrew. Don't expect he'd tell me anyway. Andrew Geddes is a policeman. Doubt he'd bend the rules for a friend, let alone an acquaintance.'

'That's that then.'

Well…not quite.'

'Why? What else is there?'

'I followed Blair tonight.'

Monica pulled herself up straight. 'You did what?'

'A couple of nights ago Adele asked me to follow him. I wasn't keen. But when I heard he was taking a lawyer that convinced me.' Gavin played with his fingers and avoided looking at her. 'I was waiting when they came out of the police station and trailed them into the city. The lawyer dropped him at the Lorne Hotel in the West End.'

'Did he see you?'

'Don't think so, but by the time I got inside there was no sign of him. I asked at reception. They don't have a Gardiner staying with them. Maybe he did see me and left by another door.'

'Or the room's registered under another name?'

Gavin stroked her cheek. 'Why didn't I think of that?'

She smiled. 'You're a man. When it comes to deception, you're all amateurs. Where do you go from here?'

'That's easy. For the next few days I'll take your car. Blair's never seen it.'

'And what about Derek, will you tell him?'

He thought about it. Derek Crawford pointing the finger at his brother-in-law had sown the seeds of mistrust, poisoned the water for all of them. 'Not yet, he's fired up enough. Besides we still aren't sure what's going on. But if Blair's with Mackenzie it'll tear the family apart.'

Day Eleven

The next time she wakened, the heater was off and the room was in darkness. Mackenzie tensed. Had he come back? Was he in the chair? She listened for the sound of his breathing and heard nothing. She was alone. But he must have returned, otherwise the light would be on.

Had he touched her when she was sleeping? The thought sickened her.

Mackenzie's tongue felt thick in her mouth and her brow was on fire. She needed water. It took three tries, each one more demanding than the last, before she could drag herself into a sitting position and pull on the tracksuit bottoms. Getting to her feet was the next challenge. The first attempt ended in failure. She collapsed on the floor, the cold stone soothing her burning skin. How easy it would be to close her eyes and surrender.

She blindly felt her way. Something jagged cut into her knee and Mackenzie cried out: the prong of the belt he'd used to beat her. It gave her an idea. But first she had to have water. Disorientation threatened to overwhelm her and she fought a constant battle against panic. In a strange way, the chain rattling, knowing where it led, reassured her. Mackenzie crawled on, blotting out the pain wracking her body.

Her fingertips traced the bristles of the toothbrush and the smooth tube beside it; she almost cried. From there, finding what she wanted was easy. She unscrewed the top, put the bottle to her lips and drank, then, using the chain to guide her, she retraced her steps.

Returning to the bed was like meeting an old friend. Mackenzie tied the harsh reminder of what she'd endured round her chest, pulling it as tight as she could to bind her ribs. Employing the weapon that had been used on her was ironic but it helped and she could breathe more easily. As she fastened the buckle an idea almost too futile to contemplate came to her.

She sat on the edge of the mattress, working the prong in the keyhole, hoping against hope it would spring. Nothing happened. She tried again with the same result: it had been a long-shot, a stupid notion born of desperation, but she kept at it. Just as she was about to give up a miracle happened. With a click, the lock released and Mackenzie was free. She rubbed her wrists, savouring the moment, realising it was only a beginning.

Crossing the cellar was the next move, and the hardest. In her mind's eye she pictured the staircase on the other side. If she moved in a straight line she would reach it. Mackenzie put the torn tracksuit top on, tied the belt around her chest again, and got on all fours using the chain to guide her as far as it would go. After what seemed like hours, her fingers touched the rough wood of the bottom step and she rested, physically and emotionally spent, her breath wheezing in her chest like an old woman.

It was taking too long. If her jailer returned and discovered her like this, he'd kill her for sure.

And he'd have won. She couldn't allow that.

Her resolve to escape came back and she went on. Halfway up, she almost passed out. Only by telling herself that every step was a step closer to freedom was she able to continue. Somehow she reached the top and struggled to her feet, elated. She felt for the light switch, turned it on and took her first real look at her prison. Viewed from this angle, the room was surprisingly small, the bed no more than a dozen yards away. Not how it had seemed on the floor in the darkness. She nervously tried the door, praying it was unlocked. If it wasn't, it had all been for nothing.

The handle turned and she stumbled along the hall into the grey early morning, shielding her eyes, breathing air sweeter and cleaner than any she'd ever tasted.

She scanned the horizon searching for the white van, seeing only hills rising and falling on every side, broken by a distant line of wind turbines, silent sentinels in the dawn. The stalker hadn't lied: there was no one to hear her scream.

She limped towards the road. When she looked back she couldn't see the derelict house where she'd been held captive.

The growl of a diesel engine broke the quiet and a flatbed truck with a white-haired man in his seventies behind the wheel came into sight. Mackenzie waved. The farmer waved back and drove past. She shouted but the truck rolled on by. The tracksuit – what was left of it – had made him think she was a jogger out for a run. After all she'd been through, the disappointment was crushing. Mackenzie sat on the grass and wept, unable to recognise herself as the woman she'd been only days ago.

She felt light-headed, her vision blurred, and every breath was agony. Her tired eyes registered something on the horizon coming towards her. With the last of her strength, Mackenzie struggled to her feet and staggered into the middle of the road. This might be her only chance, her only hope, she couldn't lose it.

The car dipped out of sight and she prayed it hadn't gone another way. When it reappeared, gratitude like she'd never known surged through her. She raised her arm to attract the driver's attention. A frail voice, not her own, whispered on the breeze.

'Help! Help! Please help me!'

The vehicle drew up and a man got out. Mackenzie sank to her knees, tearing her hair, wailing in anguish.

He was wearing a black coat.

* * *

The stalker looked down at her, his features distorted with rage. 'What the fuck!' He dragged her to her feet and slapped her, splitting her lip. 'Ten out of ten for effort. Give you that much.'

Mackenzie hit out. He punched her again, dragged her by the hair to the rear of the vehicle and threw her in the boot. The door closed. He didn't secure her wrists, assuming it wasn't necessary. His prisoner was weak, her spirit broken, barely holding on. Mackenzie lay on the floor, devastated and exhausted. Escape had seemed impossible, yet she'd come so close. If only the farmer had stopped or she'd walked in the other direction. All the effort had been for nothing, and the thought of going back to the underground prison was more than she could stand. She drew on reserves of strength and determination she hadn't known existed.

It couldn't be over, she wouldn't let it be over.

She would fight this monster with the last breath in her body.

She struggled to unfasten the belt – the only weapon she had. In the front seat, the stalker whistled tunelessly as if he hadn't a care in the world. The car stopped, the boot opened and he hauled her into the morning.

'Home sweet home,' he said, and laughed at his joke. 'Good to see the old place again, isn't it?'

This was the moment of truth. If she let herself be taken to the cellar she wouldn't be coming out again.

His hand tightened round her left arm and led her to the door. Under her tracksuit Mackenzie gripped the buckle in her clenched fist so the prong stuck through her fingers and readied herself. There would only be one opportunity to hurt him. She had to make it count. Over-confidence made him careless. He didn't see the blow coming and didn't realise what was happening until the prong pierced his flesh and buried itself just below his ear.

He screamed and staggered away. She followed, stabbing him again, in the chest this time. The stalker stared in disbelief at the belt in her hand. For seconds neither of them moved. Mackenzie lunged at him trying to get his eyes. He took the blow on his arm, deflecting it and kicked her legs from under her. She lost her grip on the leather belt and he seized it, raging out of control. 'You cunt! You fucking cunt!'

He pushed her inside the house. At the top of the stairs, Mackenzie made a final attempt to fight back, throwing herself at her tormentor. He punched her in the face and forced her down the stairs into the place she'd hoped she'd left forever.

She shut her eyes as her clothes were ripped from her body. The last thing she remembered was lying naked on the bed with the man in the black coat standing over her, breathing hard, turning the belt in his hands.

He smiled for the first time. 'Think of this as your reward. Enjoy it. I will.'

* * *

Gavin Darroch had assumed bringing the police in on his sister's disappearance would help. Arguably, it had made things worse: two marriages were in the balance and he doubted they could be saved. Mackenzie's performance at Adele's birthday party convinced the family the Crawfords' relationship was doomed. It had certainly looked like it. Discovering Blair's infidelity was more shocking. Honest, reliable Blair – backed into a corner – and forced to show up at Cathcart police station with a lawyer to defend himself against accusations yet to be made.

Things had taken a turn for the better with him and Monica and Gavin thanked God. They'd lain beside each other, sharing a pillow, whispering and giggling in the darkness, finding love while others lost it.

When Alice woke for her feed, they were still talking. He sat on the edge of the bed marvelling at the miracle they'd created while Monica held their daughter, the joy outweighing the responsibility. Alice was their child, their little girl, and they were her mum and dad.

Dawn broke over their naked bodies, locked together with a passion which had been so much part of their life before. Later, Gavin showered and dressed. At ten-to-seven he was driving through an almost-deserted Glasgow in Monica's car towards Sauchiehall Street and the Lorne Hotel.

He ordered coffee, croissants and a newspaper and settled himself in the foyer near the door to wait. Half an hour later, guests started to arrive for breakfast. Gavin kept his eyes on the lift, expecting at any minute to see Blair and Mackenzie.

Something Monica had suggested came to him.

registered under another name

This morning, two receptionists, both female, were on duty. The serious lady from the previous night wasn't there. One of them raised her head when she realised he was waiting.

'Sorry to bother you. Could you check if Mr and Mrs Darroch and Mr and Mrs Crawford are still in their rooms?'

The girl studied the computer screen in front of her, eyes narrowed in concentration. 'I don't see them. When did they arrive?'

Gavin couldn't begin to guess and feigned annoyance. 'Bloody idiots have got it wrong again. Have to wait until the office opens to get the correct information.' He pulled out his mobile and made an imaginary phone call for the receptionist's benefit, pretending to be irritated. 'Too early. Nobody's there yet. Thanks, anyway.'

Back in his seat, he considered a second cup of coffee and changed his mind. Through the plate-glass window the city was going about its business. He lifted *The Herald* but couldn't concentrate, his racing mind wouldn't let him. So much had happened since the party, even in the last twenty-four hours: Adele angrily accusing him of playing favourites and her distraught implication '"– Blair Gardiner isn't the "good old Blair" you think he is – ";' Andrew Geddes' bombshell that his brother-in-law was coming to the interview in Cathcart with a lawyer; following them to the Lorne and losing Blair; and finally, more important than everything else, where others were foundering, his own marriage turning the corner.

Now he was here, skulking behind a newspaper in a hotel foyer like a Cold War spy. A lot to take in. He considered calling it quits, thinking Blair must have spotted him last night and used the hotel to lose him.

At five past eight, the lift doors opened and Blair Gardiner walked out, guiding his companion towards the restaurant and the buffet like the gentleman he'd believed him to be.

it'll tear the family apart

The woman smiled at the gesture and Gavin saw her face.

* * *

It wasn't his sister. It wasn't Mackenzie.

Gavin's initial reaction was relief. Whatever else, Adele would be spared the humiliation of her husband betraying her with her own flesh and blood. The feeling was short-lived. There were no winners here. Taking sides was never a good idea. These things happened, but he'd been accused of favouring one sister over another. It wasn't true and this was his chance to prove it.

He stopped at the restaurant door, scanning the tables until he spotted them in the far corner, holding hands. Blair was spooning cereal into his mouth and didn't see his brother-in-law until he was standing over him. Gavin tried to keep his voice down and failed.

'What the hell do you think you're playing at?'

Conversation died in the dining-room. The shock of discovery made Blair falter. 'Gavin, why..?'

Gavin ignored him and spoke to the woman. 'I assume he's told you he's married.'

Blair apologised to his companion. 'Sorry about this, Martha. I'll deal with it.' He turned back to Gavin. 'This isn't the time or the place…'

'Really? Then when is? Next, you'll be asking me to believe it isn't what it looks like.'

Blair wiped his mouth with his napkin. 'I don't have to explain myself to you and don't intend to. It's between Adele and me and none of your damned business.'

Gavin was stunned. This was Blair, a good guy. Suddenly it was like talking to a stranger. He was aware of a waiter at his shoulder, drawn by his raised voice. People were watching. He didn't care. He leaned across the table until his face was inches from Blair Gardiner's.

'Your wife made it my business.'

Blair pulled away. 'What do you mean?'

'Adele isn't stupid, Blair. She asked me to follow you.'

Blair blanched. 'We should discuss this outside.'

'No, no. Right here's fine.'

Martha threw in her twopenceworth. A mistake. 'Whoever you are, you're embarrassing yourself. And yes, Blair's told me everything.'

'Everything? I doubt it. Has he mentioned his two sons? Has he shown you pictures of Adam and Richard? Nice kids. And you're comfortable ruining their lives, are you?'

Her expression answered for her.

'Didn't think so.'

'You can behave any way you want, Blair. It's allowed. If that means being with somebody else, okay. But don't sneak around. Don't leave your wife worried out of her mind. Do the right thing.' He pointed to Martha. 'And tell this woman the truth.'

Blair stared ahead, waiting for the lecture to end.

Gavin said, 'By the way, why bring a lawyer to an informal interview? What's that about?'

So far, Blair had let his brother-in-law do most of the talking. Now, it was his turn.

'*Again*, none of your business, though since you ask, I'll tell you. The other night I got the message, loud and clear. Your family thinks I've something to do with Mackenzie leaving.'

Gavin didn't deny it.

'Then I'm told the police want to "eliminate me from their enquiries". Too fucking right I'm bringing a lawyer with me. Be a bloody fool to do anything else.' He stood. 'I'll tell Adele when I'm ready to tell her. When she's ready to hear it. Now, if you'll excuse us, we have work to go to.'

Gavin wouldn't be brushed off so easily. 'Could've done it clean. It didn't need to be like this. You've got a day, Gardiner. You tell her or I will.'

* * *

Derek Crawford locked his office door. He didn't want to be disturbed. He dialled the number and waited for Adele to answer. When she did, her tone was hesitant, cautious, as if she was reluctant to speak. '… Hello.'

'Adele, it's Derek.'

'Derek. Is there news? Has Mackenzie contacted you?'

'No. No, she hasn't.' He heard the disappointment come down the line. 'That isn't why I'm calling.'

'Then why?'

'To apologise. I was out-of-order the other night. Bursting in. Fighting with Blair. I'm sorry it happened.'

Adele was sympathetic. 'I appreciate it but there's no need, really there isn't. You were upset. This must be a nightmare for you.'

'It is. Bringing the police into it put me over the edge. Truth is, I was pretty close to it before that. I'm either a cuckold or I've done away with my wife. Not the greatest choices.'

'Nobody's saying that.'

'Maybe not saying it. They're certainly thinking it.'

His sister-in-law didn't give him an argument.

'Blair deserves an apology, too. I'm working up to that one. He's always been protective about Mackenzie. Isn't there, is he?'

She was tempted to unload and decided against it. Telling Derek that Blair hadn't come home the last two nights would only make things worse. 'No. It's just me, and I shouldn't be here, either. I asked the school for a few weeks off. They were very good about it. Now I wish I hadn't. Mooching around the house worrying doesn't help.'

'Know the feeling. I'm calling from the office. Was going crazy staring at the phone hour after hour, willing it to ring. Have to accept it, she's gone. Mackenzie's gone. Been eight days.'

'That's not long. I'm hoping that wherever she is she'll come to her senses. The sooner the better.'

'That's the thing. The more time passes the harder it is to put it behind us, even if I could. Even if I wanted to. Told the police I wouldn't take her back. That isn't the truth. Been doing a lot of thinking. Maybe I was wrong for Mackenzie from the start. That's always been Gavin's opinion. And Blair's.'

'Maybe, but I disagree. You made her happy.'

'Did I, I wonder?'

'Yes, you did. Alcohol changes people. Nobody can help an alcoholic or anyone addicted unless they can admit they have a problem. Mackenzie hasn't reached that place. Until and unless she does…' She heard herself getting carried away and stopped. 'I'm saying you aren't to blame. What's happened isn't your fault.'

He sounded subdued. 'Just wish I could believe it.'

'Believe it. You've given that girl everything. What she does after that is up to her.'

'I miss her, Adele. I really miss her.'

'We all do. Mackenzie's a giant pain and always has been, but we love her.'

Derek couldn't let it go. 'What if she doesn't contact me? How can I live knowing I could've done more?'

Comforting Derek Crawford was helping Adele. Her own troubles seemed less significant compared to what he was going through. Under her breath she cursed her sister for the hurt she'd caused. Not only to her husband, to all of them.

'It'll be all right. She'll turn up at the door full of the promises we've heard before. Perhaps this time she'll keep some of them.'

* * *

Gavin had intended to go back to work but after the confrontation at the Lorne Hotel, he couldn't face it and went home. Monica took one look and didn't question him, immediately understanding it hadn't gone well. He'd talk about it when he was ready.

The day passed with little conversation and she was afraid the progress made the night before was in danger of being lost. She dismissed the thought: they couldn't go back there – not for Mackenzie, not for Blair, not for anyone.

She overheard Gavin calling the office, telling them he needed another few days. He was the boss. Nobody asked him why. By necessity, small businesses were lean and Jamieson Coburn was no exception. Deadlines didn't just go away. Clients were only interested in how their design was progressing. Everything else came second. He had other responsibilities besides a wayward sibling and couldn't step back for very much longer.

Monica brought coffee for both of them and set the cups on the table. 'How you doing?'

He told her the truth. 'Not great. This morning...' He didn't finish the sentence. 'Not great, Mo.'

'Anything I can do?'

'Why do people make life so complicated?'

Did he mean them?

'We can't help it. It's who we are.'

'Why do we always want what we haven't got?'

'Thought we were putting the last few months behind us?'

Her husband moved from the couch and took her hands in his. 'We have. I'm not thinking about us.'

'Derek and Mackenzie?'

'Derek and Mackenzie, Blair and Adele, the whole bloody world. Relationships have to be simpler than that.'

He gathered his thoughts. 'Blair's having an affair.'

Monica almost shouted. 'What! Blair? Seriously? Please tell me it isn't with Mackenzie. Our Blair? I know I said it was possible but I really didn't think it was happening.'

'Apparently he isn't "Our Blair" anymore. I knew they weren't getting along but I didn't realise how bad it was. Dismissed it as one of those troughs every marriage goes through. Well, it isn't. He was at the Lorne Hotel with a woman, having breakfast together.'

Monica struggled to take it in. 'Surely it's a mistake? Something to do with work, maybe? Not what it seems.'

Gavin could see her reaching for an explanation she could live with and was glad they'd come to their senses. A day earlier this conversation would've been too close to home.

'He didn't deny it, Mo. They were holding hands. The only good thing is it blows him having a thing about Mackenzie out of the water.'

'Poor Adele – does she know? She'll be devastated.'

'Not the details. But she will. He's going to tell her.'

'And those boys. What's got into him?'

'Damned if I know. Told you, the world's gone mad.'

She looked up at him with fear in her eyes, needing his reassurance. 'Thank God it isn't happening to us.'

Later, he was on the phone again. She heard him say 'Andrew'. When they met in the kitchen he was wearing his jacket. 'Got to go out. Meeting Geddes for a pint. He's going to bring me up to date, whatever the hell that means. If Adele phones don't say you know anything about it.'

* * *

Andrew Geddes leaned against the bar in Blackfriars at the corner of Bell Street in Merchant City and read the posters on the walls advertising live music. In the nineties he couldn't see past the Red Hot Chili Peppers or, at a push, Guns 'N' Roses. A long time ago. He swirled the dregs in the bottom of his glass and thought about having something to eat. Chicken Balmoral caught his eye until he read the ingredients: haggis stuffing. Geddes hated haggis. Beer-battered fresh haddock got the vote but just as he was about to order Gavin Darroch came through the door, waved and joined him.

The DS said, 'What're you drinking?'

Gavin pointed to the empty glass in front of the detective. 'What's that you're on?'

'Brooklyn Black Chocolate.'

'Any good?'

'It's all right, yeah.'

'Then that'll do.'

Geddes paid and they carried their drinks to a table over by the wall. 'Don't mind if I eat, do you?'

'Suit yourself.'

The DS went to the barman and came back.

Gavin said, 'Tough day?'

Geddes shrugged. 'Fighting evil wherever it raises its ugly head. You know, the usual.'

'And where does it raise its ugly head?'

'In Glasgow? Fucking everywhere.'

'So what've you got to tell me?'

The policeman set the scene. 'When you came to the station to report your sister missing, have to admit I didn't reckon there was much to it. The clothes and the stalker made me change my mind. That sounded suspicious.'

Gavin Darroch listened, wondering if some bombshell was about to drop. It was bombshell season. He needn't have worried. The DS said, 'In the last few days I've spoken to your wife, your sister Adele, to Blair Gardiner – though his lawyer did most of the talking – and your brother-in-law Derek C rawford, as well as their cleaner and Mackenzie's boss and colleagues at the garden centre.'

He interrupted himself to drink his beer and wipe a froth moustache off his top lip, giving Gavin a glimpse of what the detective would look like thirty years down the line.

Geddes returned to the feedback. 'Be nice to be able to report I made some big discovery. But it wouldn't be true. Every one of them tells more or less the same story. Mackenzie was a problem drinker. They're all agreed on that. An unhappy woman with a track record of – and I'm aware this is your sister I'm talking about – being "economical with the truth"'. He tried to gauge Gavin's reaction. 'What I'm saying is, I haven't found anything that suggests foul play.'

'Not taking her clothes?'

The policeman waited for the barman to lay a place mat and cutlery on the table before he went on. 'Maybe she never intended to take them. Maybe her new man's got money and she didn't need to take them. Maybe it was symbolic – a fresh start away from Crawford. Who knows? She's a woman. Can't predict any bloody thing with them.'

'What about the stalker?'

Geddes lifted the knife in one hand and the fork in the other and rested his arms on the table. 'You mean the stalker nobody saw except her?'

When the fish and chips arrived, the policeman examined the plate with his eyes then dropped his conclusion into the conversation. 'I've changed my mind.'

Gavin took a deep breath. 'That surprises me.'

'Surprises me, too. But the more I talked to people the clearer it became that the stalker was probably a fairytale. Consider this: who actually saw this guy?'

'Derek. In Buchanan Street. He described a man wearing a black coat.'

Geddes used the knife to emphasise his agreement. 'Correct. A man in a black coat who Mackenzie later confessed was her lover.' He forked haddock into his mouth. 'Do you see where I'm going with this? All we have is her word. Unfortunately, that isn't enough.' The detective gave his dinner his attention. 'Bloody good, by the way. Should try some.'

Gavin wasn't hungry. 'I'll pass if it's all the same to you.'

'When your other brother-in-law showed up with a lawyer, must admit I thought he'd something to hide.'

'He does.'

'Who doesn't? But nothing he told me connects him to your sister's disappearance.'

The detective chewed and swallowed. 'So why come lawyered-up?' He answered his own question. 'My guess is he's having an affair and didn't want anybody to find out about it.'

Gavin Darroch stared across the table in disbelief. 'How the hell did you figure that out?'

Geddes tapped the side of his nose. 'Copper's instinct. Came over as a straight guy. But even straight guys have secrets. So I'm right?'

'Absolutely. The night the family got together to discuss Mackenzie ended pretty badly. Derek had made it clear he was done with her and wasn't invited. He burst in to have it out with me for involving you and accused Blair of fancying Mackenzie. They fought. It wasn't good. But we all thought there was more to it.'

'You thought they were involved?'

'Yeah. Turns out he wasn't, but that's why he came ready to defend himself. He knew he was innocent and was afraid you might pin something on him. I understand it's been known.'

Andrew Geddes half-emptied his glass and burped. 'Has it? Anyway, I heard enough to know that whatever he was keeping dark had nothing to do with your sister. Will say this for him: he spoke about her like a friend. More than could be said for some.'

'So you're telling me nothing criminal's going on.'

Geddes finished his drink. 'No, I'm telling you there's no evidence of anything criminal. A big difference.'

Day Twelve

The Baxter House
Lowther Hills

Across the room the chair was empty. He wasn't there. Even the rats had gone quiet. They knew what he knew – it would soon be over, and she'd never understand why. Mackenzie drifted in and out of consciousness, beyond hurt, beyond pain. One regret stayed with her: Alec. If she'd listened to him, done what he'd wanted her to do, how different it might've been. But she'd lacked the courage and had paid the price. Her eyes fluttered and closed and she drifted into dreamlessness.

* * *

The voice on the phone had the same bitter edge as when he'd burst into the meeting at their house, except now it was joined by something he couldn't put his finger on. Derek Crawford spoke slowly, deliberately, keeping his anger in check, savouring the words. 'I've seen him, Gavin. I've seen the bastard. I'm following him.'

The line went dead. Gavin called back. Nobody answered. Ten minutes later the mobile rang again. He managed to get off a question. 'Where?'

Derek didn't reply, and in that moment his brother-in-law realised the only thing that existed for him was his wife's lover. He tried a second time, almost shouting. 'Tell me where you are?'

Derek snapped out of it. 'Going south. Almost at Bothwell.'

'Is he alone?'

Crawford steadied himself before answering. 'Yes.' His focus was absolute as he whispered to himself. 'Got you, you bastard'. And Gavin knew he'd forgotten he was even there.

'Listen. I'm on my way. Stay back. Whatever you do, don't let him see you.'

The smouldering rage coming from him told Gavin he wasn't going to wait – for him or anybody else. Derek intended to have it out with the man who'd stolen his wife and there was nothing anybody could do to stop him.

Crawford said, 'He'll see me. He'll see me all right.'

'If he does he'll run. Any chance we have of finding Mackenzie will be gone.'

Crawford didn't answer and Gavin dived for the door shouting over his shoulder to Monica. 'Derek's found the guy from Buchanan Street. He's following him. Need to catch him before he does anything stupid. They're near Bothwell, heading south.'

'Why? What?'

'He thinks he'll lead him to Mackenzie.'

She didn't understand. 'But what's the point? I mean, if she doesn't want to be with him, it's better to leave her alone.'

'Christ knows what's going on in his head. He sounds completely out of it. Doubt I can catch him. Got to be at least twenty minutes in front of me.'

At a set of traffic lights, Gavin's mobile rang. The hard determination in Derek's voice was unmistakable, yet he seemed more in control. 'Still on the motorway. Lesmahagow coming up. No sign of him turning off. Where are you?'

'Leaving the city.'

'That's a good way behind me.'

The anger in Derek's voice worried Gavin. This might be the chance to sort out this whole mess. He said, 'Don't lose sight of him and for God's sake don't do anything daft.'

Derek laughed a grim laugh. 'Not a chance. I'm having the bastard.'

Gavin swerved to overtake a driver in a red Mondeo loitering in the fast lane. He blasted his horn and got the finger in return. Thirty seconds later the Mondeo wasn't in his mirror. Near Uddingston, he had a shocking realisation: Derek was so wound up he might kill this guy.

The accelerator pressed the floor and the SUV surged forward, shooting past a line of vehicles in the middle lane. He felt the steering-wheel tremble in his sweating palms. 'Not if I can help it,' he said out loud.

Minutes later, Bothwell – home to footballers and businessmen – appeared on a hill to the right. Gavin's mind raced. What if it's a mistake? What if it wasn't the same guy? His thoughts fell silent and he concentrated on the road.

The mobile lay abandoned in the well between the seats. Gavin glanced at it, willing it to break into life. It didn't. Time passed. Five minutes became ten. The Central Belt was left behind, the scenery changed: hills dotted with sheep replaced houses and, in the distance, wind turbines appeared on the horizon. Derek could be anywhere. The only thing to do was to keep driving.

Thirty-odd minutes after he'd left Glasgow, traffic on the motorway thinned to heavy lorries and the occasional car. His mobile rang. The scary-calm had gone from Crawford's voice. Something about him wasn't right; he'd cracked. Gavin wasn't sure he understood he'd been out of contact with him, that he'd lost him. Or did he even care?

'He's pulled into Abington service station.'

'For God's sake don't get too close. He can't see you now. We need him to lead us to Mackenzie.'

Crawford didn't agree or disagree. He drifted in and out of awareness, conscious enough to make the call then seeming to fade into another world. Little about him said he knew he was talking to anyone. What did that say about his state of mind? For sure, nothing good. Gavin wondered again if the whole thing wasn't a case of mistaken identity. Derek had been under enormous pressure – more than anyone appreciated – he might be suffering some kind of emotional collapse.

'He's gone inside. Said something to the woman behind the counter, she's laughing. Must be a funny guy. Won't be so funny when I'm finished with him.'

'You're sure it's him? You only saw him for a couple of seconds in Buchanan Street. How can you be so certain?'

'Still wearing the fucking black coat. Wait a minute, he's out again and he's bought two coffees. Now he's sitting in the car drinking one of them. So the other one must be for Mackenzie. We're going to find her, Gavin.'

The accelerator took the brunt of Gavin's impatience. 'I'm coming. Stay back. I'll be as quick as I can.'

Abington Services sat at the edge of the village round a long curve in the road. Gavin arrived just as a gang of long-haired bikers revved their engines and pulled away. Two vehicles were at the pumps filling up, another sat on the forecourt.

Derek's car wasn't one of them.

He got out. The air was clear and still, the scenery lush and verdant, like a landscape painted by one of the Masters. Even with the backdrop of traffic noise it was impressive.

Inside the shop, the fair-haired woman behind the counter couldn't help. 'Can't remember serving anybody in a black coat. Leather jackets, yes. Just had a bunch of them in. Maybe I was too busy keeping an eye on the bikers.'

'But he was here.'

She shrugged. 'Well, I didn't see him.'

It was understandable. She was on her own. Harassed out of her head. Not easy having a bunch of Hell's Angels land on you.

The chase from Glasgow had been frantic. He'd done well to make up the distance. But if he lost them now it would all have been for nothing. The mobile rang in his hand. Derek sounded far away although he couldn't be more than a couple of miles.

'He's heading towards Leadhills. Hurry up.'

Gavin followed a sign and crossed to the other side of the motorway. Immediately the road rose in front of him and climbed as Abington disappeared in the rearview mirror. He drove between steep rounded earth-coloured mounds while shallow crystal streams broke and bubbled over grey rock.

Ten minutes further on he hadn't seen another living thing. Not a sheep, not even a bird. It was beautiful but he couldn't picture a city girl like his sister living out here. Too many creepy crawlies for a start.

It was mamba country – miles and miles of bugger all.

The village of Leadhills broke the monotony: rows of miners' cottages crowded together, some whitewashed and well-cared-for with welcoming smoke trailing from the chimneys, others ramshackle, rusted corrugated roofs and clumps of weeds growing in the guttering, leaning into their neighbour like teenage girls at the end of a wild night. Inside they'd be cramped and damp. It took a certain kind of person to want to stay here.

Derek's car still wasn't in sight. Gavin kept to the main track and drove on to Wanlockhead, the highest village in Scotland. He hadn't heard from his brother-in-law since the service station. Maybe he couldn't get a signal. If that was the case, the race from Glasgow had been in vain.

When the mobile rang it startled him. Derek had gone back to the eerie detachment of earlier, disturbing to hear. 'He's stopped.'

'Where? Where is he?'

'Old house on the other side of Wanlockhead.'

Gavin heard himself shouting. 'Wait for me, I'm right behind you! We don't know anything about this guy, he could be dangerous!'

Crawford ignored the warning. 'I'm going in.'

Gavin changed down gears and gunned the engine. 'No! Hold on!'

He was talking to himself again. Derek wasn't there. Minutes later he came across his Audi parked at a crazy angle, the engine running, the front wheels in a ditch, the back-end high. Its flowing metal beauty incongruent in the rustic setting. He got out, and started running.

The grey stone building was hidden by a hill at the front and another at the back. Crawford's directions hadn't given much but his car had shown the way. Without it, he would never have found him.

The house was derelict. Boards had been nailed over the windows, the roof had sagged scattering broken black slate tiles and the rusted nails that had held them in place. Nobody could live here and nobody had in a very long time.

Gavin spoke to himself. 'Christ, what is this?'

He touched the bonnet of a mud-spattered Toyota sitting outside the open door. It was warm, or maybe he was cold.

'This is where she is? Not possible.'

He edged down a narrow corridor, every movement a gunshot in the silence as tired timbers cracked and sighed beneath the old linoleum. The staircase to what had been the floor above had collapsed, and not recently. On top of the rubble, a brown rat – the biggest he'd ever seen – sniffed the air and watched him, unafraid.

'Fuck.'

Across the hall, a wooden door swung on its hinges. Angry voices echoed from below; Derek's was one of them. Steps descended into the bowels of the house, the dank smell of sour earth growing stronger with each rung. A spider's web caressed his face. He dragged it away. Whatever he'd expected to find, it wasn't this.

A battery-powered light illuminated the crazy scene. Derek Crawford had his hands round the other man's throat, their shadows dancing like crazy marionettes on the rough walls as they staggered, locked together. Mackenzie lay unconscious on a single bed, chained by her wrist, her face swollen and her body bruised where she'd been beaten, a line of dried blood, like a scar, running from the corner of her mouth to her chin.

She was naked.

And in that moment Gavin understood. Everything his sister said had been true.

The bastard was real.

He ran to her side, gently draping his jacket over her body which was covered in livid purple and yellow marks. But thank God she had a pulse. Behind him, the two men punched and kicked at each other, cursing and growling. The stalker slammed Derek against the wall, pounding him with his free hand. Gavin jumped to his feet as Derek got hold of the stranger's lapels and threw him to the floor, then fell on him. Suddenly, the man who'd abducted Mackenzie cried out and the struggle ended.

Gavin dragged his brother-in-law to his feet. His eyes were wide and wild and scared, like a lost child who didn't know where he was or how he'd got here. The life went out of him. He slumped and burst into tears. 'Is he dead? Have I killed him?'

Gavin saw the knife buried in the unknown man's abdomen and didn't answer. Derek got to his feet and rushed at the stalker. 'Let me finish it. Let me finish the bastard!'

Gavin hauled him away. 'Leave it alone. It's over.'

He bent over the fallen man, uncertain if he was alive or dead, tearing at his clothes, his one thought to find the key to free his sister. Crawford dropped to his knees beside his wife, crying uncontrollably, crushed with remorse. He turned towards his brother-in-law, on the edge of losing it again. 'I didn't believe her. I didn't believe her.'

The reply was harsh. 'For God's sake get a grip. That doesn't matter now. We need to help Mackenzie. I'm calling Andrew Geddes.'

* * *

DS Geddes was at his desk in Cathcart and lifted the phone after one shrill ring. Gavin quickly filled him in. Geddes said, 'Listen to me. Stay calm. Otherwise you're no use to Mackenzie. Keep her warm and don't move her. Don't move either of them.'

When Gavin came back into the cellar Derek was holding Mackenzie's hand in his, whispering. 'I'm sorry. I'm so so sorry. Please forgive me, I didn't know.'

The body on the floor hadn't moved. Gavin looked across at him, beating down the desire to finish what Derek Crawford had started. Instead, he went outside and called Monica. As soon as he heard her voice, he broke down.

'What's wrong? What's wrong, Gavin? Tell me.'

Through tears he managed to say 'Mackenzie. It's Mackenzie.'

'Oh God! What's happened to her?'

From somewhere he found the strength to answer. 'She wasn't making it up. It was all true.'

Monica felt sick, afraid to ask the question. 'Is she..? Is she... alright?'

'No, she's in a really bad way. We're waiting for the ambulance.'

'Where are you, I'll come?'

'No, you can't. I'll call you as soon as we know which hospital they're taking her to. Get a hold of Adele. She'll be out of her mind with worry.'

'Okay. Gavin...Gavin...'

'I know. We didn't listen to her. Blair was the only one who believed her.'

'Wasn't she with Blair?'

This wasn't the time to tell her. 'No, she wasn't.'

He sat on the grass, eventually able to bring himself to go back down into the basement.

Thirty minutes later, two police cars pulled up outside the house and six men got out – four uniformed officers and a couple of plainclothes detectives. This remote part of the country was covered by Lanarkshire division. Geddes had contacted Control at Motherwell who had sent men from Wishaw, the nearest hub.

A fresh-faced detective inspector called Taylor listened to what Gavin had to tell him without commenting, while the uniforms secured the crime scene. Then the other detective took a preliminary statement. As he finished, the forensic examiners arrived, followed by two ambulances with their lights flashing. The place had been deserted an hour ago. Now it was overrun.

Andrew Geddes arrived next, his car crunching to a halt. He got out and walked over to Gavin Darroch. 'How is she?'

'Alive.'

The DS let his relief show. 'Thank God for that.'

He left and went into a huddle with DI Taylor, now and again glancing in Gavin's direction. The detectives disappeared inside for what seemed like a long time. When Geddes emerged from the house his face was stone. Battle-hardened policeman though he was, what he'd seen in the basement had affected him. He wiped the corners of his mouth with his fingers. 'No woman should have to go through an ordeal like that, it's a wonder she's still breathing.'

Uniforms put handcuffs on Derek Crawford and guided him into the backseat of a police car. His sleeve was rolled up showing his bandaged arm and there were bloodstains on his shirt. He moved like a man in a trance, his empty eyes staring at something only he could see. From their first meeting Gavin had been convinced he wasn't right for his sister – that hadn't changed – but he felt for him, in the circumstances it was impossible not to.

He went to the car. 'Hang in, Derek. Just hang in there.'

Derek didn't look at his brother-in-law and Gavin wasn't certain he'd heard. The assured persona he found so irritating was gone. A broken man was in its place. Like the rest of the family, he'd been wrong: there had been a stalker. He would have to live with that.

He already was.

The sun had dipped behind the hill when the paramedics carefully carried an unconscious Mackenzie Crawford and her unnamed abductor out of the house in the Lowther Hills, their faces covered by oxygen masks. In the gathering dusk, blue light from the ambulances made the tragedy surreal and after the adrenaline rush, Gavin wanted to lie on the ground and sleep. 'She told us somebody was following her. We didn't believe her.'

Geddes put a hand on his shoulder. 'Can't blame yourself, it doesn't work that way. Your sister's problems made it hard for anybody to believe her.'

He scratched the side of his nose, on the point of saying something, then changed his mind. Whatever it was passed. 'Best thing you can do is go to the hospital. We'll be here a while yet. I'll catch up with you.'

'Which hospital is it? Where've they taken her?'

'Wishaw.'

'I'll need to let Adele know. What about Derek, what's going to happen to him?'

Rain, the thin kind that goes all the way to the bone, chose that moment to come on. Andrew looked up at the sky. 'He'll be charged, but a half-smart lawyer will make a case of self-defence. Up to the PF. No matter what the decision, it's going to be a long road back for him.'

'For all of us.'

Gavin called Adele and gave her an update, leaving out the details; she'd hear them soon enough. Alone in the car on the journey back up the M74 to the hospital, he went over everything. The call from Derek felt like weeks ago. He'd followed the guy he'd seen in Buchanan Street with no idea where he was heading, taking the chance he might lead him to Mackenzie – the poor bastard must've intended to beg her to come back to him. But the unnatural composure in his voice on the phone had been a clue he was on the margins, straddling the invisible line between sanity and madness psychiatrists had argued over for a hundred years.

In mamba country, he'd crossed it.

* * *

Adele and Blair Gardiner were at Wishaw Hospital when the ambulance carrying Mackenzie pulled into A & E. The back doors flew open and she was taken inside. Nobody told them what was going on. Nobody knew. Gavin was in time to see the second ambulance arrive. The irony of his sister and the person who'd abducted her being treated in the same emergency room didn't escape him.

He found them sitting in the hall, Adele resting against Blair's shoulder. She'd been crying. The last time the men met they'd been on opposite sides. Mackenzie had brought them together. Blair looked up at him and shook his head. 'No news. Somebody will speak to us as soon as they can.'

Adele threw her arms around her brother. 'Why does it take this before we realise what's important?' She searched his face for the answer she needed to hear. 'Will she be okay? Tell me she'll be okay.'

Gavin was tempted to lie and changed his mind. 'I don't know. I really don't know.'

'What happened?'

'She's been through hell. If you'd seen where he was keeping her. If you'd…' His voice faltered, unable to describe the pictures in his head. 'Derek… went crazy.'

'Where is Derek? Is he ok?'

'The police have taken him in for questioning.'

'What'll happen to him?'

'We'll have to wait and see. It was awful, Adele. Really awful. I'll never forget it.'

Blair stepped between them. 'You don't have to go into it. This isn't the time. It's too raw.'

Gavin said, 'Has Monica been told?'

'Already done. Called her myself. She's dropping Alice off with her sister.'

'Thanks for that, Blair.'

Adele's way of coping was to talk about it. Blair held her close and let her get it out. Soon after, Monica arrived, rushed to her husband and hugged him. 'Are you all right?' He nodded. 'Thank God. What about Mackenzie?'

'They're examining her now.'

'Have they said anything?'

'Not yet. All we can do is wait.'

She kept her voice low. 'What about Derek? Did he intend to kill the guy?'

'Maybe, I don't know. But I saw what he did to her. I wouldn't blame him, Monica, I really wouldn't.'

Adele asked, 'So where is he?' Gavin knew who she was taking about and wasn't sure how to respond. 'My God. Don't tell me they brought him here. How could they do that?'

'They have to try and save his life too.'

His sister voiced what all of them thought. 'Why? Why do they have to? After what he did to Mackenzie – they should've left him to rot.'

The anger went out of her and they sat quietly, each with their own thoughts.

Inside A & E, high on the wall, a television with the sound turned down fascinated the dozen people waiting for a doctor to take a look at them. A guy in his late teens with a tattoo on his forehead pressed a blood-soaked cloth to the sleeve of his denim jacket. Next to him, his grinning mate whispered out of the corner of his mouth. Gavin guessed gang violence had brought them here. Tomorrow this would be a war story for the troops. Further along, a woman and a girl huddled together. The girl's left foot was in a plaster cast which had cracked open. Their dull expressions said they'd been waiting a while. A nurse appeared and called a name. The denim youth made faces behind her back to amuse his pal and followed her.

Monica said, 'Anybody want coffee? I'll get it.'

Blair had a different suggestion. 'Why don't we go to the tearoom? Better than staying here. Don't need to be gone long.'

They made their way to the cafeteria. Blair bought four coffees and carried them on a tray to the table. Nobody spoke until Adele said, 'Can you talk about it?'

Her brother nodded. 'I got a call from Derek. He'd seen the guy from Buchanan Street and was going after him.'

'Hoping he'd lead him to Mackenzie?'

Gavin glanced at his wife. 'That's what I imagined, but he was different.'

'Different how?'

'Hard to explain. Not the Derek Crawford any of us know. Like he wasn't quite there.' He shrugged the inadequate description aside. 'We were on the M74, heading for the Lowther Hills, although we didn't know that at the time. He had about twenty-odd minutes on me. Fortunately the stalker stopped at Abington services otherwise I'd never have caught up.' Gavin looked at his family. 'I'll tell you what I won't be telling the police – I was scared.'

Blair leaned forward. 'Scared of what?'

'About what he might do when he caught up to him.'

'You thought he'd kill him?'

'I don't know but it didn't feel good. For a while I thought I'd lost him. But I kept on going. Then I saw Derek's car outside a derelict house. The engine was still running, and there was another car, a Toyota.' Gavin was visibly affected by the memory. 'The house was literally falling down. The windows were boarded, doors were hanging off their hinges, and the roof was caved in. I knew this couldn't be where Mackenzie was staying, it didn't make sense. There were raised voices coming from the basement, so I went down.'

Under the table, Monica took his hand. He sipped his coffee and swallowed before he went on. 'It was the worst thing I've ever seen. It was a dungeon. Mackenzie was naked, chained to a bed.'

The women gasped and Monica squeezed her husband's fingers tighter.

'Her face was so white, at first I thought she was dead. Derek was fighting with the guy in the black coat in the middle of the room. Seeing what he'd done to Mackenzie...I guess something in him just snapped.'

Nobody pressed for details and he finished his story. 'Then the guy was lying on the floor with a knife in him and Derek was... out of it.'

Blair steered them away from the picture Gavin had painted onto safer ground. 'So you called the police.'

'Yeah, I called Andrew Geddes. He told me to keep Mackenzie warm and not to move her.'

'What did Derek do?'

'He was devastated; destroyed. If I hadn't been there he would've finished what he'd started.'

'You mean, he'd have murdered him?'

Gavin paused before he answered. 'I'm sure of it.'

'Why did he phone you?'

'No idea, but I'm glad he did.'

Monica said, 'Did you manage to speak to him before they took him away?'

'I tried, but he wasn't taking anything in.'

Blair asked what none of them had even considered. 'Did the knife belong to Derek? Because if it did…'

'I can't be sure though I wouldn't have thought so. Carrying a knife? Doesn't sound like Derek, does it? Anyway, Andrew seemed to believe a case could be made for defending himself.'

'But if he dies..?'

A good question. 'We'll be in uncharted waters. We already are.'

They sat in silence as the true horror of it sunk in. Eventually Gavin said, 'Let's get back.'

It was close on two hours before they saw a doctor. He was tall and black; prematurely balding. The face was young but the eyes were old, and when he spoke there was Africa in his voice. The name-tag pinned to his white coat read: Dr Chilolo. He led them down the corridor into a room and got straight to the point. Clearly he'd already been given the background by the police.

'Mackenzie has a punctured lung, cracked ribs, heavy bruising to her throat and body and cuts and abrasions, some of them infected. She's in the ACCU – the Adult Critical Care Unit.' He let seconds pass then added 'She's also been sexually assaulted.'

He stopped short of adding 'brutally', it wouldn't help.

Chilolo allowed the family to register what he'd said before he gave them the worst of it. 'Her physical injuries are severe but not grave. She should recover from them. I'm more concerned with her mental state. In certain circumstances, when the body's under attack, the brain reacts to protect itself. In other words, it closes down.'

'Isn't that good?'

'In theory, yes.'

'When will you know?'

The doctor made eye contact with each of them in turn. 'The next twenty-four hours are critical. My advice would be to go home and get some sleep. There's nothing to be gained by staying here.'

Gavin asked what was on all of their minds. 'And what if it's permanent? What if Mackenzie doesn't come out of it?'

Chilolo drew on his years of dealing with family members at moments like this.

'Let's cross that bridge when we come to it.'

* * *

Adele had been Mackenzie's biggest critic so it was hardly a surprise that the doctor's guarded reply affected her most. He was telling them to be prepared for the worst, that she might not regain consciousness because of a man Adele had refused to believe existed. If she could turn the clock back, she would, without a moment's hesitation, and give Mackenzie the support sisters are supposed to give each other. Hindsight was a bloody fine thing, wasn't it?

Gavin was the only one with any idea of what to expect, but even he was shocked. Mackenzie was in a private room, a bank of machines monitoring her vital signs. Against the ashen pallor the bruises seemed even more vicious than in the dimly-lit building in the Lowther Hills. Seeing her sister like that was too much for Adele. She burst into tears. Blair held her then guided her out. Gavin and Monica followed them into the corridor and Blair suggested they leave. Adele insisted on staying.

'I can't leave her like this. I want to wait a little longer. But you go, you all need some rest.'

None of them disagreed.

Blair said, 'I'll keep you company.'

She turned the offer down. 'No thanks. I'd like time alone with Mackenzie if you don't mind. Besides, the boys can't be left by themselves too long or we'll have no house to go back to.'

When they'd gone she sat by the bed holding her sister's hand, caressing it, quietly asking to be forgiven. 'I'm sorry, baby. I let you down. I didn't know. I didn't know.'

Adele listened to the rise and fall of Mackenzie's breathing, anxiously studying her bruised face for a sign of recognition – the flicker of an eyelid, the tremble of a fingertip – anything.

There was nothing.

She wasn't a religious person. Religion was a crutch for weak people and, whatever else, nobody had ever accused Adele Gardiner of being weak. But she was weak. And she was tired of pretending she was strong. She rested her head on the bed and prayed.

A nurse asked for ten minutes to attend to Mackenzie. Out in the corridor, laughter got Adele's attention – a policeman stationed by a door was joking with a porter. Coffee was mentioned. A minute later, he passed her on his way, she assumed, to the tearoom.

Adele didn't stop to think about it. *HE* was in there, the monster who'd caused her sister so much pain. She opened the door and went inside.

There were two beds in the room. One of them was empty. In the other, a figure lay unconscious, his face covered by an oxygen mask. In her mind, the man who had abducted and abused her sister was an animal. It was shocking to discover he didn't look like a monster. In fact, he couldn't have been more ordinary. His eyes were closed as if he was only sleeping, his skin had a healthy pink glow, and in the muted light, Adele took in an IV line running from his wrist to a saline drip and a bank of machines recording his vital signs.

But it didn't matter how he fucking looked, did it? He'd done what he'd done to a defenceless woman. She pictured her little sister's broken body yards away and heard the doctor's uncertain prognosis in her head. Mackenzie might not recover. Prepare yourselves. That was what he'd been saying.

let's cross that bridge when we come to it
let's cross that bridge when...
let's cross that...

She glanced nervously over her shoulder towards the door and gently removed his mask. The pillow from the other bed felt cool and fresh and crisp. Adele held it inches above his face, savouring the moment, wanting to remember it.

From behind her a voice said, 'Trust me, Mrs Gardiner, that wouldn't be the best decision you've ever made.'

It was DS Andrew Geddes.

* * *

Geddes walked from the door, replaced the oxygen mask and gently took the pillow out of Adele's unsteady hands. In the bed, Joe Melia not long back from theatre, was oblivious to how close he'd come to paying the price of his cruelty. The DS glanced at Adele Gardiner, remembering how certain and how wrong she'd been about her sister's claim she was being stalked. '" – A cock-and-bull story – "' she'd called it.

then you didn't believe it?
not for a second
why?
Mackenzie's an attention-seeker

When he'd interviewed her at her house she'd been impatient and dismissive and Geddes could only imagine how deep her guilt ran now. She choked back a sob and he put a comforting arm on her shoulder. 'I want to kill him, is that so wrong?'

The DS chose his words carefully. 'To kill him? Yes, that would be wrong. To want to?' He shook his head. 'How could you feel any other way?'

'If you hadn't come in...'

Geddes defused the bleak speculation knowing there was nothing worthwhile down that road. 'Don't be so hard on yourself. Even good people do bad things sometimes.'

She turned to him. 'All I think about is how badly I let her down. I didn't believe her. I didn't believe my own flesh and blood. What does that say about me?'

'It says you're human. It says you made a mistake.'

'But…look at me…' Adele raised the hands that had held the pillow inches from Melia's face. '…what have I become?'

'You haven't become anything. You're the same as you've always been.'

'And what's that?'

'A woman who loves her sister. Mackenzie's lucky to have you.'

Adele smiled a sad half-smile. 'Thanks for saying that, and thanks for stopping me.'

The policeman feigned ignorance. 'You've lost me. Nothing happened here.'

'Thank you anyway.'

It was time to end this. Geddes said, 'I want you to go home. If there's any change you'll be the first person I call.'

'Promise.'

'I promise. The very first.'

* * *

The detective was alone in the room with the sounds of Joe Melia's breathing and the machines monitoring him. He hadn't realised he was still holding the pillow. A picture of the dank cellar in the Lowther Hills flashed in front of his eyes and his fingers dug into it. For a moment he hesitated then put it back where it belonged and went to find out why the fuck nobody was guarding the door.

Day Thirteen

DI Taylor and DS Geddes were anxious to question Derek Crawford. The interview never got started because, in the police doctor's opinion, he was in shock and therefore in no state to answer. The detectives agreed to postpone the conversation until later in the day.

Andrew Geddes headed back to the hospital. Two things had happened since he'd last been there: security had been stepped up and a young police officer's career had crashed and burned. He wouldn't be going any higher and would probably leave the service when the message got through to him he'd be better off in another job. Now, in the ACCU, not far from the woman Melia had abducted and abused, a uniformed constable sat beside the knife-victim's bed.

According to the driver's licence in his wallet, Joseph Melia was thirty-six years old and living at an address in Shawlands. Officers had already visited the flat. It was unoccupied – a bleary-eyed neighbour confirmed it had been for months.

The knife had entered Melia's abdomen on the right side, missing his liver by a fraction, damaging his intestines and causing massive internal bleeding. An emergency operation to stem the blood loss and repair the wound had been only partially successful and the trauma brought on a stroke. He remained critical.

Geddes watched the figure in the bed, his complexion a picture of health thanks to three blood transfusions, asking himself what kind of monster would do what he'd done. The scene in the basement was as grim as he'd come across in twenty years on the force. Like something from a horror movie: the iron bed, the chain, the smell of decay. And, in the midst of it, Mackenzie

Crawford's beaten body. The detective detested this creature for the suffering he'd caused and, hardened professional though he was, he still hadn't come to terms with it.

He was at the door on his way out when the constable shouted. 'Sir!'

Joe Melia's eyes were open, unblinking, staring at the ceiling. Geddes put his revulsion aside – this may be the only chance he'd get. He bent to whisper in his ear. 'Joe. Joe. Tell me why you did it.'

Melia didn't respond and the policeman couldn't be sure he'd heard him, or even knew he was there. The stroke had pulled one corner of his mouth down so he seemed to be sneering contempt for the naive notion his nearness to death would convince him to reveal secrets only he knew.

Geddes tried again, coaxing him to speak. 'C'mon, Joe, tell me why. Why Mackenzie Crawford? Do yourself a favour. Do the right thing while you still can.'

He almost blurted out the old cliche about it going easier on him but stopped himself.

Joe Melia would never leave this room.

Melia's bottom lip quivered, his twisted mouth producing sounds more animal than human. The DS stayed with it. 'Why her? What did she do to you to make you hate her so much?'

'Cccoaddaawth.'

Geddes altered his approach using a gentler tone which wasn't in his heart. 'Take your time. Take your time, Joe. There's plenty of time. I'm here.'

The eyes darted in Melia's head. 'Hhhhththth. Kkkkadd.'

'You and I know you're not a killer so help me understand. Why take it out on the woman?'

The reply was mangled, unrecognisable as language. 'Kkkkkaaaaa.'

Across the bed the constable observed his superior uncomfortably. 'Think we should get a nurse, Sir. I really think we should.'

Geddes ignored him. 'Joe. Joe. For God's sake man. Tell me why.'

Suddenly, Melia's back arched violently as if some giant hand had taken hold of him. He thrashed under the bedclothes. His jaw fell slack, his pupils turned up into his head and his body shook uncontrollably while a moan, long and thick, came from deep within him. His tongue protruded from between his bared teeth before they snapped shut, severing the tip, filling his mouth with blood. A red spray landed on Geddes face but he didn't stop. He put aside his shock and stuck to his task, conscious of the manic urgency in his own voice, knowing he was wasting his time: Melia was having a second stroke and would be lucky to survive – the opportunity was slipping away.

If the bastard died the truth would die with him.

'Why? Why her? Why there? Fucking tell me!'

Suddenly the room was filled with nurses and the detective realised the constable must have pressed the emergency call-button. The last thing he saw before he was pulled away and forced to leave were the metal paddles attached to Melia's bare chest and a doctor leaning over him calling 'Clear!'

Then Andrew Geddes was in the corridor with the white-faced officer giving him a strange look, no nearer understanding what had brought Joseph Melia to the house in the Lowther Hills.

* * *

Gavin Darroch hadn't slept much during the night and guessed he wouldn't be alone. None of the family were proud of themselves and he imagined Adele would take it especially hard. He drew into the car park and walked to the hospital entrance with Monica at his side. Blair and Adele were already there. Visiting hours didn't apply to them.

Adele said, 'I phoned before we left. She's still unconscious but stable.'

He nodded; he'd made the same call.

They dreaded what was waiting for them. What they found was no change in their sister although some of the tension had left her features and she almost looked like herself again. If only it was that easy. Gavin asked if Doctor Chilolo was available. He wasn't and he had to settle for a doctor who'd just come on duty who was sympathetic but answered his questions in general terms.

Unaware of the nurse stripping the empty bed that had held Joseph Melia, they trooped back downstairs no wiser than they'd been.

* * *

Geddes took a call at his desk in Aikenhead Road. He listened, his lips a tight line, then went to look for Taylor. The Detective Inspector was in his office. When Geddes stuck his head round the door, Taylor misunderstood.

'Ready to go, are we?'

'Not yet.'

'Then what?'

'Joe Melia died five minutes ago.'

* * *

Derek Crawford had agreed to speak to the officers but was clearly still shaken. Roxburgh, his lawyer, had updated him on his wife's condition and assured him they had a solid defence: a stranger had kidnapped her from outside their home and tortured her in the bowels of a derelict building. If he hadn't acted, she'd be dead. He'd saved her life. He was a hero. No jury in the country would convict him. Crawford believed him.

Taylor and Geddes came in and sat down. The man they were about to interview had suffered a terrible experience but whatever they were feeling they kept to themselves; their expressions gave nothing away. When Gavin Darroch told the familiar face from the five-a-sides about his missing sister in a room not thirty feet away, the DS couldn't have imagined what it would become.

Taylor recognised Geddes' existing knowledge of the case and had asked him to lead. He began gently. 'I'm aware this is a difficult time for you, Mr Crawford. It isn't my intention to make it any worse. Having said that, I do have some questions. As your lawyer has told you, the man we suspect of abducting Mrs Crawford has died in hospital of his injuries.'

Crawford whispered through his teeth. 'Bastard. Got off scot-free.'

Geddes didn't comment. 'Which makes it all the more important we understand exactly what happened. Tell me how you came to be in the house in the Lowther Hills?'

Roxburgh said something to Derek Crawford the detectives didn't hear.

'I followed him from Glasgow.'

'Did you know him?'

Crawford fingered his bandaged arm. 'Know him, no. I'd seen him before.'

'Where?'

He took a deep breath. 'In Buchanan Street. I told you this.'

'You did, but we need it for the record. Describe the circumstances and take your time.'

'I can't think about it, can't go there, it's too painful.'

The DS encouraged him. 'Try. Do it for Mackenzie.'

Crawford covered his face with his hands. 'She told me. She pointed him out. I wouldn't listen to her.'

Roxburgh shook his head at the detectives. 'Obviously this is upsetting. Can my client have a minute?'

Geddes announced they were taking a break, turned the recorder off and the policemen stepped into the corridor. The DS said, 'This guy's fragile. Going to take a while. Haven't even got to the crime scene.'

Taylor voiced what both men understood. 'Still have to charge him and pass it to the PF. Let it be somebody else's shout.'

Geddes' mobile rang; he answered it. When the call ended he turned to the DI.

'Well, well.'

Taylor raised an eyebrow. 'What?'

'Joe Melia wasn't working.'

'So?'

'His last job ended four months ago. He got sacked.'

The senior detective wasn't in the mood. 'Tell me.'

'From Crawford Cars, would you believe?'

Taylor said, 'Get somebody over there to take a statement.'

'Already done. Lawson's on her way.'

* * *

Crawford sat forward, shoulders slumped, eyes heavy, but he seemed calmer. Geddes turned the recorder back on and was about to pick up where he'd left off when he thought better of it. In the seat next to him DI Taylor folded his arms across his chest. For now at least, it was Geddes' show.

The DS said, 'We'll come back to how you came to follow him to the Lowther Hills.' He looked at his notebook. 'How many dealerships do you have, Mr Crawford?'

Crawford paused before answering. 'Twenty-four.'

'Where are they?'

'Nine in Glasgow, seven in the Edinburgh area, two in Aberdeen and one each in Ayr, Dundee, East Kilbride, Paisley, Motherwell and Hamilton.'

'So it would it be fair to say you're a successful man.'

It wasn't a question. Crawford answered it anyway. 'In 2017 I was voted businessman of the year by the Glasgow Chamber of Commerce. So yes.'

'How many people do you employ?'

'All told, including the service division, rental and leasing: three hundred, three-fifty, something like that.'

'How well do you know them?'

Crawford was unfazed. 'Apart from a handful of guys who've been with me for years, I don't. The managers manage the units, I manage the business.'

Roxburgh earned his corn. 'I'm at a loss to understand where this is going. In case you've forgotten, my client is the victim here. His personal circumstances have no relevance.'

Geddes ignored the lawyer and spoke to Crawford, reading from his notes. 'So you're not familiar with a salesman who joined the Airbles Road showroom in Motherwell last October and was let go in February?'

Crawford said, 'You've lost me.'

Roxburgh interrupted in lawyer-speak. 'How is this germane, Detective?'

Crawford gestured to silence the lawyer and nodded at Geddes to continue.

'A bit of a rising star before he got found out. The top salesman in January.'

'So why did we let him go?'

'Turns out he was in business for himself; cutting the margins to the bone and doing side deals with some of the customers. Nice scam while it lasted. Bound to catch up with him and it did.'

Crawford was defensive. 'His references must've checked out or we would never have taken him on.' He made a dismissive sound in his throat. 'Mind you. References? These days? Telling the truth means opening a can of worms. Employers keep their comments neutral and kick the problem down the road for somebody else to deal with.'

Geddes doodled on the pad in front of him. 'Melia wasn't prosecuted. I wonder why?'

'That's a no-brainer. Can answer it without moving out of this chair. The manager who hired him was covering his arse. When what this guy was doing was flagged up he decided to get rid as quickly and quietly as possible. Don't blame him. Would've done the same to protect the business. "Conman Car Dealer" isn't the sort of publicity we need. Though I don't understand what this has to do with anything.'

'Would it surprise you to know that salesman was Joseph Melia?'

The policemen could almost see the wheels turning behind Crawford's eyes, demanding his memory reveal anything he might know about this man. The lawyer seized on what he was hearing. 'So you're saying the abduction was motivated by revenge?'

Geddes wasn't prepared to concede that much. 'I'm saying the man who abducted Mr Crawford's wife was a former employee.'

'But if this ne'er-do-well had an axe to grind, then surely it isn't a stretch to assume this was a reprisal?'

The detective ignored him and turned to Crawford. 'Did you receive a demand for money?'

'Obviously not or the police would've been brought in.'

'Not everyone goes down that road. So what did Melia hope to achieve?'

The lawyer jumped in. 'How can my client possibly answer that?'

Geddes let it go. 'Buchanan Street. Let's get back to it. You were saying your wife pointed a man out and you wouldn't listen to her.'

Crawford drew a weary hand over his face; his head went down. He looked up at the policemen, willing them to understand how it had been. 'Mackenzie's a lovely person, but when she drinks she changes. The things she says. Talks as if she hates me. Threatening to leave is par for the course. I suppose I'd had enough of it. I'm ashamed to say I lost patience with her.' The recorder would capture his story but not the expression on his face. 'She ran out of the restaurant. I caught up with her in the street. She was shouting. People were staring. Then she saw him. I saw him too.'

'Melia?'

'Yes. Mackenzie said he was following her.'

DI Taylor spoke for the first time. 'So why didn't you believe her?'

'He waved. He waved at her.'

'And you assumed they knew each other?'

Desperation choked him. 'I thought it was a set-up. I thought he was waiting for her.' Crawford's eyes were wild with regret. 'Later at the party she confessed he was her lover in front of everyone. They all heard her, ask them. When we got home she screamed it at me. The next day she announced she was leaving.'

He threw up his hands, frustrated and angry, appealing to them. 'What the fuck was I supposed to think?'

Geddes waited a moment before lobbing a hand grenade into the interview. 'Do you always carry a knife, Mr Crawford?'

The lawyer seized on the question. 'I demand you retract that. May I remind you again my client's wife is the victim here?'

Geddes didn't miss a beat. 'Why did you have a blade with you?'

Roxburgh banged his fist on the table. 'That's an outrageous assumption.'

Crawford put his hand on his arm; his eyes met the policeman's. 'The knife wasn't mine. It belonged to that bastard. If I hadn't got there when I did we'd be having a different conversation.'

* * *

Blair and Adele Gardiner needed to talk, and it wasn't going to be easy. While Mackenzie remained unconscious they avoided it. Gavin watched his sister sitting by the bed, noticing the strain she was under and understanding why. Adele had been Mackenzie's harshest critic, irritated by what she believed was the adult manifestation of parental over-indulgence. The events in the house in the Lowther Hills had changed her mind. She held her sister's hand, gently caressing it, whispering. Blair stood behind her. She wouldn't have to search to find him – he was there.

Monica wasn't. She was at home looking after Adam and Richard and Alice. Gavin missed her. Suddenly, Adele cried out and startled them. 'She moved! She moved her fingers!'

Blair knew the guilt his wife was suffering and how much she needed it to be true. He chose his words. 'Are you sure?'

She turned to Gavin. 'She moved her fingers.'

Mackenzie's unlined features said it wasn't so. Adele saw the doubt on his face and reacted. 'You think I imagined it. I didn't. I really didn't.'

Frustration turned to anger. 'Call the nurse, Blair.'

He pressed the buzzer by the side of the bed. A moment later a nurse arrived and made a show of taking Mackenzie's pulse. The others waited for her verdict and were disappointed.

'We'll keep monitoring her.'

* * *

Mackenzie Crawford was still unconscious in the ACCU in Wishaw Hospital. Her husband should be at her bedside instead of a room in Aikenhead Road police station. The last time he'd seen her was in the basement in the Lowther Hills. Geddes and Taylor had no desire to drag the interview out.

The DS said, 'Describe how you came to be at the house.'

Tiredness made Crawford irritable. He barked his reply. 'I saw the guy from Buchanan Street...Melia...in Glasgow. Behind the wheel of a Toyota at traffic lights on Cathedral Street. I made a U-turn and went after him.'

'Why?' In light of what came later the question seemed stupid.

'Why?' Derek Crawford spat out the word like it had a bad taste. 'Why do you think? Mackenzie was with him.'

'But you'd washed your hands of her, hadn't you?'

He smiled a sour self-deprecating smile. 'Did I say that? I suppose I did. I was worried about her. The whole family was worried.'

'You wanted to be sure she was all right?'

'No, there was no reason to think she wasn't all right. Mackenzie's family has been torn apart by this. It was a chance to put their minds at rest. For me...I just needed to know.'

'So that's when you called your brother-in-law?'

'Yes.'

'What was going through your mind?'

Crawford drew Geddes a sharp look. 'I wasn't thinking of killing him if that's what you mean.'

'I'm not suggesting you were, Mr Crawford.'

Roxburgh touched his client's arm and he got himself back under control.

'It's hard to remember. The further we went the more I wondered where the hell he was taking me. When he turned off at Abington and headed into the back of beyond...it's another world...couldn't imagine Mackenzie living out there. I saw the car parked outside a house with the bloody roof caved in.'

Crawford took a minute before he went on. 'You've been there, you've seen it.' He shuddered and rubbed his injured arm. 'When I went to the basement he was standing over her with a knife.' He looked at Taylor and then at Geddes. 'Christ only knows what he was going to do.'

'Did he attack you or did you attack him?'

'He came at me, and I knew I had to take that knife away from him before he had a chance to use it.'

'What happened after that?'

The lawyer started to speak and changed his mind.

'There was a struggle, that's all I remember...until Gavin pulled me away. That's when I saw what he'd done to Mackenzie.'

Crawford bent over the table and broke down, sobbing uncontrollably. Andrew Geddes didn't wait for the DI's say-so, he switched off the recorder.

The interview was over.

* * *

An hour later, DS Geddes explained to a shattered Derek Crawford what was going to happen. Crawford's eyes were empty and lifeless. Geddes said, 'You'll be formally charged with the murder of Joseph Melia.'

'Murder? You're doing me for murder? You saw what he did. Doesn't that matter?'

The detective put a reassuring hand on his shoulder. 'In a case like this the police always bring a murder charge. Standard procedure. The procurator fiscal will make the final decision.' He looked hard into Crawford's ravaged face. 'And to answer your question – it *does* matter. In fact, it matters a great deal. Under the circumstances we won't be opposing bail. This time tomorrow you'll be able to visit you wife.'

Crawford didn't raise his head and was taken to the cells. The next afternoon he would appear in court. Out in the corridor, the three men were sombre. What they'd witnessed had been rough – on all of them. Roxburgh spoke to the detectives with more than a trace of flint in his voice, appreciating they had a job to do but not liking them any better for it.

'We'll be entering a plea of not guilty and of course, requesting bail. The physical and psychological trauma Mrs Crawford has suffered may well have repercussions which publicity would exacerbate, inhibiting her recovery, and taking into consideration the damage to my client's business reputation, I'll also be asking the judge to impose a reporting ban.' Roxburgh nodded stiffly and left.

Geddes checked his watch. DI Taylor said, 'Caught me off-guard with the knife, have to say. Wasn't expecting that approach.'

'Just making sure, Sir. If Melia had been his wife's lover, Crawford would've had quite a resentment going. In the circumstances it was a whole lot worse. According to PC Lawson, the manager who fired him clearly remembers that when he told him he was out, Joe Melia was calm. Derek Crawford played no part. He wasn't involved.'

Geddes asked his superior for direction. 'When do you want me to get the brother-in-law in? He's an eye-witness.'

'We have his initial statement, don't we?' Geddes told him they had. 'Then there's no rush. Let's see how it goes after tomorrow.'

'Any idea what side the PF will come down on?'

'My guess is they won't proceed. It's an open and shut self-defence. Culpable homicide at best.'

'You sure about that, sir?'

'Not sure about anything these days. Are you?'

Day Fourteen

Derek Crawford walked out the side entrance of the court building and took a deep breath. The taste of freedom was a cliche but even after one night in the cells it was true. And it was sweet.

Not far away, traffic raced from Trongate down Saltmarket, while across Clyde Street the river sparkled in the afternoon sunshine. It had gone well. His lawyer's request for bail had been granted, unopposed by the police and, by order of the magistrate, a reporting ban was in place. And thank God. The last thing he needed was to have this plastered on the front page of every bloody rag. The fewer people who knew the sooner they could get past it.

Roxburgh joined him full of cheerful reassurance and placed a friendly hand on his shoulder, pleased with the work he'd done on his client's behalf. Crawford shrugged it away. The rejection didn't register. Roxburgh said, 'Only the first obstacle but it's better to have it behind rather than in front of us, eh?'

'What happens now?'

'Depends on the procurator fiscal. If he decides to proceed to trial we'll start preparing our defence. I believe – and it's only my view – he'll conclude there's no charge to answer and drop the case. In any event, I wouldn't be overly concerned if I were you.'

'But you're not me.'

Crawford took off his jacket and untied the bandage on his arm; the wound was already healing. His lawyer hadn't learned his lesson and offered an unwelcome opinion.

'Safer with it on I should've thought.'

Crawford ignored him and threw the soiled cloth on the ground. 'Reminds me of what I want to forget.'

Roxburgh pretended to empathise. 'Quite so.'

'The policemen were in court. Is that significant?'

'Not particularly. It's not unusual. No role at this stage, of course. Whether they ever do will be determined by others. You haven't got a car. Can I give you a lift anywhere?'

'Yes. Wishaw.'

DS Geddes saw them leaving and hurried to catch up. 'Mr Crawford?'

It was too soon to have forgotten the interview and Crawford eyed him suspiciously. Geddes said, 'Got good news for you. Your wife's regaining consciousness.'

* * *

Gavin and Adele had stayed in the hospital overnight, taking turns at trying to sleep. Neither had managed more than a few minutes and they were exhausted. The sight of their sister blinking at them made it worthwhile.

It had been a long vigil, spent mostly in silence. At 2am. Mackenzie's fingers tightened round Adele's hand and this time Gavin saw it, too. Nothing else happened until a quarter to six when she moved her head – not much; a fraction. But enough to breathe hope into their tired bodies.

Adele was elated. 'She's coming round. She's coming out of it. Thank God.'

Gavin held his enthusiasm in check. He'd been in the basement. He'd seen what Adele hadn't. She couldn't know the horror Mackenzie had endured or begin to guess the aftermath. The hospital staff were cheerful and gentle but wouldn't be drawn on their patient's condition. While Gavin went to make a few calls. Adele stayed by Mackenzie's side until Doctor Chilolo arrived on his rounds and a nurse asked her to leave.

Downstairs in the tearoom she talked excited gibberish for Scotland. Her brother listened, understanding that more than any of them she needed it to be all right.

'How soon do you think they'll let her go home?'

The question was unrealistic, impossible to answer, and an indication of how divorced from the reality of the situation she was.

'No idea. We have to understand how serious this is. She was in that dungeon for nine days. Whatever the damage is, it may not be only physical. It'll take time.'

Adele brushed her brother's dark speculation aside. 'Of course. But love will make her well, and there's no shortage of that.'

Gavin recognised denial when he heard it. If only it was so simple. His fears were rooted in the memory of the derelict house: coming down the wooden stairs, seeing Mackenzie unconscious on the bed and Derek in a fight to the death with the man who'd abducted his wife. Dwelling on what she'd suffered before they arrived was more than he could handle. He said, 'The doctor will decide. We'll be led by him.'

That wasn't enough for her. 'Yes, but I'm asking what you think.'

He struggled to be patient, knowing she wasn't ready for the truth, whatever it turned out to be. 'Honestly, I haven't a bloody clue. She's coming round. Let's take it one step at a time, eh?'

* * *

Upstairs, Doctor Chilolo was waiting. 'Your sister's sleeping. For the moment the most important thing is rest. Allow the body to heal. The tests we did when Mackenzie was brought in show no life-threatening injuries. That isn't to say she's free and clear. Once she's fully conscious we'll begin a new round.'

'But you think she'll be all right?'

'I'm hopeful, yes.'

Adele picked up on his reluctance to commit himself. Driven by her fear she said, 'There something you're not telling us.' Her imagination got ahead of her. 'Brain damage. You think she's got brain damage, is that it?'

'I've seen no evidence to indicate that. I'm suggesting we need to be cautious.' He spread his arms. 'The early signs are good. But your sister hasn't spoken yet. When she does we'll know more than we do now. I understand your anxiety. I'm saying we need to give her time. And she isn't the only one who could use some sleep. Go home. Come back this evening. If anything changes we'll get word to you.'

Good advice, though not advice Adele was willing to take. 'No, I prefer to stay. I wouldn't sleep. How could anybody sleep when she needs us here?'

It was the reaction the doctor anticipated – he'd seen it more times than he could remember. In the end people did what they wanted and, beyond giving them the benefit of his opinion, there was nothing else he could do. He nodded. 'Of course, it's up to you.'

'Can we go back in? I have to be there when she wakes up.'

'Just don't expect too much, too soon.'

Adele wasn't listening. The doctor spoke to Gavin. 'You understand what I'm saying, don't you?'

A look passed between them. Gavin didn't answer.

* * *

One minute Mackenzie's eyes were closed, the next they were open. And everything Doctor Chilolo had said was forgotten. Adele threw her arms around her sister. This time the tears were tears of joy. Gavin caught hold of her hand and got her to sit down. For a terrible few seconds Mackenzie seemed not to recognise them and Adele's wild conclusion looked to be real. Then her lips moved and she spoke. 'Where am I?'

Adele moved closer. 'You're in hospital but you're going to be all right.'

The answer seemed to satisfy her and she drifted off to sleep until she woke again and startled them with a question. 'Where's Derek?'

Gavin and Adele looked apprehensively at each other. Which of them was going to tell her?' Adele lied for both of them. 'Don't worry about that. He'll be here.'

Without warning, Mackenzie's features crumbled as the memories flooded in. She panicked, tore the IV drip from the back of her hand and tried to get out of the bed.

'No! No! Noooo!'

Gavin caught hold of her, so thin under the dressing-gown. 'It's okay. It's okay, sis. We're here.'

Two nurses rushed in and took over. One said, 'Give us a few minutes to settle her down, will you?'

Adele would've argued but her brother led her away. Out in the corridor she told him how close she'd come to killing Melia. 'It wasn't some aberration. I knew what I was doing. If it hadn't been for your detective friend I would have. He stopped me.'

Gavin held her close. 'Good thing Andrew was there. I can't lose you as well. Ever since I saw her in that awful cellar I've thought of doing the same.'

The nurse found them with their arms round each other. 'She's calmed down. You can go back in. Please, don't tell her anything that might upset her. She's asking about her husband. I wasn't sure what to say.'

Gavin wished Monica was here.

They returned to the room they'd so hurriedly left. Mackenzie was lying on her side, as if she was hiding. Her first question wasn't about Derek. 'How did I get here?'

'An ambulance brought you.'

'When?'

'Two days ago.'

Mackenzie started to shake. 'Where is he? Where is he?'

'Derek will be here soon.'

'Not Derek.'

Gavin touched Adele's hand: this was his responsibility. 'You're safe. He can't hurt you now.'

She tried to sit up, her voice rising. 'But I need to know where he is.'

Her brother put his arms round her.

'How did you find me? Did Derek pay them? I knew he would.'

Gavin kissed her forehead and pulled the bedclothes round her. 'It's over. It's really over. I'll tell you everything when you're well. Right now you need to rest.'

* * *

But rest would have to wait because Derek appeared and rushed to his wife's side. He dropped to his knees and took her hand. 'Thank God. Thank God you're okay. I've been worried sick.'

Seeing him was too much. Mackenzie broke down. She tried to speak and couldn't. He put a finger to her lips then folded his arms around her, whispering words only she could hear. Gavin and Adele gave them time to themselves and went to the café. Later Derek joined them, visibly more relaxed than when he arrived.

'They've given her a sedative. She's sleeping.'

Adele reached out to him. 'She's been through so much. She'll be fine now she's got you.'

The men didn't comment; they understood only too well what Mackenzie had gone through. Derek said, 'As long as I live I'll never let her out of my sight. Thanks for being here when she woke up. I was frantic she'd be alone. That would've been terrible.'

Gavin had last seen his brother-in-law in the back of a police car in the Lowther Hills and remembered his gaunt, bone-white face: shock had made a ghost of him.

'What happened with the police?'

Derek wiped something from his eye. 'They charged me. I've just come from court.'

Adele was outraged. 'Charged you? What with?'

'Murder.'

She exploded. 'That's ridiculous!'

He shook his head. 'It's not as bad as it sounds. Apparently it's how they do things in Scotland. But a man died, that's the bottom line. Nothing will change it. I've been released on bail. I'm free. For the moment. Where it goes next is up to the procurator fiscal.'

'But after what he did to Mackenzie…'

Derek spoke softly. 'It's not about that at this stage. The police have a job to do.'

'But it's crazy.'

'Have to admit it certainly feels like it but that's the way it works.'

Gavin said, 'The guy, what about him? Do they know who he is…was?'

Derek paused. 'His name was Melia. Joe Melia. Apparently, he worked for Crawford Cars.'

The news shocked Adele. 'What?'

Gavin cut across his sister. '*Apparently*? What does that mean? Did you know him?'

He shook his head. 'Be easier to understand if I did. Don't recall a bloody thing about him.'

'Sorry, I'm not getting this. He worked for you yet you didn't know him?'

For a moment the Derek of old surfaced. 'A lot of people work for me. People come and go all the time in my business. He was in the showroom at Motherwell. The manager discovered he was running a scam and sacked him. Abducting Mackenzie was his way of hitting back.'

'So he was a stranger?'

'A stranger with a grudge.'

'What does your lawyer say?'

'What you'd expect. Reckons the fiscal won't go ahead. And even if he does, we have a strong case.'

'What about you?'

'Haven't given it a thought. All that matters is Mackenzie.' He looked from Gavin to Adele and back and tried to put the last twenty-four hours into words. 'Still can't believe any of this is real, except it is. In the cells… not knowing…you've no idea… the worst night of my life. Appearing in court this afternoon was almost a relief.'

Gavin said, 'I'll be giving a statement later.'

Derek nodded. 'Just tell them what you saw.'

'I'm not sure what I saw.'

'Then that's what you have to say. The truth is the best defence.'

Day Sixteen

Doctor Chilolo had a progress chart tucked under his arm and seemed almost pleased to see the police officers again. 'In an ideal world I'd ask you to leave it a little longer. That said, Mrs Crawford's a good deal better than she was and, as we agreed yesterday, we all have our jobs to do. Follow me.'

Behind his back DS Geddes raised an eyebrow at the constable and PC Lawson almost laughed. Maybe DI Taylor had known what he was doing when he'd handed this part of the investigation over to his sergeant.

The doctor smiled. The day before he hadn't been so welcoming, keeping them waiting outside his office. The delay was entirely intentional. When it came to the best interests of his patients, Chilolo could be a difficult man. He intended to refuse the them permission to interview Mackenzie Crawford for at least another twenty-four hours, and nothing or no one would change his mind.

The Tanzanian doctor had trained in the USA, but there was only one place he wanted to work. As a committed hill-walker, Scotland was an easy choice. In two years he'd managed to climb seventy-four 'Munros', the Scottish mountains higher than three thousand feet. Modest compared with Kilimanjaro, a challenge nevertheless. Before he moved to another country, Chilolo was determined to 'bag' all two hundred and eighty-two of them. The previous weekend he'd added Ben Hope, the most northerly Munro, to his list. Number seventy-five. After that, imposing his will on a couple of police officers was easy.

The officers sat down and came to the point. Geddes introduced himself and PC Lawson.

'We're anxious to speak to Mrs Crawford. We believe she may have important information regarding a serious crime.'

Chilolo had rested his arms on his desk. 'I'm afraid that won't be possible, not today. She's been through an ordeal. She needs time to recover. Questioning her at this stage will set her back. I can't allow it.'

Geddes jaw tightened. 'I appreciate your position and ask you to appreciate ours. We're looking at murder. Your patient is crucial to our enquiries.'

Chilolo wasn't persuaded. 'Is she a suspect?' He knew the answer. 'A witness? Then I can't agree. tomorrow we'll see how she is. Come back then but I'm not making any promises.'

Walking towards their car they were tight-lipped. Andrew Geddes started the engine and pulled away. He tried to sound unfazed. 'A good man to have on your side, isn't he? Can't say I blame him. Mackenzie Crawford was unconscious during the fight. Don't expect her to have much to say.' He glanced across at the young policewoman. 'But you never know.'

* * *

Now, a day later, outside the ACCU, Chilolo stopped to let the corridor clear before he spoke, the apparent good humour of earlier gone, his expression warning them to listen because he was serious.

'Let's establish the ground rules. As you are aware, this woman is the victim of serious physical and sexual assault. However well she may seem to be, let me assure you she's fragile and will need professional counselling. Apart from her injuries the psychological trauma has been devastating.'

DS Geddes bristled. He'd conducted interviews like this hundreds of times and didn't appreciate being lectured. 'We respect what Mrs Crawford's been through.' He gestured to his young colleague. 'That's why PC Lawson is here. And, of course, we'll take it slowly. Upsetting her is the last thing on our minds, believe me, Doctor.'

Chilolo drew himself to his full height, towering over them, unimpressed by Geddes' speech. 'If you distress her in any way I'll report you to your superior. I'm giving you ten minutes. Not a minute longer. If you haven't got what you need by then we'll be seeing each other again. But it won't be today. Is that understood?'

He led them to a private room in the corner of the ACCU where Mackenzie was propped-up on pillows, nervously playing with the edge of the sheet. The last time Geddes had seen her was when the ambulancemen stretchered her out of the house in the Lowther Hills. She looked better, but how difficult was that?

The doctor explained who the visitors were and why they were here. On his way to the door he reserved his final words for the senior officer. 'Ten minutes. No longer.'

Geddes had no doubt he meant it.

They sat down on opposite sides of the bed and Andrew Geddes introduced them. 'This is Constable Emily Lawson and I'm Detective Sergeant Geddes. We'd like to ask you a few questions. Think you're up to it?'

Mackenzie nodded, uncertainly. 'I'll try. But first I need to know: where is he?'

She meant her abuser. The doctor's warning came back to the detective. He chose his words carefully. 'Don't worry, we've got him.'

'He has to pay. He has to pay for what he did to me.'

Lawson leaned forward to reassure her. 'He will. I promise you he will.'

Geddes said, 'We understand some of what happened. Tell us about it from the beginning. There's no rush.'

That wasn't true.

Mackenzie Crawford's refusal to be a victim gave her the strength to tell her story, beginning with the first time she'd seen the stalker in the supermarket. Speaking so softly they had to strain to hear, she described the incidents in Buchanan Street and the day she'd run from him, faltering only when she came to the abduction and what had come after.

Geddes noted the chronology and waited until she was finished. So far she'd done well. 'I have to ask, had you met him before?'

Her voice faded. 'Never.'

He clarified the point. 'So he was a stranger?'

She answered with a nod.

An instinct prompted the policeman. 'Did you ever attend social functions connected to your husband's business?'

The question puzzled her. 'The first year after we were married we went to the Christmas party. I think Derek wanted to show me off. After that he went by himself.'

The DS moved to the events in the basement and marked the change in her but pressed on. Retelling the days in captivity was almost too much and she became agitated. Lawson used her initiative and held Mackenzie's hand until she calmed down and was able to continue.

It was a harrowing tale.

His years on the force didn't help Geddes come any nearer to understanding how resentment could drive someone to do what had been done to Mackenzie Crawford. It seemed Joseph Melia's sacking had taken him close to insanity. What he'd done was the work of a madman.

Doctor Chilolo appeared at the door, his hands in the pockets of his white coat. He made a show of checking his watch but Mackenzie interrupted before he could begin.

'I have to do this. Don't stop it.'

'They'll come back tomorrow.'

She was insistent. 'No, no. Today.'

'As your doctor, I – '

'Today.'

Chilolo shrugged and signalled for them to continue. At the side of the bed, Lawson's eyes filled with tears. The courage this woman was showing moved her. She caught hold of herself before Geddes noticed the lapse and focused on the notes she was taking. The DS wasn't immune, just better at hiding it. He said, 'A couple more questions and we'll leave you alone. The balaclava: why do you think he wore it? You'd already seen him?'

Mackenzie shuddered. 'To frighten me. To scare me. And it worked.'

The officers stood. The interview was almost over. Mackenzie Crawford had been impressive; brave and convincing. Yet something about her statement didn't ring true. Her claim to have never met the stalker didn't gel with her outburst at the party or Derek Crawford's statement.

Had there been an affair? Had it gone wrong? And was this the result?

'At your sister's birthday party you claimed he was your lover. Why?'

'I heard them all talking about me and knew they didn't believe he was real. So I lashed out. It was stupid.' Her voice faltered. 'Maybe none of this would've happened if I hadn't said it.'

Geddes would have preferred to leave it there but couldn't. 'So who was the man you were meeting?'

Behind the bruising, Mackenzie was confused. 'Man? What man?'

'When you went out at night your husband saw you get into a car.'

Her expression softened with the memory. 'You mean, Alec? He was taking me to an AA meeting. Helping me to get sober.'

The detective hadn't seen that coming. In the car he switched on the ignition and drove away. They'd just interviewed the most misunderstood woman in Scotland. He kept his eyes on the road and spoke to the constable in the passenger seat. 'You okay, Lawson, because I'm not. If Joe Melia wasn't already dead I'd kill the bastard myself.'

Day Fifty-Six

Gavin Darroch was in a good mood. The progress meeting he'd just come out of on a redevelopment project south of the river had gone well. He was satisfied the talented young guns who worked for him were on their way to delivering a design which matched the remit and was, at the same time, aesthetically pleasing. The public/private partnership committee members more often than not wasted time squabbling among themselves vying for power, struggling to agree on anything. Gavin was confident they would approve what he'd be presenting to them at the end of the month.

His mobile rang. Mackenzie. Immediately, he felt himself tense. It had been over a week since he'd visited his sister, taking Monica and Alice with him and phoning ahead as Derek asked, rather than dropping in unannounced.

Mackenzie had looked better, there was no doubt about that. The bruising had disappeared, she had colour in her cheeks and put on weight. But beyond the usual greetings, she hadn't had much to say. Derek did the talking for both of them, more vociferous than they'd known him, filling the gaps in the conversation whenever they appeared. Gavin may not have noticed how often he answered for Mackenzie, Monica certainly did. Given what his wife had been through, his over-protectiveness wasn't difficult to relate to.

When Mackenzie went to the kitchen for a glass of water Derek said, 'You've no idea how difficult it is. She's absolutely obsessed with that bloody house. Never stops talking about it.'

Monica wasn't surprised by that. 'Understandable, given what she's been through.'

Derek was on the point of adding something when Mackenzie came back.

Gavin smiled at his sister. 'Just asking if the doctor's pleased with your progress?'

She looked at her husband. He replied, speaking as if she wasn't in the room. 'Very happy. We're on course to make a complete recovery. Whenever she's well enough we're going away for a long holiday, just the two of us. Palm trees and coconuts.'

At one point during the hour with the Crawfords, Alice woke up and cried out. No louder than normal. Mackenzie's reaction was troubling. She froze. Derek moved to the arm of the chair and gently rubbed her hand, keeping the conversation going while Monica attended to Alice.

Something and nothing.

But in the car going home with the baby asleep in her cot in the backseat, Monica said out loud what her husband was already thinking. 'She isn't right, Gavin. You can see that, can't you?'

He wasn't ready to admit it was true. 'It's early days. It'll take time.'

'Of course it will. That isn't what I mean.'

Monica's concern went deeper. She wondered if her sister-in-law would ever get over it. It was the stuff of nightmares and it had come too close to home. She'd found herself on several occasions imagining how she'd cope if it happened to her and never got very far.

It was too terrifying to contemplate.

Gavin closed his office door and put the phone to his ear. Mackenzie's voice was an urgent whisper, as though she was afraid of being overheard. Not possible. For a month after she came out of hospital, Derek spent every day and night with her, telling anyone who would listen that the business could go to hell. Eventually, he'd gone back to work. Mackenzie would be alone. It didn't sound like it.

'I want you to take me to the house. I need to see the house.'

This was wild. 'Mackenzie, hold on. What're you talking about?'

She repeated what she'd said. 'Take me to the house, Gavin. Today.'

Derek's warning about her obsession came to him and he spoke gently. 'I don't think that's a good idea, sis.'

She wasn't listening. 'I have to see it.'

'Why? What good will it do?'

Mackenzie didn't explain; she pleaded with him. 'I have to. I have to go.' And Gavin knew Monica's fears were justified. His sister was nowhere near right.

'It'll only stir things up. Put it behind you. Melia's dead, he's dead, he can't hurt you again. It's over.'

'Over?' At the other end of the phone the laughter was harsh. 'You really believe it's over? For you, maybe. Not for me. It'll never be over for me. Take me to the house, Gavin. Please. Now. Right now. Come and get me.'

'But Derek – '

She cut him off. 'Derek thinks he can solve this the way he solves everything. But they're my demons. I'm the one who has to face them or it can never be over.'

The excuse was genuine – his diary was rammed. 'I can't. I've had too much time off already. We've got a helluva lot on. The business needs me.'

'I need you.'

She went quiet, the silence more disturbing than her frantic request. Her brother thought she'd hung up. 'Mackenzie? Mackenzie, are you there?'

'You ask why. I'll tell you why.'

His sister started to speak. Words he'd never wanted to hear, pictures he couldn't even think about. Gavin covered his ears but it was too late. Her voice was cold; detached. Like a narrator reading an extract from a horror story. She didn't spare him and when it ended, he was shaking.

'Shall I go on? Do you want to hear the rest of it? The worst of it? Would you understand then?'

she isn't right, Gavin

you can see that, can't you?

'Stay where you are. I'm on my way.'

* * *

They left Glasgow and drove south. Above them the sky was overcast, the default position for Scotland these days. For almost forty miles they didn't speak and Gavin was glad because he'd no idea what to say. Across from him in the passenger seat Mackenzie stared out the window, quietly humming a monotonous tune that reminded him of something. At Abington, the landscape morphed before them as they climbed into the Lowther Hills and the dissonant music faded until all that was left was the purr of the engine.

The last time he'd been here seemed like years ago. Leadhills village was as it had been. Yet there was peace here, of a kind.

They travelled on.

As they got nearer, Mackenzie sat bolt upright, one hand pressed against the dashboard in front of her, gripped by a fear too unspeakable to name. Except she had named it. Most of it. Her brother made one last attempt to dissuade her from revisiting the old house. 'Let's not do this. It won't change anything.'

She didn't reply. Whatever her shortcomings, Mackenzie had never lacked courage. Being prepared to put herself through this, to relive the ordeal, may not be wise. But it sure as hell was brave.

He drew up outside the derelict building and pulled on the handbrake. Mackenzie braced herself and started to get out.

'I'll come with you.'

She kept her face turned away. 'No. No. I have to do this myself.'

Attached to the door handle, a blue and white fragment of police tape marking the crime scene fluttered in the wind. He watched her walk towards it and go inside, wanting to run after her, to hold her and tell her it was all right. Her duty, her only duty, to herself and her family, was to get well and come back to them. Instead he stayed where he was and prayed he hadn't made a mistake in bringing her here.

Mackenzie's legs were so heavy she could barely get them to obey. She had to force her feet to move, each step taking her closer. Her heel split a tile blown from the roof. It cracked like a gunshot in the quiet. Above her, the granite house towered against the grey clouds, the hole in the roof a giant wound, and for a moment her resolve failed. She stumbled and almost fell. From the car, Gavin saw her wrestle against an invisible power, regain her balance and continue.

At the end of the corridor, at the top of the steps, she hesitated, her brother's words loud in her ears, urging her not to do this.

it's over

It wasn't a choice. She refused to spend the rest of her life tied to him. Mackenzie ignored the feeling of panic rising in her, flicked on the light tied to the handrail, and went down.

Everything was as it had been. The basement was small, much smaller than she remembered, the distance from the bed to the steps just yards. Not how it had seemed crawling towards it in the dark. She ran her fingers over the bed. The chain was missing, taken, she assumed, by the police to be used in evidence against a man who would never have to answer for his cruelty, a terrifying shadow that appeared in her nightmares and invaded every waking hour.

he's dead

he can't hurt you again

Not true. He had hurt her. He hurt her still.

The chair where he'd watched was just a chair. And the rats made no sound. But they were there, hiding behind the walls, and when night came they'd be back.

scratch scratch, scratch scratch

Mackenzie tidied the wrappers and cartons into a corner then dragged the sheets from the bed and remade it, tucking the edges under and pulling the grubby covers tight the way she'd seen the nurses in the hospital do then sat in the middle, hugging herself as if she was trying to stop the world from getting in, slowly rocking backwards and forwards, singing softly.

'Ring a ring o' roses,
a pocket full of posies;
atishoo, atishoo.
We all fall down.'

Standing outside the open door, Gavin heard and worried again that bringing her back to this place had been the wrong thing to do.

Eventually she came back to the car, moving like a sleepwalker over the rough ground. He jumped out and draped his jacket round her shoulders like he'd done before. Her skin was ice cold, her lips bloodless. The house seemed to have sucked the energy from her body in a final act of malice.

* * *

On the journey to Glasgow, Mackenzie stared through the windscreen. They were approaching Hamilton when Gavin found the courage to ask how she was.

'You all right, sis? You okay?'

She replied in a tiny voice with questions he couldn't begin to answer, tears in her eyes. 'Why would he come after me? What had I done to him?'

He reached over and took her hand. 'The police say the motive was revenge. It wasn't about you. Melia used you to get to Derek. Blaming yourself is wrong.'

She shook her head. 'No, that's not it. It was about me. I saw it in his eyes.'

'Look, you have to put this behind you. I'll do anything I can to help.'

A strand of hair fell across her face and was absently brushed away.

She turned to him. 'Anything?

'Anything.'

'Then burn that place to the ground.'

Day Fifty-Seven

Adele was a woman with an inner strength her brother had often envied. It wasn't enough. Gavin had watched her go down for weeks. She looked exhausted, defeated even, and seemed to have aged. Not bothering with makeup didn't help. Neither did the navy-blue cardigan she was wearing, fit only for the bin. Two months since the abduction and still she hadn't come to terms with her guilt over Mackenzie.

Adele and Blair had tried to work it out. It only lasted weeks before he left for good. The split couldn't have come at a worse time. He'd always been more than her husband; he'd been her best friend. Adele hadn't appreciated how much she relied on him until he wasn't there. Without him the world didn't make sense.

Gavin kissed her forehead and guided Monica and Alice inside. On the night of the birthday party, when his sister had proudly given them a tour, it had been a show house. Not anymore. Clothes were scattered on every chair. Adele saw the surprise on their faces and made a half-hearted apology. 'Sorry about the state of the place. Keep meaning to get round to tidying up. Can't find the energy.'

This was so unlike his sister. Gavin drew her aside. 'You okay?'

Her answer was candid. 'As a matter of fact, no, I'm not.'

'What's wrong?'

'What isn't wrong? Since Blair left the boys are a nightmare. Adam more than Richard. He was the quiet one. Now he's surly and aggressive. I hardly recognise him.'

'They need time to adjust. Besides, he's a teenager.'

'It's worse than that. The school's given him a final warning.'

'Why? What's he done?'

'Got caught cheating in an exam. Before that he beat a pupil up.'

'Doesn't sound like Adam.'

'One more "incident" and he'll be expelled. And he hates Blair. *Hates him.* If I even say his name he goes out of the room. I've explained things sometimes don't work out with adults. Talking to myself. He won't forgive him for what he's done to us.'

'Kids are tougher than we think, he'll get over it.'

'That's just it. I don't know that he will. At least not before he's screwed up his future.'

'Is Richard the same?'

'Coping better than his brother which isn't saying much. Stays in his room most of the time. Won't discuss it. You can see he just misses his dad.'

'Want me to speak to them?'

Adele shrugged. 'Would you?'

'Where are they?'

She pointed at the ceiling. 'Where they always are.'

Gavin climbed the stairs, knocked on the door and went in. Adam was on the carpet, his back against the bed, playing with his X-Box. He didn't notice his uncle until he was in front of him. 'Am I interrupting?'

The boy looked at him blankly.

'Where's Richard?'

'In his room, I suppose.'

'Get him, will you? It's important.'

Talking to teenagers was a waste of time, but for Adele's sake he had to give it a shot. When he had them together he closed the door.

'Cards on the table. Tell me how you're doing.'

He'd known the boys all their lives. Suddenly the years watching them growing up meant nothing, he'd become the enemy. Adam answered. 'We're all right.'

'Pleased to hear it. Really pleased. Because your mum. In fact, I'm worried about whether she'll ever be all right again.'

The boys didn't react.

'Look, when I was your age I didn't realise adults were just people. And people make mistakes. Sometimes they do it wrong.'

Adam said, 'If you're talking about him, he's a waster, and she's an idiot for putting up with it.'

'*Him* is your father. And sure he's wrong. Made a complete mess of it. Nobody knows that better than he does. But give him a chance to make it right. And *she* – your mum – an idiot? No, just a woman, a wife and mother, desperately trying to hold her family together. On top of that she's got your Aunt Mackenzie to worry about. So, believe me, your mum's a lot more hurt than you are. She's sad and she's scared and she's angry. And she needs her boys to help her get through it.'

Gavin walked to the bedroom door. 'Her heart's been broken once. She doesn't deserve to have it broken again. Time to man-up, guys.'

Downstairs Derek still hadn't arrived. Adele was in the kitchen. Monica said, 'How did it go?'

He made a face. 'Who knows? All you can do is try.'

'They could come to us once a week. Give Adele a break.'

'They'll see that as a prison sentence.'

'Okay. Once or twice a month, then. Get to know Alice. Be good for everybody.'

Gavin put his arms round her waist. 'I'm lucky to have you.'

'At last, you're starting to notice.'

He kissed her cheek. 'I never stopped noticing.'

'What does Derek want to talk about?'

The doorbell rang and Gavin said, 'We'll soon find out, he's here.'

At the last family gathering Derek Crawford had accused Blair Gardiner and they'd ended up fighting. There would be no repeat. Blair wasn't part of the family anymore.

It was rare to see him casually dressed, usually he wore a suit. Tonight he hadn't bothered with a jacket and his white shirt was open at the neck. The casualness didn't extend to his expression.

He said, 'Sorry I'm late,' and came into the lounge. Adele had made an effort and put on makeup. She forced a smile and passed a cup of coffee to her brother-in-law, wondering like the others what this was about.

On the couch, Monica squeezed Gavin's hand, her question about to be answered. Derek cleared his throat. 'I asked to meet this evening to bring you up-to-date on Mackenzie so we're all on the same page.'

To Gavin it sounded as if he was running a team meeting.

'Dr Chilolo was sure that physically there's little standing in the way of her making a complete recovery. He was right. Every day, Mackenzie is getting stronger. Mentally, if anything, she's worse.'

He took a sip from his cup. 'You love her as much as I do, which makes what I have to say harder. But I don't have a choice.'

Gavin guessed what was coming and he was right. Derek looked straight at him and said, 'What you did – however well-intentioned – was a bad idea.'

'She asked me to take her.'

Derek nodded. 'You don't have to convince me, I'm sure she did. But you have to appreciate – we all have to appreciate – there's a big difference between what Mackenzie wants and what Mackenzie needs.'

Adele was next on his list. 'Asking how she's doing, talking to her about therapy, upsets her.' He held up his hand. 'I know. She appears to be okay. Enthusiastic even. If only you could hear what she tells me. It gets so bad she's afraid to go to sleep. When she eventually does it's never for more than an hour or two. Then she wakes up screaming, convinced she can hear rats behind the walls. It's heartbreaking.'

He looked at each of them in turn. 'We all have our own thoughts about what happened two months ago. I certainly do. I've done my best but she isn't getting better.'

'I don't understand. I saw her on Friday. She told me she was feeling fine.'

Derek shook his head. 'That's the thing. The Mackenzie you see is different from the one I live with. Very different.'

Adele tried to be positive. 'I'm sorry, Derek, I still don't understand. She even talked about her plans to open a shelter for women who've been abused.'

He raised an eyebrow. This was the first he'd heard of it.

'She feels strongly about getting them out of harm's way. I think it's a wonderful idea. I told her I'd help.'

Derek lost his temper. 'You don't get it. She's worse. A lot worse. What that bastard did to her... do you really believe reliving the nightmare every day for the rest of her life is going to help? Mackenzie needs to forget it. Move on.'

Monica spoke calmly. 'I hear what you're saying Derek but I agree with Adele. It's a great idea. Working with other people, helping them, would be the best therapy she could get. Maybe you're being over-protective.'

He let out an exasperated sigh. 'She won't consider proper therapy. Flatly refuses. And without a professional in charge the kind of things you're doing and saying could even be dangerous. As for being over-protective, maybe I am. But remember, I nearly lost her.'

Gavin voiced what the three of them were thinking. 'Are you asking us to stay away from Mackenzie?'

The two men stared at each other. 'No, I haven't said that. In fact, quite the opposite. The thing is: I need to get back to work. I can't stay away indefinitely. Mrs Hawthorne, our cleaner, has been sitting with Mackenzie a couple of days a week so I can go in. But she has other commitments. If necessary, I'll hire a private nurse. But I was hoping Adele and Monica might step up. It's just really important that nothing and no one stands in the way of her recovery. We all have to realise what is and isn't good for her. As I said, that we're on the same page here.'

He sat back apparently unaware of the effect he'd had on them. 'We all have Mackenzie's best interests at heart. If she's going to recover we have to work together on this. Do you agree?'

Monica moved in to smooth the ruffled feathers. 'Absolutely Derek. We'll be there for her. I was thinking the three of us could treat ourselves to afternoon tea at Crossbasket Castle in Blantyre. What do you think, Adele? Then we could work out a rota – you know, going to the gym and stuff.'

Derek's bullish approach was ill-judged and Gavin didn't know whether to be proud of Monica or angry at him.

Derek tried to soften what he'd been saying. 'It's not all bad news. She's given up smoking and it looks as if alcohol is out of the picture. Hasn't once taken a drink. She's even talked about going back to the garden centre. I don't discourage it, though of course it won't be happening. And, as you've probably guessed, we won't be splitting up. Mackenzie needs me more than ever.'

Adele was still smarting from their difference of opinions but did her best to hide it. 'Oh, that's marvellous news. I was afraid to ask.'

Monica was more clear-sighted. 'What about the man in the car?'

Derek Crawford didn't hide his displeasure with her. 'Turns out it was my mistake, he was a friend from Alcoholics Anonymous.'

The news, delivered casually, was a stark reminder they'd chosen to think the worst. That when Mackenzie needed them to believe her none of them had. For seconds they avoided each others' eyes, not comfortable enough to speak, until Monica said, 'AA? She was going to AA? Why didn't she tell us?'

Gavin answered. 'Maybe she didn't trust us.'

Derek didn't comment. He got up and walked to the door. 'I'd better be getting back. There is one more thing. And Mackenzie mustn't hear about it.' He spoke as if it had almost slipped his mind. 'The lawyer got it wrong. Because they can't be sure who the knife belonged to the procurator fiscal didn't dismiss the charge. I'm going to be tried for the culpable homicide of Joe Melia.'

The Last Day

They say time heals all wounds. Gavin Darroch had his doubts. The meeting with Derek hadn't sat well with him. He felt he'd done the right thing by his sister though in the light of his revelation that Mackenzie was getting worse, hoped he hadn't added to the problem.

He poured himself a drink, tried to switch off and flicked on the TV. With the sound turned down so as not to wake Monica and Alice, watching was a waste of time. Gavin picked up the drawings he'd been putting off looking at for days, couldn't concentrate and found himself doodling in the margin.

Why? Why? Why?

A stranger with a grudge?

What kind of a grudge would be played out like that?

Mackenzie was certain it had been about her and he believed her. So what drove a stranger with a grudge against Crawford Cars to take such terrible revenge on an innocent woman? The question had been swimming on the edge of his mind ever since they'd been told about Joe Melia's connection to Derek's business.

Suddenly, there it was. Right in front of him.

a stranger with a grudge

Andrew Geddes was at home. The words were slurred. Geddes was drinking. 'Gavin, mate, what can I do for you?'

'Been thinking about Joseph Melia. Bit of a mystery man, wasn't he? Didn't you say he'd no history of violence? To do what he did would need a powerful motive, don't you think?'

'Getting sacked is pretty powerful.'

Gavin disagreed. 'People get sacked every day without abducting the boss's wife.'

'True, except Melia went from Salesman Of The Month to out on his arse. Losing a lot of money in the process.'

'What was he up to?'

'Stealing. Like all the best scams, his was simple: the object of the exercise in the car game is to shift stock. Over-generous offers on trade-ins are common. Just how generous is often left to the discretion of the salesman. Sometimes trade-ins need to be written off entirely. No sweat, so long as more expensive new models are rolling off the forecourt. Apparently, Joe Boy was very good at making that happen. As I say, the bastard was only in the door when he won Salesman Of The Month. Nobody guessed he was negotiating kickbacks for himself.'

'How did he get caught?'

'January's a graveyard month in most businesses. The car game's no exception. Not for Jo-Jo. He was setting the heather on fire. That was his mistake. A manager twigged his figures were just too good and started checking. Nabbed him in the act shortly after that.'

'Why wasn't he charged?'

'Should've been, no question. They settled for quietly getting rid of him. Didn't want the publicity.'

'And Derek wasn't involved?'

'No, the manager handled it.'

'This happened in February?'

'Right. Three months before he kidnapped your sister.'

Gavin let what he was hearing sink in. 'Okay, except the grudge was against Crawford Cars. Melia didn't know Derek, so why take his wife and not the manager's who'd sacked him? Doesn't make sense.'

Geddes wasn't sympathetic. 'Good question, mate, and I agree with you. Unfortunately the only guy who can answer it isn't around. Every case can't be tied in a big bow. Life isn't as simple as that.'

Maybe he was right. Gavin apologised for breaking into his evening and rung off. He poured himself another glass of wine and turned over what Andrew Geddes had said. Then he opened the PC and checked Melia's Facebook account. The dead man hadn't used it much, what was there was standard stuff, like the blurry shot of a fish lying on a riverbank. Underneath it he'd written "The one that didn't get away".

Six weeks before he'd been sacked he'd posted a slew of pro-Brexit comments and links to newspaper articles supporting his views. Nothing else, until a picture of people wearing paper hats, with their arms round each others' shoulders at the Christmas party. Joe Melia was second from the end, grinning drunkenly at the camera.

In the final entry, posted a month later, a night-time shot of King Tut's Wah Wah Hut at the top of St Vincent Street had snow on the ground. Whoever was gigging didn't get a mention. No friends either, female or otherwise, which struck Gavin as unusual.

Who went to a gig by themselves? Not anybody he knew, that was for sure.

His 'friends' list ran to only half a dozen, none of them in Scotland. It seemed selfies weren't his thing, or women for that matter, and there was no suggestion he was gay. Melia had been a man of few interests and even fewer mates. A loner. On this evidence nobody was going to miss him.

Gavin could hardly keep his eyes open. The wine, what was left of it, got poured down the sink and he made a double-espresso. The coffee tasted harsh and bitter and he had to force himself to drink it. He went back to the PC and scrolled through Melia's Facebook one more time. Trying to understand who the stalker had been wasn't easy, yet he wasn't ready to give up. The more he looked the less he saw. Maybe Andrew Geddes was right about having to make sense of it all instead of accepting what was already known. Eventually, he closed the computer down and went to bed.

* * *

But sleep wouldn't come. And in the darkness, listening to the occasional car pass on the street outside, images of his sister chained to the bed, her body abused and broken, appeared behind his eyes.

When dawn broke over the city it found him washed-out and weary and back at the computer, going over the same old ground. Nothing had changed, it was all still there: the dead fish, the Brexit stuff, the wintry King Tut's, and the gang at the Christmas party. Gavin studied Melia's boozy face guessing he'd been the star of the show that night. It wouldn't last. Just weeks later his glittering career would be over, he'd be fired – out on the street and fortunate not to be facing a prison sentence. On the surface, he seemed normal, ordinary. Dull even. But Gavin Darroch had been there. He'd seen. And what this man had done to a defenceless woman was far beyond the grudge the police had settled for.

He printed off the picture of the Christmas party group, slipped it into his inside jacket pocket and headed for the door with no clear idea where he was going. On his way out he looked in on Monica and Alice, wishing he could crawl in under the clothes and lose himself in his wife's warm body.

At twenty past seven, Great Western Road was already full-on and progress was slow. Every now and then he glanced at the print-off on the seat beside him, as if all he had to do to force it to give up its secret was say the magic words. Unfortunately, he didn't know those words. So he zoned out and let the car drive itself while Andrew's rebuke rang in his head.

tied in a big bow
life isn't as simple as that

At Hamilton, with Strathclyde Loch a choppy stretch of grey water on his right-hand side, he gradually rejoined the world like a dreamer waking from a troubled slumber. It had cost a night's sleep and there were still more questions than answers, but now he knew where he was going though he still didn't know why.

On the outskirts of Leadhills village his bleak city-boy assessment of where he was came to him.

mamba country

He drove on until he arrived at where Mackenzie had been held against her will and treated so cruelly. The collapsed roof and boarded windows revealed the extent of the dereliction, though not the terrible crimes committed here, and the ground was still pitted with the tyre-tracks of the ambulance and police cars. Gavin got out and gazed for a moment at the empty landscape, wondering how Melia had discovered this place?

Some unknown hand had made a half-hearted attempt to hold the front door closed and failed. It had fallen ajar in a final statement of dilapidation.

A noise like a child's cry came from the rusted hinges when he pushed at the rotted wood and started down what had once been the hall, stepping carefully over the old timbers. A bird flew unexpectedly from somewhere above, startling him. Flapping and squawking in the eaves before escaping through the hole in the roof. On another day, an inconsequential happening not worthy of a mention: an embarrassing overreaction to laugh about. Not today. The grim history made it portentous enough to have his heart pounding in his chest.

He made his way along the hall. At the top of the steps he stopped, found the battery light then reluctantly went down.

Over the years the space would have had many uses though surely none as inhuman as its last incarnation. On the floor in the centre of the room, a dark stain – darker even than the flagstones – caught his eye and he heard again Melia gasp as the knife slid into him.

He'd been a bad guy who deserved what he got, no doubt about that, but it was a memory Gavin Darroch could live without.

The chain which had kept his sister prisoner had been removed. Everything else was as it had been, except the bed with its bloodstained crumpled sheets had been remade and the coffee cups, soup cartons and sandwich wrappers swept into a corner. He lifted a cardboard container and read the familiar logo with the sound of Mackenzie begging and pleading so clear she could've been there with him.

The hairs on the back of his neck stood, the temperature fell. It was bitterly cold and his tongue raced around his mouth. The awful energy of the place had got to him.

This was a basement in name only, in reality, it was a dungeon.

He needed to get out.

Standing watching the pale-blue early-morning sky, the feeling passed and the house was just a house again. Behind it, the hill rose steeply. Climbing it wouldn't be easy because the sun hadn't had a chance to do its work and the grass was wet with dew; Gavin had lost his footing several times on the way up. At the top, barren hills stretched for miles patched by mist floating like islands of smoke above them. A welcome breeze cooled his face and, after the dank cellar, the air was fresh in his lungs. No other dwelling was visible but, from this height, lines of dark-green moss rooted between the grey slate tiles and the ragged edges of the collapsed roof were starkly defined. Through the sagging tear he was able to look into the dark heart of the neglected building. Given its state of decay, spending time in it, even during the day – as he'd discovered – was an unpleasant experience. In the dead of night, manacled and terrified, waiting for the stalker to return to do his worst was beyond imagining.

It was a hellish place.

To his right, the ground fell away, gently sloping, disappearing into a gully. Gavin started walking. Five minutes further on, the horizon was as far away as it had ever been.

Where was he going? What was he looking for? He didn't know.

Until he found it.

The wooden stake had been washed clean by the waters of the shallow stream it lay across, the sign warped and cracked, though the lettering was legible. He turned his head to read it and immediately understood. Joe Melia hadn't reinvented the wheel to find somewhere so perfectly suited to his purpose. He'd taken the obvious route and been rewarded.

CUNNINGHAM AND McCLURE
ESTATE AGENTS
LANARK
01555 964142

* * *

What had brought him back to that God-forsaken house a third time was the nagging doubt his sister had planted on their last visit. At first, scaling the hill, slipping and sliding on the dewy grass, he'd truly no idea what he was looking for. Another man would have seen the Lowther Hills melding with the sky in every direction and turned back. He wasn't that man.

There was no reason, no excuse. The stalker was dead. Everybody was satisfied. Everybody but Mackenzie. And now him.

There were no other vehicles on the forecourt at Abington when he pulled up to the pumps. He filled the tank with fuel he didn't need to the hum of lorries and trucks going south. With the sun warming him it should've been hard to hold onto the memory of the house, or dismiss it as the lingering fragment of a nightmare.

It wasn't. It had happened. It had been real.

Inside the service station he added a cup of muddy coffee from a machine to the petrol and went into his act with the fair-haired woman behind the counter, the same one as before, guessing she wouldn't remember him. It was two months and she hadn't recalled the guy in the black coat minutes after he'd been in the shop.

'Beautiful day, isn't it?'

'It certainly is.'

'I'm a city guy but, on a day like today, I envy you living here.'

She smiled and handed him a receipt, pleased by the admission. 'It's not everybody's cup of tea, but I like it.'

Gavin turned away and turned back, feigning uncertainty, drawing the Christmas party print-out from his pocket like a spur-of-the-moment decision. 'I wonder. Do you recognise anybody in this picture? I'm supposed to meet somebody here – one of these guys – but I'm not sure which one it is. All I know is he's a local.'

She glanced at it then at him, her willingness to help tinged with a shadow of distrust. The smile disappeared. Seconds passed before she answered. 'As a matter of fact I do.' Her fingertip settled on Joe Melia's drunken grin. 'Him. But he's not local. Seen him a few times. Hasn't been in recently though.'

'You're sure?'

'Absolutely.'

He started to fold the sheet and was about to thank her when she touched his arm, her hand hovering over the group. 'And him right at the back. Came in together a few times.'

Gavin couldn't speak. He'd been so focused on Melia and the people near him he'd paid no attention to the crowd at the back by the bar.

'Sorry, you say they came in together?'

'Once or twice, yes.'

* * *

The Clyde Valley runs through countryside which, in its own way, is as glorious as any in Scotland. Lush and green, peaceful and ordered. None of it registered. Gavin gripped the steering wheel, driving faster than was wise and, for a short stretch early on, almost winning a race he was always going to lose with a train from London heading to Central Station in Glasgow. Unfamiliar villages with unfamiliar names: Roberton, Wiston, Thankerton and Carmichael, came and went unnoticed. It was only when traffic lights at the single file Hyndford Bridge halted his progress that the full implication hit him. He'd come, hoping someone or something could offer an insight into why Melia had done the terrible thing he'd done. Instead, he'd uncovered a crime too bizarre to believe. And try as he might, he couldn't get his head round it.

But he did believe it. He knew it was true. The lady at Abington's confident identification meant it could be no other way.

Four miles further on he hoped an estate agent would finish it. The accelerator hit the floor and the engine roared as the SUV shot up Hyndford Road towards the Royal Burgh of Lanark.

At the top of the hill, golden shards of sunlight pierced the branches of dense fir trees on either side of the road, the temperature dropped and he was reminded again of the dungeon in the Lowther Hills. Gavin glanced at his watch; it was still only ten o'clock in the morning. Further on, the Inn On The Loch and then a row of detached houses on one side of the road told him he was almost there.

With no idea where he was going it made sense to take the first parking option that came his way, which turned out to be the car park at Morrisons, off Whitelees Road. He found a space between a green Renault and a black Citroen, got out and started to walk.

History wasn't his subject though he was familiar enough with Lanark to know it had been a market town since medieval times. Unfortunately for the local traders, impressive though that boast was, it counted for nothing in the 21st century and the High Street was faring no better than most.

This wasn't his first visit. Once, when he was a child, an uncle brought him to the cattle auction. He remembered sitting beside him while, in the ring, monsters with huge heads pawed the ground, snorting steam, saliva foaming at the corners of their mouths as farmers in overalls and tweed jackets appraised the beasts with critical eyes and listened stone-faced to the auctioneer rattling through the bidding.

On another day the memory would've been a thing to savour. Today his need for answers sucked the pleasure from it.

Now, apparently in this part of the world, selling houses was the business to be in. He came across three estate agents on the High Street. Cunningham and McClure wasn't one of them and Gavin Darroch had a terrible thought. What if they weren't in business anymore? At the bottom, in Wellgate, their office was sandwiched between an Italian restaurant and a dry cleaner promising twenty-four hour turnaround. The agent's windows were filled with properties, mostly flats and bungalows to buy or let. No sign of the house in the Lowther Hills.

A woman in her late-thirties looked up when he went inside. Across the room, a male colleague was talking on the telephone, the top button of his blue shirt open and his tie loosened. He saw him, turned away and lowered his voice. Confidentiality, it seemed, was valued. The woman smiled and spoke. 'Good morning. How can I help you?'

'Are you the agent who deals with the Lowther Hills?'

'No, that's Megan.'

She pointed to a desk, neat and tidy apart from sunglasses on top of a pile of folders. 'She's late. Won't be here 'til eleven. One of her kids is sick.'

'But she's definitely coming in?'

'Yes. You can wait if you like.'

It was a nice offer; he turned it down. 'No, I'll come back.'

'It wasn't something I could help with, was it?'

'I don't think so, but thanks anyway.'

He called Geddes and heard his message go straight to voice mail and for the next forty-five minutes walked around the town centre, up one side of the High Street and down the other: four circuits and still had time to kill. What he'd learned was almost beyond belief. Too shocking to take in.

Where Wellgate met High Street, he stopped and called Andrew again. The detective's phone stayed switched off and Gavin had to stop himself from throwing the mobile away in frustration.

He settled for cursing Geddes out loud. 'Answer for fuck's sake!'

He loitered anxiously outside the old tollbooth near the provost's lamp, turning over what he'd learned so far, unable to completely believe it. When the clock on St Nicholas church above a statue of William Wallace struck eleven, he raced round the corner to Cunningham and McClure.

As soon as he went in he realised Megan hadn't arrived yet; her chair was still empty. The woman he'd spoken to earlier was about to launch into an apology when the door opened behind him and a petite blonde burst in looking flushed and flustered.

'God what a morning, you wouldn't believe it. Sorry I'm late. Jake was sick all over the bed. Twice.'

Her colleague's brow furrowed with concern. 'Are you sure you should be here? How is the poor wee soul?'

'Seems okay now. Can't always tell with children.'

Her colleague pointed to their visitor. 'This gentleman's been waiting. He wants to speak to you.'

Megan moved past the window and shrugged off her jacket. 'Let me get myself settled. Have a seat, Mr...'

'Darroch. Gavin Darroch.'

'Have a seat Mr Darroch. Can I get you a coffee, I'm having one.'

The hospitality annoyed him. He struggled to keep irritation out of his voice and just about managed it. 'I won't, thanks. It'll only take a minute.'

'Then the coffee can wait.'

'I've just come from a property in the Lowther Hills with your sign outside it. The windows are boarded and the roof's caved-in. Do you know the one I mean?'

She screwed up her face. 'Yes, for my sins. The Baxter house. The original owner emigrated to Australia – or maybe it was Canada. He died, I understand. It belongs to his nephew. Spoke to him on the phone once. He lives in Antigua. Never even seen the property. Couldn't care less about it. Over the years, as no doubt you noticed, it's fallen deeper and deeper into disrepair. Are you interested in it? Do you want to put in an offer?' She got up. 'I'll find the schedule. Pretty certain he'd accept just about anything to get shot of it.'

'No, please, I don't want to buy it. I wanted to know if you'd had any interest in it, any interest at all.'

She pursed her lips, considering how to answer the question, caught the tension in him and became defensive. 'Why're you asking? Why do you want to know?'

The truth would take too much time to tell and, if he was right, there was no time. Gavin looked over his shoulder and lowered his voice. 'I'm afraid I can't answer that at the moment but I will say this: either you tell me or you tell the police. Sorry to be so dramatic. It's very important.'

'I've already spoken to the police about this. They showed me a picture of a man and asked if I'd ever seen him.'

'And had you?'

'No. Never.'

The turn the conversation had taken rattled him. He recovered and deliberately misled her. 'Some new information has come to light. So, are you saying there hasn't been any interest?'

She hesitated. 'As a matter of fact there was.'

'When?'

'I had a viewing with a man but it was months ago. I'd have to look it up.'

'Do you remember his name?'

'Not off the top of my head. Took him round a few places. The Baxter house was the only one he got out the car for. Wasted an afternoon on him.'

'He didn't buy?'

She almost laughed. 'Would you?'

'What did he say?'

The estate agent shook her head, searching for the words. 'He didn't talk much. Shouldn't really tell you this. I didn't like him.'

'Why?'

'There was something…odd. Hard to describe. He was remote. Aloof.'

'Would you recognise him again?'

'Maybe.'

He took the print-off out of his pocket and placed it on the desk. 'Is he in this picture?'

Megan's eyes wandered over the Christmas party revelers. 'Yes.'

This harassed mother held the final piece of evidence. From here on there could be no going back. He needed her to be absolutely certain.

'Which one? Which one is he?'

Her finger stabbed the paper. 'The man at the very back.'

* * *

He ran, half-staggering, his skin clammy and his chest so tight he might have been on the edge of a heart-attack. People who saw him assumed he was drunk and got out of his way. Later, he'd have no memory of getting to the car. Outside Morrisons, his fingers wouldn't work and he fumbled for his keys. Driving was out of the question; he wasn't fit. He waited until his pulse returned to normal before turning on the engine, at a loss what to do or where to go. It was bizarre. Twisted beyond anything he could've imagined.

He knew. He didn't understand, but he knew.

The stranger with a grudge didn't exist. Had never existed.

No matter how far-fetched it sounded, it was true. Derek Crawford had had his own wife abducted and used a disgraced former employee to do it.

Had he promised him money? Or was it the threat of going to prison that swayed it? Either way, from the beginning, Melia's fate was never in doubt. Mackenzie could identify her captor and Gavin was certain the stranger who was his brother-in-law wasn't the kind of man to leave a witness to his twisted plan, or open himself to blackmail.

Silencing him was inevitable.

But why? What could Derek possibly hope to gain?

The estate agent had unwittingly found the right location for him. The derelict Baxter house couldn't have been more ideal. After that, it was simply a case of fitting-out the basement and setting the plan in motion. Melia had played his part well, making his unwelcoming presence obvious, creating the illusion of a stalker. Mackenzie's erratic drink-fuelled behaviour at Adele's birthday party and her lie about a lover couldn't have served Derek better. Far from humiliating him, it convinced the family he was the victim.

But again, why? Why would he do that to her?

The chase from Glasgow was a sham, orchestrated to lure Gavin to the house in the Lowther Hills to witness the fight to the death: Melia's death. Crawford must have been sitting in his car somewhere, calling the shots. Toying with him. Getting him in position to be able to testify to his innocence.

The perfect murder. The perfect plan.

Could he actually put his wife through that kind of hell to keep her? Could anyone?

Gavin banged his fist on the steering-wheel. It was too much to take in. Every possible answer threw up more questions. He couldn't make sense of it by himself and called Andrew Geddes again. Still no reply. This time he left a message.

'Get to Derek Crawford's house as quick as you can. It's him.'

He broke the speed-limit and raced to Wellgate, fighting down panic – past the statue of William Wallace and on towards the motorway, with only one thought in his mind. Right now, why didn't matter anymore.

Derek Crawford was a madman. He had to get Mackenzie away from him.

* * *

On the drive to Glasgow, he tried to put the pieces together. The nearer he got to the city the more he realised he was out of his depth. None of it added up. He overtook a long line of cars, one after another, and glanced at his silent mobile on the passenger seat. Where the hell was Geddes?

Heavy traffic on the Kingston Bridge slowed his progress. He thought about his sister and his wife. Adele and Monica had never understood Mackenzie's unhappiness. Married to a man who gave her everything, who adored her, what more did she want? To them, Derek was a loving husband who worshipped his wife. Impossible to believe he was anything else. And they hadn't. Only Blair had realised something more fundamental was wrong. Blair, whose own relationship was in pieces.

In Whitecraigs, the silver Audi – Derek's pride and joy – was outside, and Gavin's hope Mrs Hawthorne would be with his sister died. Derek opened the door before he reached it.

He smiled a thin smile. 'What brings you here in the middle of the day? Monica thrown you out, has she?'

Gavin faked a smile of his own. 'Not yet, thank God. Finished early. She suggested Mackenzie might like to spend a couple of hours with Alice. Do her good. Give you a break as well.'

Derek was convincing, his disappointment came across as genuine. 'Should've called to let me know you were coming. Mackenzie's asleep. Better if I don't wake her.'

'Didn't Monica ring you? She was supposed to. I'll wait 'til she wakes up. See if the idea appeals. You could go out if you wanted.'

They were still at the door. Derek hadn't moved to let him go in. 'That's all right, I'm good. She didn't have a great night. Doubt she'll be up to it.'

Gavin stepped past him and Derek followed. 'Worth a try. Besides, I'm here now.'

The lounge was showroom-tidy apart from his sister sleeping in an armchair. Her eyes fluttered open. 'Gavin.' She reached up and kissed him.

He felt Derek's presence behind him. 'Monica had a notion you might like to see Alice. Getting to be a big girl. Only right she knows who her Aunt Mackenzie is.'

Mackenzie fussed. 'I'm a sight. Look at me. I'd have to get ready.' Her eyes went to her husband for approval. 'Should I make an effort and go? Haven't seen Alice in ages. She'll be wondering if she even has an auntie.'

'Don't think it's a great idea. You know how tired you get.'

'As soon as she starts flagging I'll whisk her back.'

Mackenzie was unaware of the danger she was in. She answered brightly. 'But I'm feeling fine. Babies cheer you up.'

Derek's voice took on a firmer tone. 'You're better off here.'

Gavin stepped between them. ''Fraid I'm going to have to play the big brother card. My little sister could do with some colour in her cheeks.' He spoke without taking his eyes off Derek Crawford. 'You're fine as you are, let's go.'

There was something Mackenzie didn't understand. She forced herself between them. 'What's happening? Will somebody tell me what's going on?'

Her brother answered. 'Just get in the car.'

'She's going nowhere.'

'Yeah, she is, Derek. She's going with me.'

Derek lost it. 'She's my wife, Darroch! She's staying with me!'

Mackenzie started to cry. 'What's wrong! Tell me what's wrong!'

Gavin didn't see the punch coming. It caught him on the chin; his head rocked back. Derek lunged at him and pinned him against the wall. Gavin shouted 'Get to the fucking car! Go! Now!' Crawford's hands closed round his throat. He dragged them away. 'It was him, Mackenzie!'

'What?'

'The stalker, the house. All of it.'

Her husband spoke quietly. 'Don't listen to this lunatic. I'll deal with him. He's had a few too many or something. Go upstairs and don't worry. Doctor Chilolo said you mustn't get stressed.'

She wasn't listening to him. 'What are you talking about, Gavin? It was revenge. The police said it was revenge.'

'It wasn't. They were in it together.'

Mackenzie's arms dropped to her side. The horrific realisation of what her brother was saying dawned. 'He kept the balaclava on. He kept it on because it was you. You were there.'

Crawford dropped the pretence and turned on her. '"Til death us do part". Remember? I wasn't going to let you leave me. No fucking chance. Not then. Not ever.'

Shock drained the little colour she had. 'You did that? You did that to me?'

'He was never meant to hurt you. You know I could never hurt you. Melia was only supposed to scare you. That's what I told him.'

'Why? Why, Derek?'

'You'd forgotten how much you need me. I had to make you remember.'

She didn't hear. 'That awful house...the rats...him.'

'I can explain. Just come with me. Come with me now. We'll go away. It'll be all right. I'll make it all right.'

Gavin shouted. 'Mackenzie! Don't listen to him! He's insane!'

Crawford's free hand stretched towards her; she backed away and fell to her knees.

'I was chained. Chained! Do you understand what he did to me?' She screamed. 'Do you!'

Gavin Darroch punched Crawford on the side of the head. The bigger man staggered back and stumbled, regained his balance and ran to the door. Gavin rushed to his sister and helped her to her feet. 'Stay here. Stay here. The police are coming. I'm going after him.'

The Audi reversed into the street and shot away in a crazy zigzag just as Andrew Geddes pulled up and jumped out. 'What the hell's going on? Crawford almost ran me off the road.'

Gavin answered angrily. 'Took your fucking time, didn't you?' He started the engine. 'Get in or we'll lose him.'

The back door opened and Mackenzie scrambled inside.

'I asked you to stay. He's dangerous.'

The look she gave him told her brother he was wasting his time.

* * *

They were on the motorway, racing towards the city.

Crawford's silver Audi was in the outside lane, its lights flashing to intimidate the drivers in its path. Some moved aside to let it pass, others stubbornly held their ground, stopping its progress, among them a black Transit van which refused to go faster or give way. At times, their bumpers were no more than inches apart. Forced to accept it wasn't on, the Audi cut in front of a bus. The driver braked hard and it edged into the gap. Seconds later it was on the move again, crowding out a beat-up Ford. Gavin kept his eyes on the road and told Geddes what he'd found out in the Welcome service station at Abington, confirmed by the estate agent in Lanark.

Geddes listened in silence, recalling a lecture he'd attended as a young detective: The Killer Within. One afternoon at Tulliallan Police College near Kincardine, he'd learned that given the right conditions, we were all capable of brutality beyond imagining. Everyone had a trigger. In a Polish town in 1940, a Nazi uniform had turned the village postman into an executioner. Innocent men, women and children died, their bodies buried in a ditch they'd been forced to dig themselves.

With Melia, an abandoned house and the role of abductor unleashed his monster. Why was chillingly obvious: because they could.

Geddes had been repulsed by the bitter truth then and was repulsed now.

Gavin weaved between cars, somehow managing to stay in touch with the faster Audi. On a clear road it would be a different story. Thanks to the traffic he had him in his sights.

But unless he drove as crazily as Crawford, he'd lose him. That knowledge spurred him on. One foot pressed the accelerator into the floor while the other tapped the brakes in time to avoid hitting the car in front. Gavin changed down to fourth, determined to find something extra under the hood and heard the engine complain. The driver waved an angry fist at him.

In the passenger seat, Andrew braced himself against the dashboard with his outstretched arm; they swerved round a Honda Civic, missing it by inches.

'Fuck's sake. You're going to kill us!'

That wasn't Gavin Darroch's plan. He gripped the steering wheel so tight his knuckles threatened to break the skin as the outside world raced by. Geddes spoke urgently into his personal radio. He covered it with his hand and shouted across the car, his voice hoarse with tension.

'A team's on the way. Don't lose the fucker. Stay on him!'

Gavin sensed his sister leaning forward between them and looked at her. Mackenzie's eyes were locked on the Audi and the stranger who'd been her husband. There was hate in them.

Inside the A5, Crawford hunched forward, completely focussed on escape. Blue flashing lights in the wing-mirror and the distant sound of sirens signalled they'd been joined in the chase. Derek Crawford would hear them too and know the net was closing in. As the police cars roared by in the outside lane the Audi seemed to slow, drifting to straddle the middle of the motorway. The police caught up and boxed it in and Gavin was certain it was almost over.

But he was wrong.

The Audi swung right, smashing the outside car against the crash barrier. The car flipped on its side and slid into the centre of the road, losing its exhaust in the process. Crawford turned his attention to the second police car; like a mad bull playing the same manoeuvre on his other side, hitting the driver's door and pinning it against the rails. The car burst into flames, the noise of tearing steel incredible. Anybody directly behind didn't have a chance. Screeching brakes and the smell of burning rubber rose in the air as vehicle after vehicle piled into the one in front.

The sheer audacity of it took them by surprise. Gavin was going too fast to stop and had no time to consider the options. He did the only thing possible, threw the steering wheel one way then the other, somehow squeezing between the lines of crashed vehicles. When he looked again, Crawford was still ahead of them.

Their brush with death had stunned Andrew Geddes. He hadn't spoken since the first police car came to grief, his thoughts with the policemen. But what was there to say? He was fortunate, he was alive. By the end of today that wouldn't be true for everybody.

For what seemed like forever, yet could only have been minutes, they kept pace with the Audi, neither losing nor gaining. Drivers, recognising the danger, shrank from it and let it pass. Geddes had the radio stuck to his ear, his expression frozen on his face. Whatever he was hearing wasn't good. He shared the news. 'Tanker carrying hazardous material has jack-knifed at Easterhouse, going west. Christ knows what's in it but it's all over the road: a major incident. They've blocked off the carriageway. They'll do the same the other side.'

'What're you saying?'

'Closing the bridge is out of the question. It isn't going to happen. They won't get there in time. We're on our own.'

The statement fell like a hammer blow and for the first time since the chase began, Geddes realised Crawford might get away. 'Stay with him. Just stay with him.'

'I'm trying, but he's crazy. Got nothing left to lose.'

Derek Crawford had destroyed two police cars and more than a dozen others. At this stage, it was anybody's guess how many people were injured or dead. Gavin zigzagged between lanes, dodging in and out, living every boy racer's dream, while Geddes gave a commentary of what was going on to someone in the control room, someone with an overview and the authority to send officers to calls. Frustration marked the corners of his mouth, the stark reality of his words echoing around them.

we're on our own

The sign for the Tradeston turn-off appeared on the left and the motorway rose towards the Kingston Bridge, high above the brown water of the River Clyde.

Geddes said, 'He might not be ready to give up but he can't know what's ahead. If he stays where he is we've got him.'

Gavin was less confident; he gritted his teeth. 'If the bastard takes the City off-ramp and ditches the Audi, he could lose himself in Glasgow.'

When his next attempt to bully his way to the inside lane failed, Crawford did as he'd done with the police cars and intentionally crashed into the side of a green Fiat. Metal scraped against twisted metal, the Fiat's front tyres blew out, it rolled over, raked the barrier in a shower of sparks, then spun like a toy on its roof. The driver behind ploughed into it. Sixty yards back they saw his body fire through the windscreen and land in a shower of shards, two lanes over. Gavin Darroch swerved to avoid the wreckage and shuddered.

Mackenzie covered her eyes and moaned.

In the seat in front the policeman said, 'Cold-blooded murder.'

But the Audi hadn't escaped unscathed. Crawford lost control and they stared in disbelief as it mounted the sloping back of a Volkswagen Beetle like a mating insect, for a moment welded to it, before shooting over the safety barrier and clipping the top of a Renault on the SECC turn-off, somersaulting into space. At one point, it seemed to glide, then, dragged down by its own weight, it lost height, descending in a lazy roll with the sun glancing like bolts of lightning from its battered silver chassis until it entered the water nose first, throwing spray into the air.

On the bridge, people abandoned their cars, keen to witness a lunatic on his journey to the bottom of the river. Gavin was already running, Andrew behind him, shouting 'Can you see him? Can you see him?'

The Audi's tail hung suspended by an invisible force before it disappeared into the Clyde. Geddes' eyes were hard. When he spoke he was thinking of Mackenzie's ordeal and the carnage this monster had caused.

'We've been robbed.'

Gavin legs were close to buckling under him. Suddenly, he was dog-tired. It was finished but his emotions hadn't got the message. Geddes' features were white with anger. 'The bastard fucking robbed us.'

Gavin didn't agree or disagree. He went back to the car, parked at an insane angle and spoke to his sister. 'It's over, Mackenzie. This time it really is over.'

'It can't be. He can't get away like this. Not like this.'

She leapt out and ran to the barrier where DS Geddes was talking into his radio.

'Let him live. Please, let him live. It can't end like this.'

* * *

The Finnieston Crane was a black mangle against the cloudless sky.

It had been a long day and it still wasn't over. The crowd patiently watching from Lancefield quay hadn't got what they'd come for, not so far, but they wouldn't forget what they'd seen. This was Glasgow. Stuff like this happened in New York or L.A., mostly in crime movies, not here. Except it had.

The Police Scotland Marine Unit launch appeared. Shortly after, the arrival of a boat owned by an independent specialist contractor, lying low in the water with a winch rising like a phallus from its deck and SANDERSON in red letters on the hull, suggested it wouldn't be much longer. Three divers in wetsuits and facemasks did a recce to establish where the Audi was and to come up with a plan to retrieve it from the murky depths. In one of his frequent calls during the afternoon, Andrew told Gavin that, just three feet down, visibility was close to nil.

'They say you can't see your hand in front of your face. No use hanging around. It's a slow process. Won't be much going on for a while.'

Gavin read between the lines. 'You're saying we should leave, Andrew?'

'I'm saying you should leave.' He softened his tone. 'It's better your sister isn't here when the car comes up.'

Good advice. But Mackenzie wasn't ready to hear it.

'Geddes thinks we shouldn't be here.'

'You mean he thinks I shouldn't be here?'

'Yes.'

She bowed her head. 'I can't. I just can't. This won't be finished until I see it myself.'

Her brother didn't argue. He understood.

Closing the Kingston Bridge had caused serious disruption all the way to Ayrshire and it would reopen only when the crime scene examination was complete, a decision that lay with the men by the side of the river. DS Andrew Geddes was one of them.

Meanwhile, chaos reigned: people crowded behind the police barrier, and from the flats along the Quay eyes followed the excitement from every window and balcony. TV crews jostled for the best positions while press reporters interviewed everyone and anyone. On the evening news and in tomorrow's headlines, this would be the number one story. It seemed like the whole of Glasgow was squashed into a quarter mile and all around phones and cameras flashed, attempting to get the shot which would guarantee fifteen minutes of fame.

Gavin and Mackenzie had made their way to the walkway. Further along, Geddes stood in a circle talking with DI Taylor, the lead officer from the Marine Unit, and the senior diver while two more divers floated in the muddy water. It was an animated conversation, lots of pointing and shaking heads. Even from this distance, Gavin could read Geddes' body language. He was on edge. Eventually, he stepped away and took a long look towards them, dug a hand into his coat pocket and brought out his mobile. A moment later, Gavin's rang.

'Is she listening?'

'No.'

'Okay.' He sounded weary. Gavin guessed the long hours weren't the reason. His tiredness went beyond physical. 'They've finally got a line they think will hold on the back axle. They're ready to bring the car up.'

Gavin imagined Crawford's car rising from the river, water cascading from the plush interior of the most expensive scrap metal in the city. The detective hesitated, the words when they came, falling like stones dropped from a height, each one heavier than the one before.

'Pitch dark down there. Just shapes. Not even shapes.'

'And what?'

Geddes realised he should talk to the brother and sister face to face and broke away from his colleagues. What he had to say wouldn't reassure anybody.

* * *

The detective joined them and drew them aside. Gavin was impatient. 'Spit it out, Andrew.'

Geddes tried again with Mackenzie, his characteristic brusqueness gone. 'It would be better if you weren't here. Really it would. We've no idea how badly he's been injured.'

'You mean he's not…'

Gavin had to take hold of her arm to keep her from falling. She stared at the policeman, her voice trembling. 'He has to be dead. He has to be.'

The DS saw the fear in her eyes. Until Crawford was on a mortuary slab his wife wouldn't feel safe. Clearly, she didn't understand what he was saying. Her brother did. He said, 'So it could be bad, then?'

Geddes let the question go unanswered.

Mackenzie was on the verge of a panic attack. 'I have to get out of here.'

'I'll come with you.'

'No. I need to be by myself. You stay…please. I need to know.'

He didn't argue.

She pushed through the throng excitedly waiting for the car to be brought to the surface, shielding her face from the unwanted attention of strangers. For them this was an event, an entertainment, for her it was a tragedy. Mackenzie had to get away.

Under an arch of the George V bridge, she stopped and tried to process this latest horror; too much to take in. Derek had done this to her in a desperate attempt to keep her. A strong woman was a woman he couldn't control. He needed her to be weak, weak enough to depend on him totally. And he'd almost succeeded.

She couldn't run from the pictures in her head. Suddenly, she wanted a drink. The craving gnawed at her, as powerful as it had ever been. Her fingers tingled. She started to shake. A film of sweat broke on her brow. Desperation overwhelmed her. She didn't know this part of Glasgow: where could she get one?

A cheer went up behind her and brought her back. They'd raised the Audi. Bitter bile burned her throat. Her stomach turned over. The man in the balaclava flashed in front of her eyes. Sitting in the chair. Watching her. A hand went to her mouth in a vain attempt to stem the vomit spewing between her fingers. She leaned on the railing where the giant foundations ended and let it happen.

Who cared if someone saw?

On the other side of the bridge recovering the Audi was cause for celebration. Applause broke out, scattered at first, building to a cheer as the lines tightened and the silver tail broke the surface and hung suspended above the water, both doors open like twisted wings, no longer the sleek machine it had been.

Gavin Darroch heard the reaction and didn't share it. There was little to feel good about.

'Fucking ghouls.'

Geddes ran towards him to give him the news. 'Crawford isn't in the car.'

'So where is he?'

'We don't know. The Marine Unit officers are good lads. Give them time. They'll find him.'

'Could he have survived?'

'Wouldn't have thought so. Even if he was thrown from the car, you'd expect the damage to his body to be fatal.'

'How deep is it down there?'

'About twenty-eight feet.' Geddes looked towards the river. 'Tide's coming in so maybe deeper.'

'Could he be on the bottom?'

'Stuck in the silt? Not likely.'

'So where can he be?'

The detective leaned towards him. 'Fucked if I know.'

* * *

The jetsam of the city – scraps of newspapers, plastic bottles, rags and leaves and worse – floated on the dirty-brown surface. Mackenzie wiped her mouth, about to turn away when she saw him.

Derek Crawford's hair was matted above ashen skin, his face cut and bruised. One eye was a bloody hole the other closed as he blindly grasped the wall, trying to get a hold. Mackenzie fell back, unable to believe he was there.

She whispered. 'Derek. Derek.'

Crawford didn't respond. She spoke again, louder. 'Derek.'

The remaining eye opened and her heart missed a beat. His lips moved. 'Mackenzie, help me. Help me.'

Realising she could save him she climbed over the railing and balanced on the cold stone ledge, stretching her leg towards him as far as she could. Not close enough. She tried again, holding on with one hand, reaching until her foot rested on top of his head. Derek let go of the wall. His fingers closed round her ankle. He mouthed a silent 'Thank you.'

An unnatural calm washed through her. She looked into the baleful eye that had calmly watched her pain, saw her terror and let it go on.

The man who had put her in harm's way.

The memory gave her the strength she needed. She pushed down until his head disappeared. Crawford thrashed the water and tightened his grip and Mackenzie felt her hand slip; he was going to take her with him.

'til death us do part

With a strength borne of loathing she leaned forward, prised his fingers from her foot and held him under. A line of bubbles broke the surface, then less, then none.

no one saw

like a leaf falling to the ground, it went unnoticed

Epilogue: The Lowther Hills, South Lanarkshire

Mackenzie was standing alone on the pavement opposite the Mount Florida Bowling Club, a fragile figure in the pre-dawn darkness. She'd been careful not to wake Adele and the boys when she slipped out. This wasn't about them. Better they weren't involved.

A day after his car had gone over the Kingston Bridge, Derek Crawford's body was dragged from the River Clyde. His wife was the wrong person to identify it. Gavin confirmed it was him.

The human spirit was reckoned to be remarkably resilient and it was true. Moving in with Adele and Adam and Richard had been good for all of them, Mackenzie especially. Once or twice, in random moments, Adele caught a glimpse of the sister she'd known. Then the barrier came down and she retreated into silence, sometimes lasting a week.

How he could help came from an almost forgotten promise. Gavin dialled the number. The conversation was brief and one-sided. Explanations were unnecessary.

'5am. Be ready.'

She didn't ask why or where they were going.

He turned off the M74, nosed past a stand of trees and on through a silent Abington before crossing to the other side of the motorway to begin the final part of the journey from Glasgow. He felt the road rise under him and changed down through the gears. In forty miles they'd seen less than a dozen vehicles. Thinking was the enemy – if he allowed doubt into his mind he'd come to his senses and wouldn't go through with it.

And Mackenzie would be denied the closure she craved.

Leadhills village was asleep. Beside him, she said nothing.

The Baxter house was a shadow against the lightening sky and when Gavin brought the petrol cans from the boot they felt heavy in his hands. He opened the car door and spoke to his sister.

'Do you want to do it?'

She shook her head. He nodded and walked to the front door.

His footsteps on the stairs sent a rat scurrying to its lair. Gavin turned on the light in time to see a long brown tail disappear through a crack. The familiar dank smell filled his nostrils, images of what he'd witnessed here filled his head and he went down into the basement, sloshing fuel up the walls and over the bed, dousing everything; gagging on the fumes, retracing his steps, cursing quietly. On the ground floor he did the same until both cans were empty, then he tossed them in a corner.

Outside, he sheltered a flickering match in the palm of his hand and glanced towards his sister. God alone knew what she was feeling. He threw the match inside. Nothing happened and he thought it must have died. Then it exploded into life.

Gavin didn't notice her until she was next to him. He anxiously searched her face, hoping she was strong enough. He needn't have worried. She put her hand in his and let it rest there.

Tendrils of yellow and red flames crackled over the building, devouring everything they touched. The gap in the roof became the rim of a cauldron, pouring a black cloud into the new dawn. The fire roared and the building burned. The heat was intense, flushing Mackenzie's face, making her eyes water. But she didn't move away.

Suddenly, the Baxter house sighed and fell in on itself, throwing dust and sparks and charred fragments into the air.

Gavin led his sister to the car and drove towards the morning. Behind them a line of smoke drifted to the sky. They didn't see it. They didn't look back.

Acknowledgements

Many people have contributed to this work and I am indebted to my Beta readers on In Harm's Way: Elizabeth Condon Campbell, Mary Snaddon, Sandra Fay Jones, Catherine Campbell, Kirsty Adam Elsever and Craig Stolarek, for so generously giving me their time and their feedback.

My editors, – John Hodgman and Ben Adam who brought invaluable insights and superior language skills and shielded me from the multitude of errors I otherwise would have made. And Linda Wright, for her local knowledge and eagle-eyed proofreading. Thank you.

Everyone at Bloodhound Books, especially Betsy Freeman Reavley for putting on one of her many hats and designing the cover. I loved it from the moment she showed it to me.

DS Alasdair McMorrin of Police Scotland for once again keeping me right on the procedural elements of the story and for always being just a phone call away. Really appreciated, Alasdair.

The unfettered imaginations of Devon and Harrison Carney. I remember the three of us on the banks of the River Clyde, discussing how the story should end. Thanks guys.

And my wonderful wife, Christine, the most talented woman I know. With me from the first word to the last. Without her this book would not exist.

Owen Mullen
Crete 2018

Lightning Source UK Ltd.
Milton Keynes UK
UKHW040819021118
331645UK00001B/67/P